DYIN

23rd June 2017

Dying for Power

R. Pearl and G. Bamford

To Jean,

With very best wishes,

Ros Pearl

LARCHWOOD
PRESS

First published in Great Britain in 2017 by Larchwood Press.

ISBN: 978-1-910990-19-3

Cover design by George Bamford

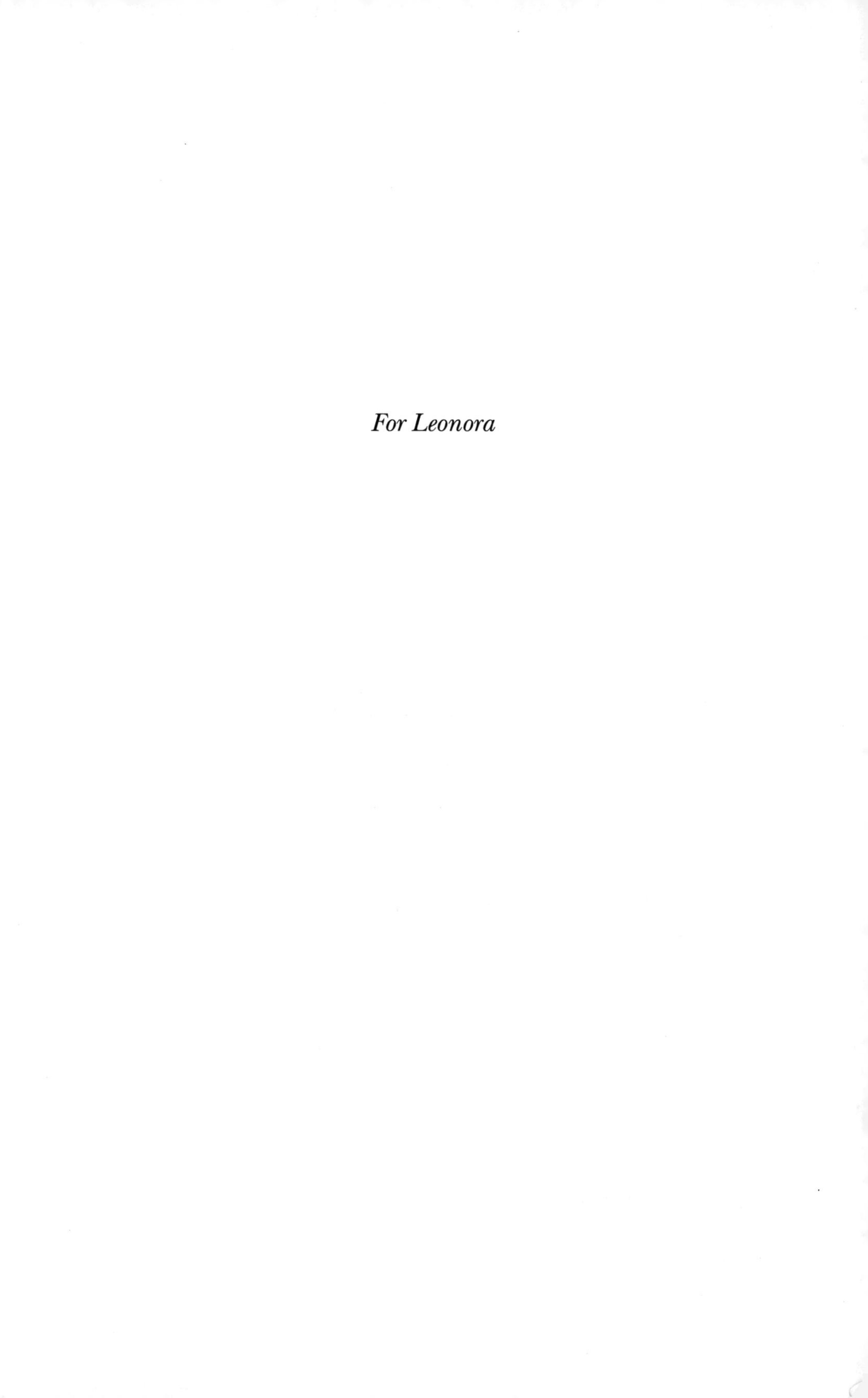

For Leonora

List of Characters

ALPHA and OMEGA (aka Bo Huáng)	Two of Quan's female bodyguards
MICHEL BONNARD	Young boy
BREDA	of The Mustard Seed
LIAM CALLAGHAN	Irish entrepreneur
DAI CHAVET	Young Japanese Secret Service agent
OKI CHAVET	Japanese Secret Service agent
JOHNNY DASHU	Japanese Secret Service agent
HENRI DAVOUST	Friend of Maurice Duval
LAURE DAVOUST	Henri Davoust's widowed sister
ARISTIDE DE LAMERIE	Head of French Internal Intelligence Service
MAURICE DUVAL	A master baker
PĖRE YVES DUVAL	Maurice Duval's brother
JOHN EDWARD	of The Mustard Seed
CAPTAIN ENDO	Quan's chief helicopter pilot
CAPTAIN FÉNG	Captain of Quan's yacht the *Sappho*
ORLA FLYNN	Irish airline pilot
MINSHENG GĀO	Junior attaché at the Chinese Embassy, Tokyo

PASCAL GARNIER	Friend of Maurice Duval
CAPTAIN AKI HARA	Private pilot
MISTER HIGUCHI	Manager of the Tawā complex, Tokyo
MIDORI ITO	Japanese Secret Service agent
MISTER JOHNSON	Private investigator on Quan's payroll
INSPECTOR BILL KEARNEY	Kinsale Garda officer
ADA KUCHINSKY	American owner of IT company and golf fanatic
KYUJI	A Japanese Secret Service I.T./electronics expert
MADAM CHOW LEE QUAN	Chinese tycoon
SIR JOHN AND LADY LISTER	Guests on Quan's yacht the *Sappho*
ARTHUR LYSAGHT	Owner of Fort Rufus Golf Club
MAI-LI	Tiger Tanaka's P.A.
SORA MORI (aka Natsumi Nomura)	Japanese super model and sister of Jiro
BAKU MORI	Japanese Secret Service agent
DAN MULLANE	of The Mustard Seed
AGENT MURATA	Japanese Secret Service agent
YORI NAKANO	Tiger Tanaka's second in command
NING	One of Quan's female bodyguards/ hired killers
AGENT NIN-PO	Japanese Secret Service agent
JIRO NOMURA	Weapons inventor
HUGO O'CONNOR	Irish airline pilot

ATSUSHI OGAWA	Chairman of a Japanese armaments company
MOLLY O'GORMAN	Irish ex soap star, now in PR
AGENT ONISHI	Japanese Secret Service agent
JAVINDA AND PURNA PATEL	Guests on Quan's yacht the *Sappho*
GENERAL PENG	Chinese general
AGENT SUN	Japanese Secret Service agent
HIROSHI (H) SUZUKI	Anglo-Japanese Secret Service agent
WASSIM TALEB	Algerian suicide bomber
TIGER TANAKA	Head of the Japanese Secret Service
MISTER UCHIDA	Jiro Nomura's immediate superior
GENERAL WEISHENG	Chinese general
BRIGADIER SIR HARRY WETHERALL	Head of MI6
GENERAL WU	Chinese general
ZHENG	Quan's senior female bodyguard

In the 2014 World Economic Forum, held in Davos, Switzerland, the Prime Minister of Japan likened the tense relationship between his country and China as being, 'similar to the situation between England and Germany before World War 1'.

Prologue

Japan

The elderly farmer jumped to his feet, staring in disbelief. Then he began to run.

His daily routine seldom varied. After finishing his early morning jobs, he'd fill a beaker from the nearby stream, settle himself down on a fallen tree trunk and eat a small meal. His dog, well used to his ways, would lie beside him in the shade, hoping for scraps.

There he would sit waiting for the *Shinkansen* Bullet Train to pass by, on its way between Kyoto and Tokyo. It was a sight he never tired of watching. The sleek, streamlined train was a daily fascination, which filled him with awe. He'd never been on a train and could only imagine what it must be like, watching the countryside flash past.

It was 8.33 – a time which would be blazoned over newspaper headlines the following day. The farmer had no need for a wrist-watch: the slight trembling of the ground under his feet told him that the train was approaching.

He bit deeply into his anpan roll, filled with red bean paste and topped with black sesame seeds, looking towards the track, which ran less than half a mile from where he sat. His eyes told him what happened next, followed a split second later by the sound.

There was a flash of dazzlingly bright light. He blinked, and when he opened his eyes again, one of the centre carriages had imploded and those behind it seemed to be climbing over it and travelling upwards into the air. He couldn't process what he was seeing. He felt a juddering in the ground as the train faltered and slowed. The huge blast, followed by the sound of shrieking metal rolled over him. The noise was shattering.

Leaping up, his roll falling to the ground, he stumbled towards the carnage. His dog, pausing only to wolf down the discarded food, ran at his heels. The sky was filled with pieces of falling debris, but he ran on, impelled by an instinctive urge to help.

As he got closer, he began to hear a different sound. People were screaming. A large metal door thudded into the ground beside him and he dodged sideways, his breath coming in gasps. A child's doll lay sprawled on the ground and without knowing why, he picked it up and clasped it to his chest. He shuddered to a halt, his hand pressed to his mouth, as he started to see unspeakable sights. Suddenly there was blood in the air and he saw the first body part. A foot, still wearing a white trainer, landed in front of him, seeping blood into the grass. With tears pouring down his withered cheeks, he blundered on.

A chunk of debris bounced off his shoulder, knocking him to his knees. Nearby, he saw a young man lying on his back, with his eyes open and an expression of surprise on his face. The farmer felt for a pulse, which fluttered beneath his fingers. He started to give artificial respiration, but within moments he realised that the boy had died. Closing the staring eyes, he said a prayer and tried to stand.

A massive jolt of pain hit his chest like a hammer. For a moment, he swayed and staggered forward. His heart stopped beating and when the rescue parties found him, later that day, he was sprawled in the semblance of an embrace with the boy he'd tried to save. His dog lay, whimpering at his side.

Part One

Chapter 1

The Yaeyama Islands – Pacific Ocean – Japan

The rising moon reached a point where its light entered the bedroom. A silver beam illuminated a naked foot, and lingeringly exposed a long, slim leg and a body as pale as alabaster.

Hiroshi Suzuki – or simply H, as he was generally known – lay on his side and watched as the exquisite form next to him was fully revealed. Something in the pose reminded him of Velázquez's Rokeby Venus. He checked his Rolex Submariner and saw that it was almost four in the morning. Although he was on leave, he knew that he wouldn't be able to go back to sleep.

He slid out from under the sheets, pulled on a pair of shorts and running shoes and walked out of the French windows onto a small veranda, with two steps leading down onto a sandy beach. He paused to sniff the air, inhaling the scents from the tropical forest behind him and the salt tang of the sea. He spent a couple of minutes looking up into the navy blue sky, stitched with a million stars, before stretching his muscles, then setting off along the beach.

Almost an hour later he was back outside his room. His leg muscles tingled from running on the wet sand and he felt energised. The night and the stars were fading and palest pink shadows were lighting up the ocean on the horizon. The place was deserted and H revelled in the beauty and the peace, broken only by the dawn chorus of the local birds. He looked inside, but the woman slept on and hadn't moved. He grabbed a towel and walked down into the water. It was like swimming in warm milk. He floated on his back, watching the day slowly come alive. It was so far removed from the dangerous and hectic life he normally led. It was a different world.

Back in the cabin, he took a quick shower before looking to see if his companion was awake. Her long black hair covered the pillows and lay across her naked breasts. Hiroshi sat on the bed and traced a finger lazily up her calf.

She smiled as she woke up, opened one eye and said, "Come back to bed H."

Two minutes later, with incredibly bad timing, H's satellite telephone rang. Swearing under his breath, he scooped it up, clicked it on and put it to his ear. It was the familiar voice of Tiger Tanaka, his boss, honorary uncle and head of CIRO – the Japanese Secret Service.

"I'm sorry to ruin your vacation, but I need you back here immediately."

"What's the problem?" H asked, moving off the bed and out onto the veranda.

"The 8.18 Bullet Train was blown up, shortly after leaving Kyoto this morning."

Even though Tanaka was talking in his normal, composed voice, H could tell he was far from calm.

"Yori Nakano was on board and we haven't been able to reach him on his mobile. There was an international conference in Kyoto yesterday and he was accompanying the Minister for Defence and a party of important delegates back to Tokyo. Whether it was sabotage or a terrorist act is yet to be determined. As of this moment, no-one has claimed responsibility."

If the Defence Minister had been killed in the explosion, the repercussions would be enormous. Nakano was Tanaka's second-in-command at the Japanese Secret Service, and one of his closest friends. If he'd died, Tanaka would need H's support.

"I've arranged transportation, which will be with you shortly. I'll call again when you are en route, with further information as it comes in."

H clicked off the phone and stood still for a moment, before turning back into the room. He sighed as he looked at the girl on the rumpled bed. She was sitting, propped up on the pillows and making no effort to cover herself with the sheets.

"You're leaving me, aren't you?" she said.

Her lips pouted and her eyes were stormy. H knelt quickly on the bed and put his hands on either side of her face, smoothing the frown lines away with his thumbs. As she opened her mouth again, he kissed her quickly on the lips, saying, "No ... no ... no ...," kissing her between each word. "Sweetheart, I'm sorry. We've had a magical time, but, yes, I *do* have to leave. It's work and it's important. Nothing else would make me go." He stood up and turned to dress; ignoring the pillow that was hurled at his back and the sound of an angry sob.

He pulled on shorts and an open necked shirt. Everything else went swiftly into his Filson Duffle Bag and in minutes he was set to go. The smell of strong coffee briefly cheered him: she had relented. On the veranda he found a hasty breakfast on the table. He smiled and told her she was a girl in a million. He was just finishing half a local pineapple when he heard the noise, not of the motor boat engine he'd expected, but the distinctive throb of a single engine chopper.

H grabbed a napkin, ran out onto the beach and waved it over his head. The pilot had flown in over the cliffs behind the cabin and was carefully circling the small bay. As a belt of palm trees and sub-tropical vegetation came right down to the thin strip of white sand, H was relieved to see that his ride was an old Bell 47, with floats attached. Painted bright red, the distinctive bubble canopy, which gave undistorted vision and the characteristic open tail boom, made the whole machine look like a cross between a giant dragonfly and a child's Meccano set.

Realising that he was going to get soaked, H stuffed his shirt and a towel into his bag and made sure the rustproof brass zipper and storm flap were closed. He gave the girl a brief kiss and waited for the helicopter to settle.

The pilot had made many similar landings and understood the dangers. He knew that the downwash of air being pulled through the rotors would create spray on the surface of the water, which would affect his visibility, as well as the inability to manoeuvre, once on the water. He picked a spot, well away from the few rocks in the bay and, descending at a relatively slow speed, settled the helicopter gently on about three feet of water. He kept the machine running, for better control and hoped his passenger knew what he was doing.

He was concerned about the proximity of the unguarded tail rotor, but H was well aware that one wrong move might end with him being chopped into small pieces. He waited until the pilot gave him a thumbs-up and waded the short distance out, getting a fierce, impromptu shower from the spray before he pulled himself up onto the floats and climbed into the cockpit. He strapped himself in and put on his headphones.

Now that they could communicate, the man introduced himself as Aki Hara. While he prepared for takeoff, H sat in silence to allow him to get airborne, knowing that this would be moderately more challenging than the landing, particularly taking account of the extra weight of his tall, wet passenger and his bag. Hara manoeuvred away from the shoreline and pulled in power as he lowered the nose of the helicopter and gathered speed as he took off in an easterly direction.

"I'm glad we're doing this early in the morning," Hara commented, as he headed out over the turquoise water, before banking to the right and rounding the headland. "We'd have had a power problem later on in the day, when it gets hotter."

H asked where they were going.

"Only a short flip to the nearest airport on Ishigaki Island. I gather transport has been arranged to take you on to Tokyo."

H listened politely as Hara explained that he was a retired naval pilot, currently working as a part-time civilian instructor at Ishigaki, who occasionally undertook jobs for what he called H's 'outfit'. The Bell 47 G was his pride and joy. Ancient, admittedly, but a wonderful old war horse. When they landed a short time later, H towelled himself dry and put on his clothes and shoes, raking his hair back with his fingers. He thanked Hara for the ride, and believed him when he said that he hadn't enjoyed a morning as much for ages.

A New Citation X was fuelled and ready on the tarmac and after brief formalities, H was in the air, heading for Haneda Airport, Tokyo.

CHAPTER 2

Tokyo

Jiro Nomura tried to work out where things had started to go wrong. Yes, he was ambitious; he was also clever. He'd laid his plans meticulously and had honestly thought he was well on the way to becoming the millionaire he'd always felt he deserved to be.

As a weapons designer and inventor, he had achieved something quite extraordinary. Three years of working almost around the clock had finally paid-off. He'd created a revolutionary type of explosive.

Three months ago he'd taken his plans to the Board. There was no doubt that they'd been impressed. It was a unique weapon, which would make billions for the company, as well as the prestige of being first in the field with this new technology. He'd swelled with satisfaction when his chairman had invited him to his home to celebrate. In Japan, this was a great honour.

For a brief while he'd believed that all his aspirations would materialise. He fondly imagined being offered a seat on the Board, with a huge increase in his lowly salary. His sister would be so proud of him, which was an important consideration. He had taken his first week's holiday in three years, and spent it looking for a new apartment in a far more exclusive area of Tokyo.

After all his expectations and plans, nothing had happened. No fame and instant recognition. No promotion. No raise in salary. No seat on the Board and no new home. He had received a letter of commendation, signed by all of the Directors, thanking him for his work. He had asked for another meeting with his Chairman, but been denied. He went to his superior and explained his disappointment and frustration at the wall of silence, but was told to grow up and stop grumbling. It was pointed out that he was extremely fortunate to be working for such a distinguished and well respected company. It was further suggested that he start work on a new project and make himself useful. Those last words rankled deeply.

Too late, he realised that his brilliance was undervalued and that he'd been cut out of the loop. The Board and shareholders would get rich off his invention and he would get nothing.

Something had to be done. After days of thought and soul-searching he made the decision which had landed him in this mess. His own company had shown him no respect and he felt aggrieved that they had forced him to act as he had. Loyalty was important to him, but they had shown him none. The name of Jiro Nomura *would* be known throughout the world.

It was time to teach them a lesson.

After careful research into his company's biggest competitors, Nomura had made his choice. It had been hard to get to see someone sufficiently high up in the organisation, but he'd persevered. At work, he'd carried on as normal and taken time off for a fabricated dental appointment, to attend the meeting. It was vital that he arouse no suspicions whilst he laid his plans. The first conference had been conducted with great courtesy and he'd preened in the respect he'd been shown. They had definitely been excited by the outline of his invention. Without giving away too much information, he'd managed to whet their appetites and been invited back for a second meeting, with the illustrious owner of the company.

The Tokyo headquarters of Armstec International was situated in the exclusive business area of Akasaka. The modern building was a masterpiece of light and open spaces. As Jiro Nomura walked over to the sleek reception desk, he admired the 'living wall', a towering bank of hanging plants, with water cascading down into a pink marble bowl at ground level. As soon as he gave his name, he was whisked into a private, glass lift and escorted straight to the office of the Penthouse Suite, where he was to meet Madam Chow Lee Quan. Nomura had discovered that she was a Chinese entrepreneur and founder of a vast conglomerate, of which Armstec International was the flagship. She had started the company from scratch and was known as a major player in the weapons industry.

Standing guard on either side of a pair of double doors were two women, dressed in dark trouser suits, with white shirts and red ties. Their haircuts were uncompromisingly short and what little he could see of the skin on their hands and neck was covered with intricate tattoos. Without speaking, one mimed raising her hands into the air. Nomura lifted his arms and was patted down for weapons. Unsmilingly, they opened the doors.

Feeling nervous and ruffled, Nomura stepped past them into a room which took his breath away. It was vast, and decorated in an ornate and over-opulent style. There was only one person in the room: a woman who stood looking out through the wall of glass onto the panoramic view of Tokyo below. She turned to face him. Tiny in stature, but wide in girth, her age was hard to guess. Her face was chubby, with a guileless expression and small, mean eyes, like currants set into dough, which seemed to strip him to the bone. Without moving she waited for him to approach.

"Welcome," she said. "My people tell me that you are an inventor, with something to sell."

Nomura hid his surprise at her bluntness. She waved him to a chair and sat down behind a gilded, antique desk.

"Why have you brought this idea to me?" she asked.

He cleared his throat and straightened his tie. "I say, without false modesty Madam Quan, that what I have created is beyond cutting-edge technology. The firm which develops my ideas will ... "

"I asked why you have brought it to me?" she cut across his carefully prepared opening words.

"My firm has treated me with disrespect" he said. "My product is unique, so I'm now looking to offer my services where my work will be fully recognised. You were my natural first choice."

"That at least sounds honest. If I were to, shall we say, *acquire* your services, I assume your invention would be available exclusively to us?" Nomura nodded, as she continued, "time is money, so it's pointless to hedge. At the right price, your proposal is of interest to me."

Nomura was thrown off his stride. Such direct dealings were alien to his Japanese mind, where etiquette demanded a far slower and less obvious approach. His carefully rehearsed sales pitch was now superfluous and while he was excited, he was unused to the art of negotiation. He blotted his upper lip with a handkerchief and jumped in with both feet.

"I have other ideas. Now that I have completed the explosive, I will have time to develop some different concepts, which are already in my mind."

Madam Quan looked at him without speaking. She pressed a button on her desk. "You will take some tea with me?"

Without waiting for an answer, she stood and moved towards a seating area by the window. When the tea had been served, Nomura sat upright, not allowing himself to lean into the deep cushions of the sofa she'd indicated, whilst she took a similar seat opposite, on a far lower sofa. Her short legs, he noticed, hardly reached the floor.

Madam Quan got straight down to negotiations, offering him a salary almost four times what he currently received. He tried to sound nonchalant and said that this would be acceptable as a starting salary.

Nomura began to relax – which was a mistake – and gradually allowed himself to lean back into the soft cushions. Madam Quan started to talk in a friendlier tone, asking him about his family and childhood. He responded like an opening flower.

"When your worth is recognised, as it should be," Madam Quan said, "what will you do with your first pay check? You look to me like a man who enjoys the finer things in life. Perhaps you'll buy a boat or a powerful sports car? What do you say?"

Poor Nomura, with his expensive dreams reviving, agreed that he'd always wanted a Ferrari.

"Before buying such a costly toy, I presume you'd want to take a test drive? It would certainly be the sensible thing to do."

"Assuredly, Madam Quan, that is exactly what I would do." Too late he wished he'd held his tongue.

"We agree on this, and naturally, before we go any further – as you yourself would – I shall require a demonstration of your 'product'. I shall give it my consideration and inform you tomorrow as to where and when this trial will take place."

He should have seen this coming. As a scientist he hadn't even thought about the wider picture ... that his invention was lethal.

Madam Quan stood up. The meeting was over. As they shook hands, she said, "I am willing to buy your invention outright and give you a small percentage of the profits. You will continue with your work and be provided with state-of-the-art facilities. The details of your contract will be handled by my lawyers. You will find me generous, but, I demand total loyalty from my employees. Your track record in this respect scores zero. Do not cross me, Mister Nomura, or you will regret it."

CHAPTER 3

Over the Pacific Ocean

H relaxed in the luxurious interior of the Citation jet. There were eight large white leather seats, but he was the only passenger on board. He collected a bottle of iced Perrier water and a plate of sushi from the small galley before flicking through the headlines of a pile of the previous day's newspapers.

Whilst waiting for Tanaka to call, he did some mental gymnastics by completing a 'fiendish' Sudoku in record time. They had a most unusual relationship. Apart from being his boss, Tanaka was the closest thing H had to a family. He was an honorary uncle, mentor, teacher and friend, who'd always been an integral part of H's life. Mystery surrounded the father he'd never known. His mother had brought him up, but she had died young, when H has only sixteen. His 'uncle' Tanaka had swooped down and taken charge of him. It seemed he'd always been destined to follow him into the Japanese Secret Service, of which Tanaka had been in charge of for more years than anyone could remember.

After his school days ended, H was sent to England to complete his studies at Tanaka's old Oxford College. At the same time H continued his training in the arts of weapons, battle, diplomacy, secrecy and subterfuge. Over the years he'd developed into an outstandingly talented operative. He was a natural, who'd excelled at every challenge and he'd never considered any other profession.

The satellite phone remained silent. They landed at Haneda Airport three hours later and as the whine of the twin turbofan

Rolls-Royce engines faded, the door opened and the steps were let down. H put on his jacket and stepping out into the sunshine, he saw a black Lexus GX waiting for him on the tarmac. A rear door opened and Tanaka emerged and clasped him to his chest. "I'm sorry to have ruined your holiday, but... I need you with me." He held H at arm's length and looked at him closely. "Although you only had a few days, the rest seems to have done you good. We'll go straight to the crash site together," he said, as they walked back to the car.

"We still know very little, but it *has* been confirmed that the bomb was planted in the Defence Minister's carriage. No one could have survived being that close to the blast, so we must assume that he has been murdered, along with Yori Nakano." H could see Tanaka's knuckles tighten on his tumbler of water. He drained the glass and put it down carefully on the small table in front of him. "They're still removing the bodies, but the death toll will be... considerable. The whole train was checked and swept thoroughly and no one seems to understand how this could have happened."

They discussed all of the implications and before long were nearing the crash site. It took some time to get close, as the debris was strewn over a large area. It was like a scene from a disaster film. The road was clogged with ambulances, police cars and special-forces vehicles, as well as a large collection of the media.

The Lexus edged forward, pulled off the road and parked beside a small, mobile HQ, which Tanaka's team had already installed. The interior was crammed full of burly men in hard hats, all talking loudly. At the far end, they spotted Kyuji, the computer expert, with two other specialists. They were huddled over an over-heating, box-fresh, space grey MacBook and an iPad Pro, its screen criss-crossed with their finger swipes.

Tanaka asked most of the men to wait outside, while he conferred with the leader of the crash investigation team and the bomb squad. Kyuji was also requested to stay.

After a short time, Tanaka and H could see that the experts were united in one thing. They were completely baffled. In their combined experience, they'd never encountered anything like it. Judging from the remains of the train and the area surrounding it, the carriage where the bomb had been planted, appeared to have imploded, rather than radiating out as would have been the case with a conventional device. They concluded that an unknown type of explosive must have been used.

Tanaka thanked them and asked them to remain on site until further notice. Kyuji had finished setting up his equipment and his first job had been to ascertain from Kyoto station the exact number of people on the train. The figures had come back: 342 passengers and 12 crew members, including the 2 drivers – 354 people in total. He had also begun to download footage from the CCTV cameras at Kyoto station and was starting to analyse the data. Tanaka and H watched the different screens: every face was being run through facial recognition software programmes. Kyuji admitted that the process would be a lengthy one.

Tanaka asked to see the casualty figures. The harassed chief medical officer came in and handed Tanaka a list of those they had identified so far. H scanned the sheets over his shoulder, but could not see Yori Nakano's name, nor that of the Defence Minister.

"Our preliminary information puts the numbers at 108 dead or missing and over 200 wounded. Precise figures are yet to be determined, as many of the bodies are…," he cleared his throat and struggled to find the right words, "…. are not intact."

Tanaka led H outside and lent against the bonnet of the Lexus. He seemed to have aged overnight. H looked at him in concern, knowing that it wasn't just the disaster that was weighing heavily on him: when definite confirmation came in, he'd have the unenviable task of breaking the news to Reika Nakano, Yori's widow.

Tanaka's telephone rang and he straightened up as he heard the voice of the Prime Minister, wanting updated information. When the call finished, he squared his shoulders and turned back to the control centre and the queue of people who were still waiting to give him their reports.

It was going to be a long day.

Chapter 4

Tokyo

The Maitre d' oiled his way out from behind his desk to greet one of his favourite patrons. He bowed with a genuine smile of welcome.

"Miss Mori, we are again honoured by your visit. Your usual table is ready."

He led the way through the elegant restaurant – where diners paused in appreciation to watch one of Japan's most famous supermodels – to a window table, which was set for two. After personally pulling out her chair and handing her a menu, he asked what she would like to drink.

"I'll have a Bellini, please, Masato; with more peach purée than champagne."

They made small-talk, as a minion was dispatched for her cocktail. When it arrived, the Maitre d' excused himself with another bow and returned to his station.

Several more guests arrived, but he detailed an underling to seat them. A few minutes later, a tall, slim man entered the restaurant and looked around with a frown. The Maitre d' – used to summing-up guests at a glance – was unimpressed. The man was unshaven and wore a slightly crumpled suit.

"May I be of assistance?" he asked, as if he thought the idea unlikely.

The dishevelled man blinked and looked towards him.

"You have, I believe, a table for two in the name of Nomura" he said formally, before hastily correcting himself. "No ... not

Nomura, I mean Mori." He pulled out a handkerchief and blotted his upper lip.

The Maitre d' remained inscrutable, despite his surprise. "Do you mean Miss *Sora* Mori?" he asked. The man nodded.

He was disappointed. Miss Mori – in his opinion – could do a lot better for herself. Crooking a finger at a hovering waiter, he said, "Table One," before turning his attention to some new arrivals more worthy of his personal attention.

Sora checked her watch. It was unusual for her brother to be late. She listened idly to the conversations on the nearby tables. There was a buzz of shock and excitement and the sole topic seemed to be the horrific explosion on the Bullet Train. Sora sighed. This lunch had been her idea, to celebrate signing a new and highly prestigious modelling contract. Both of their parents were dead and she and Jiro had always been close. She was looking forward to sharing the good news.

As her brother reached her table, she glanced up as he dropped heavily into the seat opposite. "Bad day, Jiro?" she asked.

A waiter arrived, set down a jug of water and poured two glasses before handing him a menu and retreated to the bar. Nomura drained the glass.

"What's wrong?" Sora asked. Nomura looked into the bottom of his glass, as if searching for answers.

"Relax," she said. "Let's order first and then you can tell me. What would you like to eat?"

He flapped a hand and put the menu down without looking at it. Sora frowned, giving him a sharp glance and when the waiter returned, she ordered for them both. Her brother looked terrible. Normally, he was smartly dressed and cared for his appearance. Today, his eyes were bloodshot, his hands shook and although the restaurant was cool, he was sweating.

"Look at me, Jiro. What is the matter?"

Nomura made an obvious effort, smoothed back his hair and said, "I've had a dreadful morning and you know I hate to be late. Anyway, this restaurant looks very smart. What's the occasion?"

It was a brave attempt, but she knew him too well. Two waiters appeared and placed their first course in front of them. Sora picked up her chopsticks.

"Tell me what's wrong."

"I know you care, but I don't want to burden you with my, my, er ... problems." He kept glancing around the room, then absently started eating, looking down at his plate, rather than at her. Eventually he felt forced to look up. What she saw in his eyes made her feel the room go suddenly cold. It was a look of despair.

"I've done something ... " he hesitated, "It's something at work. I so wanted to make you proud of me, but I'm in way over my head." He pulled an envelope out of his breast pocket and pushed it across the table. "Read this when you're on your own. We'll talk later." He stood up abruptly and turned for the door.

Sora put out a hand to stop him, but was distracted by a squeal of brakes outside in the street. She looked out of the window, watching in disbelief as two masked men leapt out of a black SUV, pulled out machine guns and opened fire straight into the restaurant. Throwing herself to the floor with lightning reflexes, she huddled under the table, as shards of glass poured down around her.

The gunfire stopped within seconds. The gunmen piled back into the car and disappeared into the traffic. Pandemonium broke out inside, with panicking diners and staff screaming and stampeding for the exits. Sora looked around wildly for her brother, but couldn't see him. At the next table, an elderly man was cradling a woman in his arms. She had been shot in the neck and blood was pouring over them both. Sora stared in horror at the scene of carnage. She grabbed two napkins and tried to help the bleeding woman, tripping over a waiter, lying on the floor at her feet. He had three bullet holes in his chest and was obviously dead. Sobbing with shock and distress, she pressed the napkins against the woman's neck, trying to staunch the flow of blood.

The sound of sirens blotted out the screams and suddenly the restaurant was filled with police and paramedics. Some form of order was eventually restored and the dead and wounded were loaded into waiting ambulances and taken away. Those uninjured spent the afternoon being questioned by the police, before being allowed to leave.

Despite a frantic search, Sora realised that Jiro had disappeared. When she'd finished giving a young officer her details, she picked her way through the debris to collect her handbag. On the table was the envelope her brother had given her. There were two spots of blood on it, which she wiped away with disgust, before stuffing it into her handbag. Her knees were shaking with delayed reaction and she sank limply onto a chair. A concerned police officer, who'd recognised her, asked if she was alright and then insisted on giving her a lift back to her apartment. Her brain was reeling. Had this attack somehow concerned her brother? The idea seemed preposterous, but then she remembered his look of terror and knew that she had to find him. She rang his mobile, but it went straight to answerphone, so she left a message.

After stripping off her clothes, Sora realised that even though it had been an expensive suit, she'd never want to wear it again. Having thrown it into the bin, she spent several minutes under the steaming hot jets of the shower, trying to wash the blood and horrors out of her hair and off her body. She dressed in a track suit and considered going for a long run, but decided against it. Suddenly she remembered her brother's letter and fetched the envelope, before curling up in a heap on the sofa with a hot drink.

What seemed like hours later, after reading the letter, she sat still; the drink had gone cold. The first page had been carefully written and composed, in her brother's neat characters. After that it degenerated into a scrawl, which got harder and harder to decipher.

He began by apologising for bringing dishonour on the family. She paused, dreading what might come next. He told her that he loved her and was proud of her. What had started as a way to make her similarly proud of him, had back-fired. Oh Jiro, she thought, what have you done? He described what he had created; realising far too late what a monster he'd unleashed. He'd tried to justify the reasons for betraying his own company and outlined the steps he'd taken.

Sora could hardly bear to read on. She felt bitterly cold and got up to make another pot of tea. Her hands were shaking as she picked up the third sheet of the letter.

Even before the demonstration he'd been forced to make, his life had been threatened. He'd been told what would happen to him if he backed-out. In the immediate aftermath of the explosion, he'd considered suicide. He knew that his life was in ruins. He couldn't conceive of going to work for these people. They were evil. He told her that his only consolation was that he hadn't handed over his invention. Her eyes widened as she read on. He had copied some useless technical-looking jargon onto a memory stick and given it to his employers. It wouldn't take them long to discover the truth that what they'd been given was worthless.

Sora paused again. How *could* he have been so insane? she wondered. Why, why didn't he come to me for help? Then she realised that she had no idea what she could possibly have advised him to do. The situation was out of control.

The tears came at last. She wept as she hadn't done since she was a child. The magnitude of the problem was such that she couldn't think of a single person she could appeal to for help or counsel. Eventually, she fell asleep, curled-up on the sofa. When she woke, the room was filled with grey, dawn light. Her body was cold, stiff and aching. Apathetically she reached for the letter again. There was one final line, which she hadn't been able to figure out the night before. Now she understood. It read: 'If anything happens to me, you'll know where to look.'

Chapter 5

Boissy – A Small Town South of Paris

Maurice Duval felt glum and apathetic, which made him annoyed with himself. Two weeks before, his well-ordered life had been disrupted by a curious episode. He had saved a man's life. Now, he was finding it hard to settle back into his humdrum life of running a successful bakery and pâtisserie.

He'd been driving home early one morning, after a delivery to a local hotel, when he'd heard the sound of gunfire. After pulling-in to the side of the road and getting out of his car, he'd seen a young man topple over the wall of the local château and fall, almost at his feet. He could hear the sounds of a chase and the barking of guard dogs coming from the grounds of the Château and without thinking, had bundled the semi-conscious man into his van and driven off at speed. The stranger had been shot and was badly wounded, but he begged not to be taken to hospital, before passing out.

As he had some medical experience, Maurice took him to his home and looked after him, as best he could. There was nothing in the man's pockets to identify him, but there was a mobile phone. With no other options, and after long consideration, he pressed the redial button for the last number called. The telephone was answered at the Japanese Embassy in Paris. Maurice persevered until he was put through to someone in authority and explained the situation.

The upshot was the arrival of a young woman, Monique Lavalle, who announced herself as an agent with the French Secret Service.

Maurice was dumbfounded, but glad to be relieved of the responsibility of caring for the stranger. After thanking him profusely for his aid, Agent Lavalle had driven away with the patient, telling Maurice that the less he knew about the incident, the safer he would be. Maurice had been left with a mass of unanswered questions.

That very morning, a courier's van had delivered an unexpected box. Inside was a bottle of exquisite cognac, with a brief, unsigned note. *'Nothing could ever repay the debt I owe you, Maurice. Drink this and know that I will never forget your kindness to a complete stranger.'*

The incident had led to a few days of excitement and danger, but now he was missing the drama and adventure. You are getting old, my friend, he told himself. He opened the bottle and poured himself a drink, raising it in a silent toast, as he thought back over every moment of the affair. He poured another glass and sipped it slowly.

An hour later, he nodded decisively, picked up the telephone and called his brother Yves Duval who was a priest and the *curé* in a village between Avignon and L'Isle-sur-la-Sorgue. What he needed was a change of scenery and Yves confirmed he'd love to see him.

The following day – after making arrangements with his staff – Maurice set out on the long journey south. The drive through the countryside in his old Citroën Deux Chevaux Azu gave him enormous pleasure and he found his old ebullience and good humour returning.

The brothers were close, but their commitments made it hard for them to meet as often as they would like. They always slipped easily into their old ways together and had long talks of family and old friends. Three days later, they were sitting in the small, sunny courtyard, eating breakfast. Maurice was reading 'La Provence', the local newspaper. A small photograph on an inside page leapt out at him. *'TRAGIC DEATH OF LOCAL GIRL,'* the caption read. *'Monique Lavalle, who came from Meuron, near L'Isle-sur-la-Sorge, has died as a result of an accident, whilst on a climbing holiday in Japan. Our thoughts go out to her parents Jean and Mireille, who are well known in the area.*

The funeral will take place this Thursday at L'eglise de St. Ann, Meuron, at 2 p.m.'

Maurice had only met the girl once, but she'd left a lasting impression. It seemed monstrous that such a vibrant young woman should have died so young. There was so much he didn't know about the mysterious pair who'd come into his life so briefly.

He showed his brother the article, giving him an expurgated version of how he'd met Monique

"Do you wish to attend the funeral?" Yves asked. Maurice took a final sip of his coffee to give himself a moment to think.

"Yes," he said slowly. "I believe that I do."

Chapter 6

At the Train Crash Site

Later that afternoon, the work of sifting through the CCTV footage from Kyoto Station was already paying dividends. They'd started by concentrating on the area around Track 12, where the Shinkansen – Bullet Train had departed, exactly on time at 8.18 that morning, before widening the search. The futuristic railway terminus was so vast that checking all of the cameras on the multiple levels had been a painstakingly long task.

Kyuji and his technicians had finally come up with two definite hits. Men who both appeared on International 'wanted' and 'no-fly' lists.

The first was an Algerian assassin named Hamza Hamidou. His image was caught at 05.29 that morning, purchasing a ticket and then walking across the spotless concourse towards the platforms. He was casually dressed and had a rucksack over his shoulders. When the cameras picked him up again, he was on platform 7, where he was seen boarding a train at 05.40. At some time during those eleven minutes, the rucksack had disappeared.

The second man was Dai Lín, a known dissident and active member of one of the Chinese organised crime syndicates. He was captured on film entering the station from the Karasuma side at 07.01. He wore a shabby business suit and was carrying a small holdall. After that first sighting, he did not appear again on any other camera.

Kyuji asked H and Tanaka to look at his findings. After watching the relevant sections, Tanaka gave his orders.

"Find out where Hamidou was going and the timings. Go through all the tapes again and *find that rucksack*."

"Already done, sir," Kyuji replied. "Hamidou bought a ticket on the Limited Express Haruka service for Kansai Airport. The earliest train of the morning leaves at 05.46 from platform 7, so the timings fit perfectly. The journey takes 75 minutes, with two stops on the way: at Osaka City's Shin-Osaka Station and Tennoji Station. I've spoken to both stations and Kansai Airport and asked them to send through the tapes for the relevant times. We may still catch up with him. I've also alerted the police and requested a BOL…'be on the look-out' for him.

We've seen four people carrying holdalls similar to Dai Lín's, but tracking them down won't be easy."

While this conversation had been going on, H had been scrutinising the other camera feeds. The one that held his interest was Platform 12, where the Bullet Train was being prepared.

"Stop!" he said, putting a hand on the shoulder of the programmer running that tape. The screen froze, showing a group of cleaning staff stepping onto the platform.

"What have you seen?" Tanaka asked.

"Back up," H said. "Start first thing this morning, when the train arrived. I want to see everyone who got off or onto that train."

Kyuji murmured, "We've already reviewed it several times."

"Humour me," H said.

They all watched intently, wondering if he'd spotted something. Several times H asked for the picture to be frozen.

Finally, his eyes flashing with satisfaction, he asked to see the section where the cleaning crew had first appeared on the platform. After that he wanted to see them descending from the train.

Kyuji was the first to spot the discrepancy. "*Chikusō*," he said, disgustedly. "I missed it. Eight cleaning staff got on and nine got off!"

"Well done H," Tanaka said warmly. He gave brisk instructions that the cleaning crew were to be brought-in immediately for questioning. Images of each face were enhanced and swiped to a separate screen.

After back-tracking the footage, they scanned everyone who had boarded the train earlier. They widened the search area and eventually pinpointed someone who had stepped on board the train almost fifteen minutes earlier. He was dressed as a station guard, in a uniform and peaked cap. In his left hand he carried a satchel. There was something furtive about his movements and his walk seemed hesitant. Despite Kyuji's best efforts, they couldn't get a clear image of his face. Once again they widened the search pattern, but found nothing.

"I have something!" Kyuji said, suddenly. He'd found a camera angle showing the cleaning staff heading off duty. They walked in a group, some pushing trolleys of cleaning impedimenta and others carrying plastic bags of rubbish. One keyed in a number on a security pad beside a maintenance door and eight of them went through before the door closed. The last man in the group hung back. For an instant, he turned and looked around, before walking off towards a bank of escalators. They had him.

Kyuji's fingers played over the keyboard and in moments they had a clear head shot. He ran the image through the most obvious data bases, but came up blank. He persevered and finally found a 100% match to the photo. Jiro Nomura, 32, a scientist and inventor, who worked for KIBO, a large Japanese armaments company based in the outskirts of Tokyo.

Within seconds Nomura's whole life history was laid bare.

Chapter 7

Tokyo

From the details on the screen, H mentally noted Nomura's personal contact details. Tanaka told H to set up a meeting with Nomura's chairman and to make a discrete visit to Nomura's flat. Kyuji made the necessary call, but found that the Chairman was out of the office attending a family funeral, so he made an appointment for early the following morning. Tanaka also allocated agents to the follow-up jobs on Hamza Hamidou and Dai Lin, the two other men who'd been identified at the railway station.

H was provided with a car and decided to drive to Nomura's flat. The area was in the western outreaches of the city. It was run-down and shabby, but there was evidence that it was undergoing gentrification. Streets of dilapidated houses and shops were slowly being demolished and there were signs of building works and modern replacements. Nomura's flat was in a small apartment block, which was covered in scaffolding and in the process of being repainted. It fronted onto a busy thoroughfare, filled with small shops.

It was early evening and H managed to find a parking slot a few minutes away and approached the building on foot. As he saw no visible security cameras, he walked straight up the short flight of steps and into the small entrance lobby. The area was empty: it was not the sort of block to have a porter. There was a bank of twenty, open cubbyholes for residents' mail. Most were empty, but Nomura's number 5 contained a few pieces of ubiquitous junk mail and three envelopes. Two were obviously bills and the third was from a smart firm of estate agents. H left them unopened and pressed the time-switched light before walking up the flight of concrete stairs to the second floor. There were three, numbered doors, with Nomura's to the left. H pressed the buzzer and waited. He tried once more, with no result. Out of his back pocket, he took his key ring and selected a small implement. He listened again and had just inserted it into the lock, when he heard the sounds of a woman's voice coming from below. Ignoring it, he concentrated on the lock. Within seconds he had the door open and stepped inside, closing it quietly just before the woman rounded the bend in the stairs. Through the thin door he could still hear her talking on her mobile phone, before the voice faded as the door of the adjoining flat opened and then closed.

H took a couple of deep breaths and listened again. He could hear noises from the street outside and a television playing next door. Blocking out the extraneous sounds, he closed his eyes and stood without moving. His senses told him that the flat was empty. There was no disturbance in the air and all was quiet and still.

Dim daylight filtered through the single window, partially blocked by a fire escape outside. He stepped into the miniscule living room cum bedroom and saw the home of an obsessively tidy person. The furniture was cheap, but well made. A small television stood in one corner and the walls were covered with shelves full of books. The only personal items were two framed photographs. One was a family group of a couple with two small children: a studious looking small boy of about seven, with his arm around a pretty little toddler, who was clutching a stuffed rabbit. In the other picture, the children had grown up and showed a young man, proudly holding up a diploma beside a ravishingly lovely teenager. A work table was clear, except for a pot of perfectly sharpened pencils and a virgin pad of paper, exactly aligned with the edge. The futon was neatly made and pristine clothes were lined-up in the small wardrobe, with two pairs of polished shoes and two pairs of loafers underneath. H made a rapid, but methodical search, going through the pockets of two work suits and three casual jackets and trousers, but found nothing. The kitchenette showed a drop-down shelf, neatly laid for one and there was food in the fridge.

It was time to go. He checked his Rolex and saw that he'd been inside for seven minutes. He left quietly and met no-one on his way out. When he got back to his car, he telephoned Tanaka and asked if someone could be set to watch the flat, in case Nomura returned.

Acts of terrorism were extremely rare in Japan and H knew that this case needed to be solved quickly. He slept badly, with nightmarish visions of yesterday's explosion playing over and over in his mind. What he needed was some physical exercise. Before it was fully light, he'd begun a rigorous parkour workout in a nearby park. The year before, he'd joined a group of young enthusiasts after watching them practice. With his Ninja training, he already had a good grounding in many of the basic moves, but the *traceur*, the parkour practitioner who taught in the local club had opened his eyes to many new ideas and skills. He'd always had a keen sense of balance as well as excellent spacial awareness. He enjoyed learning fresh ways to walk or run faster from A to B and how to use his body by running, jumping, vaulting and climbing, enabling him to pass freely over and through different types of terrain.

After some stretching and basic warm-up moves, he worked his way from the park, through an empty shopping centre and back to the park again. Some of the more technical moves were dangerous and he had to clear his mind and focus completely on what he was doing, in order to pull the moves off with perfection and safety. An hour spent on simple acrobatic moves, butterfly kicks, wall spins, dash vaults, tic-tacs and palm spins, then on to precision jumps, tumbling and Kong vaults, had concentrated his mind and left him feeling clear-headed and set for the day.

He returned to his flat for a shower and change of clothes, before setting off in his car. By half past eight, he was pulling-up at the gates of the KIBO headquarters outside Tokyo. The guard at the gatehouse checked his name on a clipboard and raised the barrier. The drive meandered gently upwards and H drove through the landscaped grounds, admiring the ornamental lakes, banks of colourful azaleas, carefully placed specimen trees and sweeping, manicured lawns. He had found time to read-up on the company and knew that the imposing building he was approaching was made of COR-TEN weathering steel, which oxidized as it aged and was reminiscent of the John Deere World Headquarters in Illinois, nicknamed 'The Rusty Palace'.

H parked his gunmetal grey Nissan GTR and walked inside. His credentials were checked again by a security officer on the door, before he was allowed to approach the reception desk. An attractive receptionist found his name on her list and escorted him straight up to the Chairman's suite of offices. There he was handed over to yet another member of staff, who checked her watch before asking him to take a seat. Instead, H walked over to the windows and looked out over the grounds.

KIBO chairman Atsushi Ogawa did not keep him waiting and at nine o'clock precisely, H was shown into an airy office. Ogawa stepped out from behind his desk and they bowed to each other, presenting their business cards, held in two hands. Ogawa waved him to a chair, looking a little bemused at the lack of information on H's card, turning it over and finding simply the name Hiroshi Suzuki.

As H sat down, he briefly mentioned his credentials and saw a flash of surprise in Ogawa's eyes.

"I deeply apologise that I was unable to see you last night, Mister – or perhaps I should say *Agent* Suzuki. How may I help you?"

H was used to summing-people up quickly. Ogawa was in his early fifties and the word that sprang to H's mind was sleek. His face and body were well rounded and his expression was one of self-satisfaction. From his pristine silk shirt and tie to his polished shoes, H noted a confident man, who knew his own worth. His eyes were astute and it was obvious that he had no idea of the reason for a visit from the Secret Service.

It was not the Japanese way to cut to the chase before polite civilities had been observed, but H could not afford to waste time.

"Sir, I believe you have an employee named Jiro Nomura."

"We do indeed," Ogawa replied. "He is one of a group of bright, young scientists on our research team. If I may enquire, what is your interest in him?"

"It may be nothing, but his name has come up in connection with a case I'm working on," H said blandly. "If he is in the building, I'd be most grateful if I could speak to him and hopefully remove him from my investigation."

Ogawa looked at him for a long moment, before reaching for the internal telephone and asking his secretary to locate Jiro Nomura and send him up to his office.

Whilst they waited, Ogawa probed delicately for more information, but H deflected his questions and asked for a little more information on the Company. The intercom gave a quiet buzz and Ogawa's attention sharpened as he listened.

"Unfortunately, it appears that Mister Nomura is not in the office at this time. I appreciate that you are a busy man, so if you will allow me to look into his whereabouts, I'll get back to you as soon as I can."

H was not about to be fobbed-off. "Can you tell me a little more about what he is working on?"

Ogawa looked at him thoughtfully before replying, "With over two thousand employees here, I'm afraid that I would have to check his file, before answering that question. Some of our work here is extremely... sensitive. Before showing you his file, I really must insist on knowing why it is you wish to see my employee."

At that moment, H's mobile rang. "Please excuse me for a moment," he said, before answering the call. It was the agent who'd been assigned to watch Nomura's flat. He said he'd been provided with a photograph and that the subject had just entered his apartment block. "I'm on my way," H said and shut the phone.

H made his apologies to Ogawa and said he'd be in touch. He bowed again, before turning and walking out of the room, leaving the Chairman staring after him.

Chapter 8

H collected his Nissan from the car park and twenty minutes later, was pulling into a slot close to Nomura's apartment block. He walked through the small lobby and without bothering to hit the light switch, was half way up the first flight of stairs, when he heard the sound of three shots, in quick succession. He bounded up to the second floor and found Nomura's door ajar. He reached into the back waistband of his trousers and drew his Beretta. Standing beside the entrance, he nudged the door open with his foot.

Two men were standing over a body. One held a laptop clutched to his chest, the other held a gun pointed loosely at the floor. They were arguing so savagely that they failed to see H until he stepped into the room, gun levelled.

"Drop the gun," H said loudly. The argument broke off abruptly as they looked towards the door. He noticed with confusion, that the two men were actually women with crew cuts.

H locked eyes with the woman holding the gun. She started to raise her arm. It was no contest. H was ready to fire. Time went into slow motion and instead of going for the kill shot, he blasted the gun out of her hand. The noise was incredibly loud in the confined space of the small room. Without warning, both women turned for the window. One, still holding onto the laptop leapt, feet first at the glass, shattering it. Both assassins protected their faces with their arms, leaped through the gap and disappeared onto the fire escape outside.

H glanced at the body on the floor, before giving chase. He recognised Jiro Nomura and saw that one bullet wound had shattered his right elbow and there were two holes in the centre of his forehead.

H was careful not to expose himself as he approached the window. He could see the two women had reached the crowded street. They were getting away.

At ground level, H knew he'd be slowed down by the pedestrians, so he decided to keep above them. Using many of the same parkour moves he'd practiced that morning, he dived through the smashed window, to avoid the jagged glass which remained on the inside edges of the frame: swung through the lower bar of the scaffolding, tic-tacked onto the balcony to his right, and worked his way swiftly after them.

In less than a minute he reached the end of the row of buildings and needed to go down two levels. Stopping briefly, he saw that he'd almost caught up with the women. They're amateurs, he thought, seeing them pushing rapidly through the crowded street, glancing over their shoulders, trying to spot him. If they'd been more professional, they'd have moved slower and made themselves far less conspicuous. Also, they hadn't even considered that he might be above them.

Judging the distance and 'spotting' exactly where he wanted to be, H launched himself into the air, landing down one floor on the roof of an outbuilding. He rolled to his feet, performed a simple turn vault and then, dropping into the street below, landed right in front of them.

With looks of panic, the women split up. The one with the wounded hand turned-tail and barged back the way she'd come. The other, still hanging onto the laptop pivoted sideways, tripped off the curb and fell forward onto the road and into the path of a rickety, over-laden lorry. The driver stood on his brakes, but had no chance of avoiding her. He pulled his wheel to the right, colliding with an open van filled with crates of live poultry, which overturned, liberating hundreds of squawking chickens, adding to the chaos. The woman had bounced off the fender and the impact had thrown her over the bonnet and into the centre of the road.

Her chest had been run over by the second van and her head was mercifully out of sight underneath the vehicle. Traffic came to an abrupt standstill and a crowd of shouting pedestrians quickly gathered.

Most of the onlookers were pressing forward, but more than a few had seized the opportunity of a free meal and were moving away swiftly, scooping up chickens and stuffing them under their clothes. H pushed his way through the mêlée until he was beside the body. Taking out his mobile, he quickly snapped a couple of photos of the corpse, noting the unusual tattoos covering the back of her outstretched hand.

He needed to get hold of the laptop and spotted it lying on the road, about twenty feet away. As he struggled through the press of people, he looked up and saw the second woman on the opposite side of the road. She'd also seen the laptop and was far closer. H lost sight of her for a moment as she pushed an elderly man out of her way and made a grab for the laptop. Scooping it up with her uninjured hand, she turned and vanished into the crowd.

The road was still jammed with stationary vehicles, so H leapt onto the bonnet of the nearest car, ran over the roof and jumped onto the car behind it. Ignoring the startled shouts of the drivers, he made his way over the vehicles towards the nearest crossroads. He kept the woman in sight. She was still ahead of him, but he was closing the gap. She was looking wildly around and as she reached the corner, a small moped appeared and skidded to a halt beside her. H pounded over the last few cars, but was too late. The driver of the moped pulled her on behind him, did a skid turn and roared off down an empty side street.

H could hear the sirens of approaching police cars and ambulances. He had no way of catching her on foot and dropped back down onto the road, feeling disgusted with himself and breathing a little heavily. As he walked away, he rang Tanaka and gave him a sit-rep and the registration number of the moped. He decided to return to Nomura's flat and Tanaka agreed to dispatch a team to recover the body.

Chapter 9

As H started up the steps to the apartment block, a woman came hurrying down. She was fumbling with her handbag and missed her footing. H braced himself and caught her as she literally fell into his arms. He steadied her as he set her back onto her feet and couldn't fail to notice that she was staggeringly beautiful. She was also crying. Tears showed on her cheeks below a pair of dark sunglasses.

"Are you alright?" he asked, before letting her go.

"Yes, I'm fine. Thank you so much," she said, before turning away and hurrying off down the street. His photographic memory clicked into gear. He'd seen her face before, on a giant billboard somewhere. H looked after her for a few seconds before dismissing her from his mind and going inside

The hall was silent and H was surprised not to find it swarming with police. The earlier shouting and sounds of gunshots should have brought out other residents to see what was going on, but perhaps they were all at work. He noted that Nomura's mail box was now empty. He walked up the two flights and in through the open door of Flat 5.

H stood looking down at the body. Although he'd only seen it for an instant, he knew that it had been moved. The position was slightly different and someone had closed the staring eyes. Something was missing, but H couldn't pinpoint what it was. He shut his eyes and tried to catch the image, but whatever was missing remained elusive. His phenomenal memory rarely let him down, but he knew it was useless to force it. Perhaps it would come back to him later.

His eyes wandered over the room and settled on the two family photographs. He walked over to look at the later one more closely. It was several years old, but he recognised the girl he'd met moments earlier, hurrying out of the building in tears. Taking out his mobile, he snapped a photo and uploaded it to Kyuji, asking him to identify the girl.

Nomura's mail was lying on the worktable and H glanced through it. The two bills were of no interest, but the third was a letter from an upmarket Tokyo estate agent, confirming an appointment for Nomura to view a flat in a more salubrious area.

As he was reading the letter, he heard the sound of several people arriving at the door. He drew his gun and chanced a quick look through the spy-hole and was relieved to see that they were friends. He opened the door to the three men and one woman who were known as 'the clean-up team'. They were dressed in navy overalls with matching caps, which bore the logo of a cleaning and decorating firm. They carried authentic-looking paraphernalia, including empty paint pots, which H knew would actually be used to store evidence and samples.

He knew them all and had last seen them a few months before, when he'd killed a would-be assassin who'd broken into his Tokyo flat. They were all professionals. The fingerprint expert, the practiced searcher, the heavy-lifter and the woman photographer slipped-on plastic over-shoes, gloves and face masks before setting about their various tasks. One opened a rucksack and took out a tarpaulin and unfolded a body bag. They were used to working in confined spaces, but the small room seemed very crowded. H had a brief word with the team leader, before leaving them to it and heading back to his office.

Tanaka had called a meeting with four of his senior agents and H arrived just as they were about to begin. The leads on Hamza Hamidou and Dai Lin – the two suspects from the train station – were being pursued, but neither man had yet been apprehended. H gave his report and brought them all up to speed. Kyuji was able to confirm that the girl in the photograph was Natsumi Nomura, the twenty four year old younger sister of Jiro Nomura. He had been able to gather some background information on her, but nothing since she left university, five years earlier. There was no mention of her owning or renting property in the city, or any employment details. Kyuji said that he was widening the search parameters and hoped to have more information shortly. Tanaka assigned them various tasks and told H to revisit Nomura's boss and to lean on him for more information.

Chapter 10

On his way out, H spent a few minutes chatting to Mai-Li, an old friend who'd worked as Tanaka's PA for many years. She put through a call and made a second appointment for H to see Atsushi Ogawa.

When he arrived back at the KIBO offices and after repeating the security checks, he was ushered into the outer office, where the same receptionist smiled at him and checked her watch.

Without waiting for the rehearsed patter, he smiled back and walked straight over to the door of the inner-sanctum. The secretary lost her smile, got up from her desk with more speed than elegance and tried to stop him, but H had already opened the door and walked inside.

Five heads turned in unison as he strode into the room and he saw that he was interrupting a meeting. Although the room was cool, all five men had taken their jackets off and two had removed their ties. The board table was littered with papers, empty bottles of water and glasses. Plates of Japanese pastries lay untouched on a central platter. Open files lay in front of each person.

H had expected a frosty reception after barging in unceremoniously and was somewhat surprised to see that the expression on Chairman Ogawa's face was one of welcome and relief. He waved away the woman, who was trying to explain the intrusion.

"I am most glad to see you again Agent Suzuki," he said. After introducing his vice chairman, his finance director and two heads of departments, he asked H to take a seat.

"The news is not good. When you left earlier, I started asking questions about Nomura and his work here. It appears that he has not been in the building for two days. He did not call in sick and his mobile is on messaging. This is most unusual. Mister Uchida here is Nomura's immediate superior and the director in charge of our weapons research department. He can explain the situation to you."

Uchida was a dolorous looking man, who appeared to wish himself elsewhere and it was obvious that he would have preferred to let his chairman pass on the bad news. He cleared his throat loudly before beginning. "I hardly know where to start. Our illustrious company had always prided itself on our security arrangements. They are rigorous and stringent. Never, in our history has such a situation occurred."

Ogawa cut in, "Please get to the point, Uchida, and tell Agent Suzuki what he needs to know."

"I apologise, Mister Chairman, but this has affected me so much that… in short, I must admit that Nomura has betrayed our trust in an unprecedented way. Someone should have noticed… "

Ogawa could stand it no longer. "Recriminations and finger pointing can come later. It appears, Agent Suzuki, that Nomura has stolen vital and extremely valuable data. Uchida has just confirmed that the records of everything Nomura has been working on have been deleted from our computer system. His research notes have also vanished. We have been discussing what best to do." He paused to take a drink of water.

"What *was* he was working on and how important is it?" H asked.

"After over two years of research, Nomura had devised a totally new type of explosive. In the wrong hands, his invention could have catastrophic results."

H tried to keep his temper in check. Two wasted days in which they might have had a chance to avert the devastation of the train crash. He asked to speak to the Chairman alone. Ogawa nodded and the four men got to their feet, gathered their jackets and papers and filed out of the room.

"It is likely that your stolen data has already been used. I must tell you that Mister Nomura was murdered this morning." Ogawa's mouth fell open. "If we'd been notified earlier," H said sternly, "it is possible that we might have been able to avert the train crash and avoid the deaths of 108 innocent people and over 200 wounded." Ogawa looked bewildered. "What train crash?" he asked.

H found it hard to believe that he hadn't heard the news, but then remembered that Ogawa had been to a family funeral the day before and had probably arrived at his office early that morning. He explained what had happened and that the specialists were still baffled about the cause of the explosion.

"Make a list of your competitors who'd be most likely to want to purchase Nomura's invention," H told him, "We'll take it from there. It seems probable that Nomura downloaded everything onto a memory stick and has already sold it to the highest bidder. We must hope that it hasn't fallen into the hands of a terrorist organisation."

Ogawa looked stunned at the news. "I can hardly *believe* what you are telling me. I feel I must disclose that there *was* some bad feeling. Nomura felt he deserved more tangible recognition for his work, but it never occurred to me that he would sell-out. This is a dreadful situation and now you tell me that he is dead and is responsible for a disaster. What can I say? I am totally appalled."

As H had the information he needed, he ended the meeting and left Ogawa wondering what the effect would be on his shareholders and company share price. It now seemed certain that Nomura and his invention were responsible for the crash. The earlier suspects, Hamza Hamidou and Dai Lin were now of secondary importance. He rang Tanaka to relay the news.

Chapter 11

Tokyo

Tanaka asked H if he would accompany him and his wife to Yori Nakano's *tsuya,* the wake, which was due to take place on the following day. Before going to bed H prepared everything he needed. He laid out a black suit, a white shirt and a black tie. Nakano had been a Buddhist, so H searched through a drawer and took out a set of *juzu* prayer beads and put his condolence money in a traditional black and silver envelope.

H was a creature of habit, not of routine, which was fortunate; in his job, routine could get you killed. Two or three mornings a week he started his day with a five mile run or an hour of parkour. Some days he went straight to the well-equipped gym at HQ for a work-out, or practiced martial arts with like-minded intelligence agents. At least one day a week he used the Olympic sized swimming pool at a private members' club. He'd been brought up by the sea and had developed a remarkable lung capacity, which had saved his life on more than one occasion. His ability to stay underwater for long periods of time was legendary, but he needed to maintain that strength. Occasionally he drove across the city to a retirement home and sanctuary for special-forces and secret service operatives. He had many old friends and mentors there and liked to join them in their daily Tai Chi routines in the peaceful garden.

As usual, he got up early and decided to go for a run. He pulled on a light tracksuit, a pair of his favourite Nike Pegasus 32 running shoes and his Garmin fēnix 3 multisport GPS watch. The sun was shining.

It was a glorious, fresh morning and he was gratified to find that he'd exceeded his best time for the distance by thirty eight seconds.

When he got back to his flat, Maru, his housekeeper had given his suit a brush, prepared his breakfast and placed two daily newspapers on the dining table. He had a shower and dressed in his funereal clothes before sitting down to eat and was just taking his first sip of coffee as he unfolded the first paper. Staring up at him was a photograph of the beautiful woman he'd bumped into on Nomura's doorstep the day before.

The headline read, **DISAPPEARANCE OF TOP MODEL**.

Celebrated Japanese super-model Sora Mori was caught-up in an aggressive raid, whilst visiting a shelter for battered women yesterday. Two members of staff were injured trying to repel the surprise attack (but have since been discharged from Kitahara International Hospital).

Miss Mori (featured on the front cover of this month's Vogue Japan) was abducted in broad daylight along with seven other young women and they have not been seen since. Police are 'following up leads,' but have yet to issue an official statement. Unconfirmed reports suggest that the police may have uncovered a possible link to human trafficking.

A spokeswoman for the Shelter told our reporter that 4 masked men, carrying sawn-off shotguns had entered the building at 11.35. "They were shouting," she said, "and ordered everyone to stand against the wall. Miss Mori, our honoured guest and 7 other women were dragged out of the line. It was chaos and we were all confused. It happened so quickly and there was much screaming. The women were hustled out into the street and I could see them being bundled into the back of a waiting van. Two of our staff bravely tried to intervene, but were clubbed down without mercy. These poor women come to our shelter because they have nowhere else to go. They are abused in their own homes and come to us for safety and shelter. We pray that they will be found unharmed."

Two further paragraphs condemned the fact that such barbarity could happen in the city and were followed by a criticism of society in general for failing moral standards. The piece ended with an appeal from the newspaper for anyone who might have further information, to contact the police immediately and a strongly worded condemnation of 'this cowardly act'.

H read it through twice before ringing his uncle to tell him about the article and that this woman was Jiro Nomura's sister Natsumi. Sora Mori was her professional, modelling name.

When H and the Tanakas arrived at the *tsuya* they expressed their sympathies to the family. Mrs Tanaka comforted the widow, who was her oldest friend. Tanaka – suddenly looking much older – spent a few minutes with Nakano's eldest son, who'd organised the ceremony. When the priest arrived to speak to the family, they moved to find seats a little further back. Shortly afterwards, the priest began the service by chanting a section from a *sutra,* the traditional religious scriptures.

As Nakano had been a popular man, both at work and in the community, a large crowd had gathered to pay their respects. The men all wore black suits and the women were in black dresses or black kimonos. H couldn't wait to get away. He was well aware that the Tanaka's and Nakano's had secretly hoped that he might one day marry Nakano's plain daughter and had thrown them together over the years. Whenever he looked around, he was dismayed to find that her slightly protuberant eyes were trying to catch his, both before and after the service. He'd known and liked her for years, but she would definitely have to look elsewhere for a husband.

Finally back in the car on their way to HQ, H heaved a rather guilty sigh of relief. His thoughts turned to Sora Mori/Nomura and wondered where to start looking for her.

Chapter 12

Meuron – Near L'isle Sur La Sorgue, France

Maurice was thankful that he'd decided to pack his best suit. It would have been unthinkable, as well as disrespectful to have attended the funeral improperly dressed. It was a beautiful and moving service and the little church was overflowing with mourners and flowers.

Maurice said a silent prayer, hoping that Monique would rest in peace. He felt comforted that so many people had attended to pay their final respects.

After the service, the congregation filed past the coffin; each person sprinkling it with holy water and dropping some money into a collection bowl. Once outside, they walked down the narrow pathway to the family mausoleum, blinking in the strong sunlight, after the dim interior of the church.

He looked around, noticing the family group, with the veiled mother, weeping gently into a handkerchief edged with black lace. She was supported on one side by a distinguished looking man, who was obviously Monique's father and on the other, by a blank-faced young man of about twenty. Other relatives stood around them in a protective semi-circle. Many of the mourners had evidently been school and college friends, who banded together, many of them in tears.

Another collection of people stood together a little apart from the rest. At the front was a tall, arresting looking man, with a thin face and silver hair, who was dressed in a perfectly tailored, dark suit and sombre tie. At his side was a tiny, chic, bird-like woman. Directly behind them were four men, in less well-cut suits, with dark glasses and a watchful air. Also a part of this group was a number of serious looking men and women in their twenties and thirties, who spoke together in quiet tones. From what little he had known of Monique, he supposed them to be her old boss and his wife; several were probably bodyguards and the rest, her colleagues in the French Secret Service.

As Maurice knew no one, he decided that he'd leave after the interment. He went to pay his respects to the family and then retraced his steps to the porch of the church, where he'd seen a book of condolences, on a black covered table. He signed his name and address and walked back into the sunshine, standing aside to allow two other people to enter the porch. A few moments later, he heard a quick step behind him and turned to see the silver haired man he'd noticed earlier.

"Monsieur Duval?" he said. "I wonder if I might have a word."

Maurice put out his hand, which was taken into a firm grip as the man smiled at him.

"Are you, by any chance a Master Baker?" Maurice nodded in surprise and returned the smile. "My name is Aristide de Lamerie and Monique Lavalle worked for me. I remember seeing your name and the town of Boissy in one of Monique's reports and she spoke most kindly of you and the assistance you gave her.

My wife is feeling indisposed, so I have decided to spend the night here, to allow her to rest. We will return to Paris tomorrow. As I shall be alone, I wonder if you might like to join me for dinner?"

Maurice accepted with pleasure.

Despite the sad circumstances, the evening was a success. The two men found they had an instant rapport and were soon on first name terms. Maurice told stories of his time in the French Foreign Legion and was delighted to find that de Lamerie knew his old commander. They swapped stories over an excellent dinner and de Lamerie said that he'd known Monique since she was a small child and explained how she'd come to work for him.

After the table had been cleared, they sat over cups of coffee and glasses of cognac. Maurice felt he could ask some of the questions that had been on his mind. The newspaper article, announcing Monique's death in a 'climbing accident' had not convinced him.

"I must admit," he began, "that my curiosity has been roused about what happened to Monique and her mysterious collaborator."

De Lamerie looked at him thoughtfully and took a sip of cognac before replying. "As I'm sure you realised, the official line we put out of the climbing accident was fabricated to save the family more heartbreak. You'll appreciate that I'm not at liberty to disclose the details, but what little I *am* able to tell you must stay between ourselves." Maurice nodded.

"Monique died on active service. Her bravery and dedication will not go unremembered; but it must remain private. We believe that she didn't suffer and that her death was swift. It may be of consolation to you that she and Hiroshi Suzuki became very close. Although he is no longer in France, I have been kept informed of his situation. Largely thanks to the excellent care you gave him, he's made a full recovery from his wounds. Lives were saved, Maurice: probably many thousands are alive today due to the work of Monique and Agent Suzuki."

"Thank you for telling me and you may rest assured that it will go no further. I'm glad to know a little more. I must say that I never got to hear the name Hiroshi Suzuki. I shall not forget it."

Maurice thanked him for the evening and drove back to his brother's house. Later that night, he was lying in bed, sleepily thinking about what he'd been told. One small point had interested him greatly. In passing, de Lamerie had mentioned Hiroshi's beloved Bentley, which, he said had crashed in the Château grounds. What had happened to the car? Maurice suddenly felt wide awake.

When he returned home to Boissy, he would find out.

Chapter 13

A Derelict Warehouse – Tokyo

They could cry no more. The eight young women lay huddled together for warmth like a litter of puppies and most of them had fallen into an exhausted sleep. Sora Mori was awake and bitterly cold; her arms were numb from holding close the two girls on either side. It was almost completely dark, but she gently removed her left arm and pressed a button on her watch. The digital numbers lit up and showed her that the time was 11.57.

It was over twelve hours since they'd been abducted from the shelter. In the space of a couple of days, she'd been through two terrifying experiences. Could both events be linked? Was it possible that her abduction could be as a result of what her brother had done? Sora wracked her brains, but couldn't work out a connection.

After the gunmen had herded them into the street at gunpoint, they'd been pushed roughly into the back of a large van. She remembered shouting to bystanders, screaming for help, but the few people she saw had simply stood with their mouths open and no one had moved. One of the gunmen had punched her on the side of her head and she couldn't remember anything about the drive. The next thing she knew was being pulled out of the van. Her legs had buckled and she'd been yanked to her feet and hustled away with the other girls. They were taken to a derelict warehouse, which had a glass roof with broken panes. The men had led the girls into some kind of storage room and bolted the door behind them. It was cold and smelled faintly of fish. There was a single window, but far too high up to see out of or to escape from. In the dim light they saw that their prison contained a lavatory pan in one corner, a crate of bottled water on the floor and a few, dirty blankets. There was a brief, undignified tussle between the girls to secure the meagre bits of warmth these blankets could provide.

Several of the girls started to cry and although Sora hadn't yet said a word, they turned to her naturally. They'd all seen her in magazines and knew she was successful and famous. A little older than the rest of the group, she had an undefined air of experience and confidence, which set her apart. They crowded round her, asking what was going to happen to them.

"We'll know soon enough," she said. "For now, we really need to try and keep calm. We don't know how long we'll be kept here, so let's ration the water. Has anyone got a mobile phone?"

They told her that their phones had been confiscated and their cash and credit cards taken from them in the van, but for some reason they'd been allowed to keep what was left in their handbags. Sora realised that her own bag was still with her. The long strap had been over her shoulder and she'd managed to hang onto it, without knowing. They'd taken her phone and wallet. Also missing was her day's itinerary, listing her appearance at the shelter. Her passport had also gone.

"Let's sit close together, to try and keep warm," she suggested.

Hours later, they'd exhausted every possible avenue of conversation and some started to doze. One of the younger girls disturbed them all by having hysterics. Screaming that she couldn't stand it, she beat on the door, pleading to be let out. Her cries went unanswered and some of the others begged her to shut up. Sora got wearily to her feet and managed to coax the sobbing girl to sit down again and tried to console her.

At some stage Sora must have fallen asleep and it was light outside when she opened her eyes. Her head ached from the punch she'd taken and she was shivering with cold. Looking through her handbag, she found a couple of Paracetamol and swallowed them with a few sips of the bottled water. Gradually she became aware of noises coming from outside. Trying not to disturb the others, she crept over to the door. There was a cold draft blowing over her feet and she noticed that there was a gap between the floor and the base of the door. Lying flat and turning her head sideways, she found that she could make out three different voices.

The three men were arguing and she heard her own name mentioned. One of the girls woke up and asked her what was going on. Sora put a finger to her lips.

After several minutes the voices stopped. Now she wasn't aware of the cold or her headache anymore. All she was conscious of was fear and a rising sense of panic. The men had seen her face and name on the front page of the morning newspaper. As they now knew that she was famous, two of them were worried that the police would redouble their efforts. One suggested they kill her immediately and get rid of her body, before moving the rest of the 'stock' somewhere else. He was frighteningly persuasive. Sora was holding her breath and gave a gasp of relief when the other two disagreed. They said that it would be madness and wanted no part of it. The last thing she heard before the footsteps moved away was their decision to ring someone higher up in the organisation for instructions.

The dishevelled girls were all awake when half an hour later, the key turned in the lock and the door was banged back on its hinges. Two men wearing balaclavas marched in, shouting at the girls to get up and stand against the wall. As they spotted Sora they pulled her forcibly out of the line, whilst the other girls shrank away.

A black hood was pulled over her head and her hands were tied behind her back. One girl screamed and burst into noisy tears, but subsided when one of the captors stepped forward and punched her in the face and kicked her as she fell to the floor, bellowing at her to shut up. The other man said, "not on the face, you idiot."

Sora was dragged out. They picked her up and carried her for some way, before lifting her into the back of the van they'd arrived in the day before. As it accelerated out of the warehouse, Sora was thrown to the floor. With her hands tied, she landed awkwardly and rolled around as she struggled until she finally managed to wedge herself against something firm. She soon gave up trying to remember the sequence of turns and after about twenty minutes the van drove down a steep ramp and came to a halt.

The doors opened and the two men who pulled her out seemed to find it amusing that she'd been thrown around like a ragdoll. They took off their balaclavas and removed her hood and handcuffs. It was then that she saw that she was in an underground car park. They took her by the arms and led her into a waiting lift. It was smartly decorated, with walls panelled in wood and mirrors. She hardly recognised herself in the mirror. The elegant suit she'd put on the morning before was crumpled and dirty. Her hair had come loose from its chignon and she looked a complete mess. Before the lift stopped, she tried to tie her hair back off her face, but her hands were shaking too much. As the doors slid open, she found herself in the empty lobby of a palatial apartment. She was hustled into an unoccupied bedroom. The door was shut and locked behind her.

Almost an hour passed before they came for her.

Chapter 14

Tokyo

"The boss wants to see you," Mai-Li told H as he arrived at the office. H smiled and kissed her cheek before walking through Tanaka's door. He found his uncle standing in the centre of the room, deep in thought and frowning at a bank of television screens.

After waiting for a moment, H cleared his throat and asked, "you wanted to see me, sir?"

"I'm afraid I need to pull you off your current case," Tanaka said, turning away from the screens and sitting down behind his desk. "As you are no doubt aware, Hiroshi, our political situation with the Chinese has been deteriorating for some time, which worries me greatly. There are constant incursions into our waters and if they are not exactly sabre-rattling, they are daily becoming more provocative in their actions. We are on a precipice.

We received an approach from one of their senior generals almost two years ago and – at some considerable danger to himself – he's been able to provide us with some useful information. I heard this morning that he believes someone may be onto him and he wants to defect. However, he is being extremely cautious and will only come over to us if certain stipulations are met. I have no problem with agreeing to most of them. I want to put you in charge of bringing him in. Speed is of the essence and we need to make sure this goes smoothly. If they *are* onto him, his life is certainly in danger and who knows what he might tell them under interrogation. His wife is from The Philippines and he has had permission to join her on a visit to her family. With luck he should be on his way. Your flight leaves for Manila at 9 p.m. tonight. If all goes well, you should be back in Tokyo within a couple of days.

In the meantime, I'd like you to go and search the flat of Miss Nomura, or Mori, or whatever she calls herself. I have a feeling that she may be the key to unlocking her brother's secrets.

Before leaving HQ, H checked in with Kyuji and the others who'd been assigned to follow up leads on the Bullet Train explosion. Agent Sun had been given the job of identifying the unusual tattoos, which H had photographed on the body of Jiro Nomura's female assassin. He'd managed to establish that they were symbols of a Chinese underworld gang. After his conversation with his uncle, H had found this Chinese connection particularly interesting. He congratulated Sun, who was frustrated that he hadn't yet been able to work out how his findings tied-into the killing.

"Keep working all of our Chinese sources and see what else you can find out about this gang; particularly about female members," he told Sun.

H called for everyone's attention. "The boss has given me an assignment, which means I'll be away for a day or two, but I want to be kept in the loop with any developments."

One of the younger agents asked if he should continue trying to track down the two men whose names had been flagged at Kyoto station. H shook his head. "Put them on the back burner for now. We need to focus our attention on Jiro Nomura. Concentrate on finding out who he could have sold his invention to. Another priority is to find Nomura's sister. Who abducted her, where is she now and what do they want with her? Is there a tie-in to the bombing? We need to know quickly. Also, I saw her coming away from her brother's block of flats and when I looked at his body again, I felt that it had been moved. I'd love to know if she was looking for something in particular and whether or not she found it."

Kyuji looked up from his computer screen. "I'm looking at the police report of that restaurant shooting two days ago. Sora Mori was dining there when it happened and gave a statement. The next day she got abducted with those other girls."

"That's interesting," H said. "Get onto the restaurant and see if they have a security camera, I'd like to know whom she was having lunch with. Follow up on what she told the police and dig deeper into the shooting."

H updated Tanaka before heading off to Sora Mori's apartment. He'd arranged to meet the police there and was given free access to join the search. The inspector was a helpful man, with whom he'd worked before and there was no inter-departmental jealousy between them.

Although they didn't turn up much of interest, it gave H a better insight into Sora's personality. Her style appealed to him, from the furniture to the pictures on the walls. It seemed she had no personal vanity, as none of her modelling images were on display, but there were several family photos. The rooms smelled pleasant, but there were vases of slightly wilting flowers on various tables. Everything was tidy and spotlessly clean. It was significantly larger than her brother's place and in a more upscale location. H checked the titles of her large collection of books and found an eclectic mix of Japanese and Western novels: beauty and fashion publications, recipe books, keep-fit and yoga titles as well as some Japanese poetry and modern biographies. Her bathroom cabinet showed that the only prescription medicine she took was something strong for migraine headaches. There was an unopened bottle of sleeping pills. The rest of the shelves carried a selection of expensive bath and beauty products. There was no evidence that she was on any contraceptive pills. Although searching through people's personal possessions was something he'd had to do many times before, H felt like a voyeur, but still gave her clothes a thorough search.

The inspector showed H her engagements diary, but it was uninformative apart from the entry of her lunch appointment two days earlier, where she'd written, *'Lunch J, 12.00'*. He copied the contents of her laptop onto a memory stick, which he'd study later.

After thanking the inspector and his team for their professional courtesy, H just had time to collect his 'ready-bag' from his flat before heading off for the airport.

Chapter 15

Quan's Offices – Tokyo

Quan sat behind her desk, talking to a Chinese general on her encrypted telephone. Her feet rested on a Perspex box hidden discretely out of sight. A silver ice bucket held an open bottle of Louis Roederer Cristal and a tray of her favourite canapés was placed within easy reach of her plump fingers.

"My dear general," she said, sipping her champagne, "I *knew* that you'd appreciate my little demonstration. This was never in doubt. The Japanese defence minister will trouble us no more. He was getting tiresome and I felt that this trial run was a suitable occasion to get rid of him. As the Chinese proverb says, the demonstration enabled us to 'kill two eagles with one arrow.' "

She listened to his response with a complacent smile, but a quiet scratching at the door made her cover the receiver with her hand and shout, "I said *no* interruptions." Lowering her tone she said, "Yes, General, naturally I'm keeping abreast of the worsening political situation. It's exactly what we've been working for. Let's not misunderstand each other. You will get the credit due to you, the kudos and no doubt, a promotion. I will remain behind the scenes and make serious amounts of money providing the necessary weaponry." She allowed him to ramble on, listening to his comments with concealed impatience. "If we keep our heads, we'll both end up with what we want," she concluded.

After switching off the phone, she poured herself another glass and ate several of the remaining canapés. Stupid, stupid man, she grumbled to herself: like all men, he's conceited and never satisfied. Another tentative knock on the door enraged her and picking up the champagne bottle, she threw it at the closed door. It bounced down onto the carpet and rolled a short way, leaving a trail of bubbles.

"What *is* it?" she shouted angrily, "it had better be something important."

A nervous looking woman put her head around the half open door, expecting another missile to come her way. "You asked to be informed, Madam, when those two men of yours brought the girl here."

"And when *did* they show up?" Quan asked.

"A little less than forty minutes ago, Madam," she answered hesitantly.

"Why has it taken you this long to tell me?" Quan asked ominously.

The girl hung her head. Hoping to appease her employer she said. "I put the girl they brought with them next door, in the Dragon Suite, having received no direct instructions. Zheng is keeping an eye on her. Ning is also waiting to see you." Quan looked at her for a long time before saying, "go." The girl retreated.

The underlings could wait, Quan decided. Walking over to a small, silk painting of egrets wading in a stream, she moved it sideways to expose a two-way mirror. I should have had her killed immediately, she thought, looking at Sora, but what a terrible waste it would be.

Ning – one of a team of female bodyguards and hired killers on Quan's payroll – waited nervously for her employer to hear her report. She stood stiffly, with her injured hand behind her back, looking first at Quan and then glancing over her shoulder to where Zheng stood behind her. All of Quan's staff were terrified of the large, female mute, Zheng, who was Quan's long-term head of security.

"I regret to inform you that we had ... problems," she began. "We found Nomura in his flat, but he needed some persuading before he turned over the laptop you wanted. As ordered, once we had it, we terminated him." She paused, but Quan stared at her and made no comment. "We were about to leave when a man appeared, holding a gun. We were able to escape, but he followed us. Dongmai was unfortunately hit by a truck and killed. However, all is not lost. I have the laptop." Bowing low, she handed it to Quan, who beckoned Zheng forward, saying, "check it".

As the machine was powered up, Quan asked: "This man. What was he like?" Ning considered and replied, "He spoke fluent Japanese, but he looked more like a westerner."

Zheng clapped her hands once to attract her employer's attention. She placed the laptop on the desk, but shook her head and made a movement with her hands, indicating bad news. Quan grabbed the laptop and scrolled through the icons. Everything had been scrubbed and the data had vanished. Her eyes turned glacial and she started to breath heavily. Opening a desk drawer she pulled out a handgun and screeched at Ning. "You ... have ... failed ... me ... and you will suffer." Without a pause, she shot Ning in the left kneecap, followed by the right and then put two more shots into the woman's elbows, as she fell to the floor, howling in agony.

"Finish her off," she told Zheng. Ning was hauled to her feet with Zheng's huge hands on either side of her head. One twist was all it took to break Ning's neck.

"Clean up the mess," Quan said, before walking out of the room.

Meanwhile, when she'd been left alone, Sora had investigated her new prison. She had no idea where she was, or why she'd been brought here, but was vaguely heartened by the comparison with where she'd spent the night before. It was an exotically and opulently furnished bedroom and her feet sank into the thick rugs as she explored. A bathroom leading off the bedroom was equipped with an enormous circular bath and gold taps. She washed her hands and scrubbed a few spots of dried blood off her face, before drying her hands on an embroidered linen towel. These simple, familiar actions calmed her a little and finding a set of tortoiseshell brushes and combs laid out, she re-arranged her hair. Turning back to the bedroom she walked over to the window of the Dragon Suite, looking down on the familiar Tokyo landmarks, trying to work out where she was.

A few minutes later the door opened and someone marched in and slammed the door. Sora turned and was confronted by the ugliest woman she'd ever seen. She was a mountain, not a person. She wore track pants and a black singlet. Taller than most Japanese men, she was heavily muscled and her arms and chest were covered with tattoos. The woman smiled and looked her up and down. She pointed to an armchair as Sora asked, "where am I and why have I been brought here?" In two swift strides the mountain swooped down and backhanded her across the face. Sora gasped as she was picked up and thrown onto the chair. The mountain towered over her as she shrank back against the cushions and closed her eyes. Then she felt a gentle hand caress her smarting cheek, her eyes snapped open again and before she could do anything to resist, the woman leant down and kissed her full on the lips. She leered at Sora before turning and walking out of the room, locking the door behind her.

After two nights with almost no sleep Sora was too tired to process what was happening. She curled herself into a ball and burst into tears. When she did look up, the dragons on the wallpaper seemed to dance and writhe in front of her and by the time she heard the key in the lock again, her nerves were frayed to shreds. Another woman had come into the room; someone less overtly alarming, but no less ugly.

Chapter 16

Manila – The Philippeans

In H's experience, whenever he was given a quick in-and-out job, which sounded simple, things were bound to be anything but straightforward. This assignment proved to be no exception.

He'd arrived in Manila on a tourist visa with a false passport and a fake identity. From the details Tanaka had given him, he'd made contact with General Wu and arranged to meet him at an anonymous coffee shop in the city centre. H spent the intervening time making preparations. During a short telephone call to a private clinic in the city he spoke to a doctor who had helped the Japanese Secret Service in the past. Without mentioning the patient's name, he explained what he wanted and asked him to book the General in for some medical tests that evening. He also organised an anonymous looking hire car to take himself, the General and his wife to a small airfield.

H arrived half an hour early and checked for signs of surveillance, but saw none. He watched the General arrive and order a cup of coffee. H repeated his surveillance checks and decided the General was 'clean' and not being followed. On entering the café, H introduced himself and sat down. General Wu was sweating freely and greeted him with relief. His eyes were darting around, but he listened to H's plan with intense concentration, his head nodding as he agreed to the arrangements.

H checked that nobody was watching them and then passed him a small pill, folded inside the menu. "Take this now, with a glass of water. It's harmless, but in about twenty minutes you'll feel palpitations." He saw the General looked puzzled. "It's 4mg of Ventolin, which will make your heart beat rapidly and you'll feel a shortness of breath. It's nothing to worry about and the feelings will only be temporary. I'll ring for an ambulance and accompany you to the clinic I mentioned. When we arrive, a doctor will telephone your wife and ask her to come to the clinic. This doctor has been briefed and will see you in his consulting room. When Mrs Wu arrives, you will appear to make a quick recovery and be discharged. The three of us will leave discretely for a small airfield."

Almost inevitably it was Mrs Wu – the unknown quantity – who caused the plan to start unravelling. Although H had insisted that the General should keep the whole plan strictly confidential, Wu had been unable to resist telling his wife roughly what to expect, warning her not to tell anyone until they were safely out of the Philippines and on their way to Japan. She had only confided in her dearest friend that their stay out of China might prove a protracted one. In turn, her friend had only mentioned it, in passing, to her husband, another Chinese general, who'd thought it suspicious and reported it up the line. Unaware of Mrs Wu's indiscrete tongue, H's plan was carried out and he and the General arrived at the clinic.

When Mrs Wu arrived, H thanked the doctor and was about to leave in the waiting car, when he heard the sound of heavy boots outside. He looked through the window and saw half a dozen Filipino police officers rushing up the front steps. Without hesitation, the doctor – who was being paid the equivalent of a year's salary for helping H – hurried them along a corridor and out through a back exit. He led them round a corner to the far side of the waste disposal building, where H had asked for the hire car to be left. H opened a door of the car and told General and Mrs Wu to lie low on the back seats.

After a hurried conversation with the doctor, H took him towards the back entrance to the clinic, where an empty ambulance was parked. There was only one person in sight; one of the drivers was leaning against the bonnet, smoking a cigarette. H stood by the rear doors of the ambulance and made a strangled groan. The driver walked round his vehicle to investigate. H was standing with one arm around the doctor's neck, his other hand held a Beretta to the doctor's temple. The driver was so surprised that he almost swallowed his cigarette.

"Do exactly as I tell you, or this man dies," H said.

The driver, who knew the doctor well, saw that he looked terrified. "Drive out of here," H told him. "Head for the port. Turn left and pass the front entrance with your siren on. Put your foot down and drive as fast as you can. Don't stop for anything and don't try anything clever. Do you understand me?" The man was slow to reply and the doctor groaned as H tightened his grip round his throat. The man got the picture. Throwing away his cigarette butt and hoisting himself into the driver's seat, he did exactly what H had instructed.

H smiled as he saw the police spill out of the main doors, jump into a couple of squad cars and take off in pursuit of the ambulance. He found the doctor waiting for him, rubbing his throat. "Make it look good," the Doctor said, with a resigned look. H knocked him out with a quick uppercut, lowered him to the ground, tied his wrists with a pair of zip-ties and propped him against a dumpster, where he'd soon be found. He climbed into the hire car, reassuring the frightened general and his wife, before turning right onto the road and driving off, observing the speed limits.

Thirty minutes later, H turned through the gates of an airfield and parked by a hanger. After filling in the paperwork as quickly as possible, he shook the General's hand and saw him and his wife onto a waiting Citation CJ4. He poked his head into the cockpit and was surprised to see Captain Aki Hara going through his pre-flight checks.

"Hello H," Hara said. "Twice in one week. I didn't expect to meet you again so soon." H clapped him on the shoulder and said, "I didn't know you flew fixed wing as well as helicopters."

Hara grinned, "providing it can get off the ground, I can fly anything!"

H lowered his voice, "I'd be grateful if you could get going as soon as possible. There's some urgency here and I'll be pleased to see the back of your passengers and have them safely on their way."

He didn't add that Mrs Wu had proved to be a nightmare. All the way from the Clinic she'd bitched about the way she'd been pushed around and kept complaining that she'd been unable to bring a single suitcase. Her long suffering husband looked as if he wished that he'd been able to leave her behind with her luggage.

H watched from the tarmac as the light jet taxied slowly onto the runway before turning towards his car. He was reaching for his mobile to brief Tanaka, when he saw a jeep at the gate, approaching at speed. It careered over the grass, towards the moving jet, flashing its lights and blaring its horn. H leaped into his car and raced to head it off. The pilot had seen the approaching vehicles, but was already accelerating down the runway. Pressing his accelerator to the floor, H smashed into the side of the jeep, forcing it off the runway, where it bounced over a marker flag and flipped over. Although the impact had jarred his wrists and smashed his windscreen, he punched a hole in the fractured glass, and was able to take a look at the jet. Captain Hara had managed to lift off safely, his rictus grin visible through the cockpit window as he climbed away.

Finding that the impact of the collision had wedged one of his feet under the pedals, H gingerly extricated it, before climbing stiffly out of his car. He found two injured and unconscious men in the Jeep. H switched off the ignition before checking their pulses and going through their pockets. They both carried Chinese passports and had the look of professionals. He drove off, dumped the car in the parking area of a busy train station and called Tanaka, who agreed to organise someone to retrieve the car. In case the local police found it first, H wiped it down, to obliterate any fingerprints, before making his way back to Tokyo.

Chapter 17

South Eastern France

Maurice Duval decided it was time to end his holiday and return home to his bakery. Now that he had ideas for a bit of excitement, he was eager to get started. The week he'd spent with his brother had been an enjoyable one, but now it was time to leave.

Following a final dinner with his brother, Maurice went upstairs to pack his bag and then sat down with his address book and a road atlas. He'd need the help of a couple of old friends from his French Foreign Legion days. The first number was unobtainable and the second went straight to answer-phone. Maurice sighed and left a message. The road atlas was more straightforward. He mapped-out his route the old fashioned way, with a pencil and a piece of paper.

After breakfast, Maurice thanked Yves for his hospitality and started his return trip. After almost three hours of driving, he stopped off for lunch near Auxerre and eventually arrived in the picturesque city of Montargis in the Loire Valley in mid afternoon. He drove slowly towards the centre, over canal bridges and finally pulled into the car park of an old fashioned inn. He checked into a small, but clean room and tried his friend again. Pascal Garnier answered at the first ring and professed himself delighted to hear from Maurice. They arranged to meet for dinner that evening, when Pascal finished work at a local bank.

Maurice felt like some fresh air and wanted to stretch his legs. He explored the town and spent an enjoyable hour at Maison Mazet, the home of praline, on Place Mirabeau and came away inspired with ideas for new recipes.

Over steak frites and a bottle of Cabernet Sauvignon, Maurice and Pascal caught up with six years of news. At their last, riotous Legion reunion, thirty middle aged men had drunk themselves under the table and behaved like adolescents. Maurice was glad to see that Pascal still looked trim and fit. He said that he ran for an hour every morning and also helped out at a local boys' club, teaching martial arts and coaching their football team.

As they ordered some more frites, Maurice asked, "*A propos*, whatever happened to Henri Davoust? Do you ever see him?"

"*Mon Adjudant*! yes, I saw him about a year ago. He always was a lucky bastard and he's recently had a windfall. An uncle died and left him a house and a good business."

"*Sacré veinard,* lucky fellow," Maurice said, blotting his small moustache with his napkin. "What sort of business?"

"It had to do with cars, I think. It's either a car hire business or a garage; something like that." He pulled an iPad Mini out of his pocket and tapped a few buttons. "Here's his new address and phone number." He jotted the details onto a piece of paper and passed it across the table. "It seems you are almost neighbours. He lives at Tallois, which is not far from Boissy."

This would fit perfectly with what Maurice had in mind. He signalled to the waiter and ordered another bottle of wine.

"I miss the old days," Pascal said, digging into a tall glass of *Café Liégeois* and going on to recall some of their more hair-raising adventures. "After what we went through together, working in a bank is mundane work, if you understand me." Maurice understood only too well.

The evening was getting late. They were the only customers left in the bistro and the two remaining staff were obviously waiting to close-up. They divided the bill and walked slowly back towards Maurice's hotel.

"It's good to see you again, old friend," Maurice said. "I'm sure that your work keeps you fully occupied, but, perhaps I might be able to ... how shall I say ... give you a brief break in the tedium."

"Maurice, you old dog; what do you have in mind?"

"I miss the excitement too. I *do* have a scheme, but it's only in the planning stage at the moment. If I needed you – plus one or two of the old gang – might you consider helping me for a day or two?"

"I'd jump at the chance."

They'd reached the hotel and said goodnight on the pavement. "If I decide to go ahead," Maurice said, "I'll call you in the next few days.

Pascal clapped him on both shoulders and walked off with a light step, whistling one of their old marching songs.

Chapter 18

Secret Service HQ – Tokyo

When H limped into Tanaka's office the following afternoon, he found Kyuji in conference with Tanaka. In the heat of the moment at the airstrip, he'd hardly noticed that when he'd trapped his foot under the accelerator pedal, he'd wrenched his ankle.

"I think we'll have someone look at that, before we get started," Tanaka said frowning as he noticed blood seeping through a make-shift bandage wrapped around H's left hand.

"It's nothing, sir," H said wearily. He was ignored and within a few moments a nurse arrived and unwrapped a nasty looking gash along the outside of his hand, which he'd cut when punching his fist through the windscreen. The nurse checked that he was up to date with anti-tetanus vaccinations, then cleaned the wound and applied three Steri-Strips before covering it with a more professional dressing.

"Let's summarise what we know so far," Tanaka said after the door had closed behind the nurse. "You'll be glad to hear that General Wu arrived safely and is now going through a lengthy debriefing at one of our safe houses. What went wrong, Hiroshi?"

"I believe that the leak must have come through Mrs. Wu," H began, before bringing them up to date with what had happened at the Clinic and the airfield. "The two in the Jeep were carrying Chinese passports. I had no time to interrogate them and left before any of the local police turned up and started asking awkward questions."

"I foresee a tedious conversation with the Philippine authorities," Tanaka said, making a note on a pad in front of him. "Wu is keen to talk and is singing like a canary. His information should prove invaluable in ascertaining Chinese military plans. Well done in getting him out, Hiroshi." He turned to Kyuji and asked him to fill H in on some more developments.

"Glad to see you, more or less in one piece," Kyuji said. "We have two updates for you. We've discovered who was behind that restaurant shooting. It was organised – rather ineptly – by Jiro Nomura's superior, Mister Uchida. We had a call from the Chairman, Atsushi Ogawa. Apparently Uchida was overcome with shame that his brightest protégé had turned traitor and sold company secrets. To expunge the ignominy, he hired some hit men to dispose of Nomura. When he found that, not only had his plan failed, but other people had been injured, he saw no other course but to commit Seppuku. Ogawa informed us and the police. So that's one mystery solved.

We also have a lead on Miss Sora Mori. Her passport was used yesterday and she's on the passenger manifest of a private jet, which left Tokyo yesterday evening, bound for Cork in the Republic of Ireland."

"Who owns the jet and who else was on board?" H asked.

"The plane is registered to Armstec International. It's on our list as one of KIBO's main competitors. The Chairman, Madam Chow Lee Quan is a Chinese billionaire. She was on board, with one other woman named Zheng, who is listed as private security consultant. There was a crew of seven: her personal pilot and an Irish co-pilot, Orla Flynn, plus three stewardesses. For some reason, there were also two extra pilots on board. I queried the Irish girl and was told that she was a last minute replacement for the usual co-pilot, who came down with a stomach bug and couldn't fly."

We have no information as to why this woman Quan is going to Ireland," Tanaka said. "I'd like you to follow them, Hiroshi and find out what she's up to. Quan is our most likely suspect in the train bombing. At this time, Miss Mori is an unknown quantity. I'll call my opposite number and get permission for you to operate in Ireland. Mai-Li has your tickets ready and you leave in the morning."

After spending one night at Quan's apartment, Sora was taken on a shopping spree, accompanied by Zheng. They spent the morning in Dover Street Market,

in the Ginza area of Tokyo visiting the most expensive boutiques. Quan had provided her with a list of what she would need and told her that the budget was unlimited. Zheng didn't leave her side for a second, even going with her into the changing rooms.

Although Quan had insisted she go out wearing a headscarf and large wrap-around sunglasses, Sora's much publicised face was so well-known in Japan, she was recognised and photographed several times as she walked around. In moments the pictures would be uploaded to social media sites. In any other circumstances Sora would have been thrilled with a new wardrobe, but her pleasure was dimmed by the constant proximity of the terrifying Zheng. Designer handbags: shoes, suits, silk underwear, long evening dresses, cocktail dresses, nightwear, wraps, scarves, hats and some more casual trousers, silk blouses and cashmere cardigans were chosen and added to the growing piles. The sales assistants fawned over her and said that everything would be delivered to Madam Quan's apartment that afternoon.

The final things on the list were a dressing case: a complete selection of make-up and beauty products along with several large Louis Vuitton suitcases. Sora was then returned to her luxury prison. When her purchases arrived, Sora was given lunch alone, whilst three, uniformed maids packed the cases.

At four o'clock Zheng took her up to the roof of the building, where a Sikorsky S-76 helicopter was waiting, with rotors turning. Quan was already inside and patted the seat beside her. "We're going on a little trip together," she shouted, over the din. "I hope you enjoyed your morning and found everything you wanted."

On their arrival at the airport, bypassing the VIP and private passengers' terminal area, the helicopter pilot set down on the tarmac beside an enormous Boeing Business Jet, which was painted matt black. Sora had never travelled in such luxury. She was reminded of the film Pretty Woman and only wished that she had Richard Gere as her escort, rather than the dumpy, middle-aged horror beside her. The interior of the plane was vast and decorated with the finest of everything. Sora took in the generous seats, which were covered in black linen, flower arrangements, stacks of the latest magazines and newspapers from around the world. Two bottles of vintage champagne sat ready in an ice bucket beside a large bowl of caviar, set into crushed ice, with mother-of-pearl spoons. There were also several plates of Quan's favourite canapés on black onyx topped tables.

The Captain came through and asked Madam Quan if she was ready to depart. He mentioned that they would be landing at Dubai International Airport in about seven hours' time and an estimated time of arrival in Cork the following day. He started to mention the time differences, so they could change their watches, but Quan had lost interest and waved him away.

When they'd levelled off, two beautiful stewardesses started to prepare for dinner in a separate dining area. All of the cabin crew were dressed in bespoke black uniforms designed by the Japanese fashion house Sacai. Quan seemed in excellent spirits and throughout the meal discoursed on the benefits of private air travel and various places she had visited recently.

When the meal was over, Quan took Sora by the hand and led her through a door into a bedroom, decorated in sybaritic, but questionable taste, with a mirrored ceiling.

"Finally, my dear, we are alone and can get to know each other properly." With a sinking feeling of horror, Sora realised that this revolting woman had her completely in her power. As a famous model, it wasn't the first time she'd been approached by a woman, but her tastes were entirely heterosexual and she'd always managed to fend off any unwelcome advances.

As she stood beside the circular bed, covered in pink satin sheets, Sora shrank away as Quan came towards her. "My dear girl, it's obvious that getting into bed with a woman is something new to you, but believe me when I say that I will give you more pleasure than you could ever have dreamed of in your wildest imaginings. You may not think so yet, but in a very little time you will see that I am right. We have all night and will not be disturbed. I am prepared to be patient with you ... up to a point, but you will find it better to acquiesce freely and with a mind open to new thrills and satisfaction. As you have already seen, I can be more than generous to those I am fond of, and I find your beauty and modesty incredibly attractive." She stepped nearer and wound her fingers into Sora's hair, pulling her still closer and whispering in her ear, "Zheng wants you too. You would not find her either gentle or patient. Now, be sensible and take off your clothes."

It seemed to Sora that the night would never end. Her mind tried to block out the disgust and degradation she felt, but by far the worst thing was that she was betrayed by her own body. Quan had spoken the truth, she took things slowly and was so skilful and experienced that eventually Sora heard herself moan with pleasure, as tears of shame squeezed out from her tightly shut eyelids. At long last, she was allowed to sleep.

Part Two

Chapter 19

H collected his tickets from Mai-Li, Tanaka's P.A. and took the 11.35 JAL flight from Tokyo's Haneda Airport the following morning. He flipped through a couple of the magazines in the rack and noticed several adverts featuring Sora Mori. He needed to find out more about her, which would be no hardship. He ran a finger over her perfect features, wondering what she was like. He admired her fine bone structure: her flawless skin, her long neck, her small, neat ears and moulded lips. There was something a little lost and innocent in her expression and he sensed vulnerability, as well as intelligence in her eyes.

H had many unanswered questions. Why had she been abducted and by whom? Why was she travelling with Quan and what was their relationship? Did she know about her brother's connection with Quan and was she complicit in their plans? What was Quan planning to do in Ireland? With all these thoughts swirling around his brain, H closed his eyes and slept for several hours.

During the rest of the twelve and a half hours flight, H read a trashy novel, completed several Sudoku puzzles and belatedly found an interesting article about Quan in Time Magazine. It provided some useful background on her career. Although Quan was smiling in each of the photos, H felt repulsed by her hard featured face and gross body. She certainly had an excellent mind and was a phenomenally successful businesswoman. She was a notable philanthropist and the article listed a variety of causes to whom she'd given millions. Alongside the well-known charities, there were some which surprised H. There were organisations and shelters around the world, for abused and battered women. Remembering that Sora had been abducted from a shelter, H made a mental note to get Kyuji to investigate them for links to Quan. Another unexpected entry was a formidable donation, divided between LGBTQ groups in several countries.

The pilot made a smooth landing at Heathrow, where H disembarked and changed terminals. He spent the three hour layover walking around, stretching his legs and emailing Kyuji asking for more information. Although it was mid-afternoon in London and midnight in Tokyo, H felt reasonably refreshed and the long flight had given him plenty of thinking time. Kyuji had mentioned a temporary co-pilot on Quan's jet and H closed his eyes and dredged up her name – Orla Flynn. His starting point would be to track down Miss Flynn.

Just before six p.m. he boarded an Aer Lingus A320 for the short flight to Cork. He'd just settled into seat 2D on the aisle, when he had to stand up again. A woman had boarded behind him and was being greeted effusively by all of the cabin staff. Several passengers in nearby rows also hailed her by name and shook her hand. She smiled at H and apologised for keeping him standing in the aisle. She sat down by the window, with one empty seat between them.

"I'm Molly O'Gorman," she smiled and offered her hand. "The Irish are a friendly lot. They have long memories and are very kind. Sure you have no idea in the world who I am," she laughed as H looked bemused. "For more years than I care to remember, I was on a very popular TV soap and it seems I'm not yet forgotten." There was no way to stem her friendly, voluble reminiscences and even before the plane had taken off, H felt he could have gone on Mastermind and taken her acting career as his 'specialist subject'.

"Where are you from, yourself?" she asked.

"I come from Japan," H replied. "I'm a golf fanatic visiting your beautiful country on holiday and hope to play at some of your famous courses."

"Sure but you don't look Japanese at all. Here was me thinking you were a film star or something! Well, you've come to the right place. We have some grand courses to be sure." H changed the subject and asked if she was appearing in anything at the moment.

"Three years ago I had an argument with our producer and the bastard had me written out of the series. I was offered other roles, but the fun had gone out of it, so I decided I wanted to try something different before I got too old. I landed a great job in PR at Shannon Airport and I also do some similar work for Aer Lingus."

H's interest sharpened instantly. "Molly, if I may be so bold; congratulations! It must be an interesting job and I can see you have a way with people. I wonder if you might be able to help me?"

"Everyone calls me Molly. It's my own name and my character in the soap was also a Molly, which makes life easier. Now, how can I help?"

"I had a call from a friend just before I left Tokyo. A large, private jet flew into Cork yesterday. He was supposed to be on it, but he missed the flight. He asked me to do him a favour and track down one of the pilots, a woman called Orla Flynn and give her a message, but I have no idea how to contact her."

"Well, that shouldn't be too much of a problem and I'd be happy to help. If you've the time, I'll take you to the Crew Room straight after we land. Someone there is bound to know where you can find her."

"Molly you're an angel."

They landed ten minutes later and having cleared immigration and given the member of an Garda Síochána a wink, Molly suddenly grabbed hold of H's hand and swung right instead of left with the other passengers, through a set of heavy wooden security doors with a sign reading 'Staff Only'. She took him down a maze of corridors and through a door with a name plate 'Pilot Operations', where several pilots sat around preparing flight plans and checking screens displaying weather charts. Molly was evidently well know and popular and soon found the right person.

"Hugo O'Connor here is your man," she said happily. "He's a friend of Orla's." Hugo was an extremely tall, youngish man, in shirtsleeves, with a Captain's four stripes on his shoulders. "I saw

Orla here yesterday," he said. "I wouldn't normally give out personal information, but if Molly here says you're ok, that's good enough for me. She's got a few days off and has gone to a friend's wedding in my own village of Ballingarry. I don't have her mobile number, but you'll find her at The Mustard Seed."

"The Mustard Seed?" H asked.

"It's a famous country house hotel and restaurant, up in County Limerick."

Molly said, "*Everyone* knows The Mustard Seed. It's owned by Dan Mullane, who's a friend of mine. He's a real dote."

Hugo took out a notepad and jotted down a number from memory. "Actually, it's now been taken over by his long time manager John Edward. If you're looking for somewhere to stay, call John, mention our names and see if he can give you a room. It's a grand place and you'll be able to catch up with Orla over the week end. She's a good looking girl," he said with a wink, "and unmarried!"

H thanked them both for their help and told Molly he'd look her up and take her out for a meal one day.

He checked his watch and saw that it was just after 8 p.m. as he walked out to collect the special car Tanaka's people had organised for him. It was a brand new, Corris Grey, Range Rover Sport SVR, fitted with non-standard extras. Getting out his mobile, he rang the number Hugo had given him. He spoke to someone called Breda, who said that they only had Room 3 available; which was often used as the bridal suite. She discretely mentioned the price and H agreed and said he'd arrive in an hour or two. Ten minutes later he'd set the GPS and was driving north to County Limerick to find Orla Flynn.

Chapter 20

Ballingarry - County Limerick

On the drive, H put his foot down whenever he could. He was anxious to get a lead on Quan's whereabouts and hoped that he wasn't going off on a wild goose chase. The light was starting to fade by the time he reached Ballingarry and turned in through the gates of the Mustard Seed. A curving drive led upwards past sweeping lawns and well-tended gardens to a symmetrical Georgian house, painted in pale ochre.

Several cars were leaving, with merry voices saying loud good-nights as he parked and got his bag out of the boot. A cheerful looking man stood on the front steps and came forward to shake H's hand. "You're very welcome. I'm John and you must be Mister Suzuki. Breda told me you'd be arriving late. Unfortunately the kitchen has closed, but I can bring you a bowl of soup in the drawing room. It'll only take a moment." H accepted with pleasure and also asked for a pint of Guinness.

When John brought in the tray, he sat down and asked if H had travelled far and H mentioned meeting Molly O'Gorman and Hugo O'Connor, then remarked how popular the hotel seemed to be. John mentioned that they were full with an American party, who'd be leaving the following day, to be replaced by guests arriving for a wedding.

With the time changes, H hadn't realised how hungry he was and enjoyed the delicious home-made vegetable soup and warm soda bread. As he drained the Guinness, H asked for advice on where to go for a run in the morning. "One of the wedding guests has already arrived asked me the same question," John said. "She was out at six this morning with her dog and she'll show you the way, if you're up early enough."

"That's great. What's her name?"

"Orla Flynn."

H considered this a good omen and was glad that his instinct in coming here hadn't let him down. John checked him in and led him upstairs to a comfortable room, filled with an eclectic mix of furniture and a four poster bed and said goodnight. Within minutes H was fast asleep.

At 5.45, H was outside the hotel, stretching his muscles, inhaling the cool, damp air and listening to the dawn chorus. It was a grand misty morning, which promised to be warm later. The front door opened and Orla Flynn appeared, ready for her run and H liked what he saw. She was about his own age, with almost black, curling hair, lively, deep blue eyes and a sprinkling of freckles over the bridge of her nose. A true Irish colleen, H thought. A little whippet at her heels greeted him in a friendly fashion and danced down the steps to caper around his feet. H bent down to stroke it's silky, black coat.

Orla seemed surprised to see anyone else up so early. "Lucinda Jane," she said, "You're *such* a flirt!" H introduced himself and complimented her on her captivating pet.

It was a good ice-breaker and she seemed happy for H to join her and they set off down the drive. She led him through the village streets and up onto Knockfierna Hill. Lucinda Jane was in seventh heaven, putting up birds and chasing scents. When they reached the summit, they stopped for a while on the broad, gorse covered ridge, to admire the distant views. Orla told him that the place was steeped in local folklore and was known as 'The Hill of Truth'. They'd passed some ruined cottages and Orla said that this was common land where people had sought refuge during the famine, when they'd been evicted from their homes. They stood looking at a memorial stone and the remains of an ancient cairn and felt sobered at the thought of the suffering that had happened there. H looked up and pointed to a pair of kestrels hovering above them, which dispelled their melancholy feelings.

By the time they retraced their way to the hotel, they found they'd been out for almost two hours. They went to their rooms to bath and change, before meeting again for breakfast. They spent the rest of the morning together. Orla mentioned that she'd have to desert him when her friends arrived for the pre-wedding dinner that evening.

They asked John to recommend somewhere good for lunch and drove for ten minutes to Adare; known as the prettiest village in Ireland. Over lunch in the bar of The Dunraven Arms, H was finally able to get down to the reason he'd followed Orla to Ballingarry.

She told him how much she enjoyed her work as an airline pilot. He steered the conversation and asked where she'd been recently. Orla felt relaxed after two glasses of Chablis and her eyes sparkled as she said, "in my work I can never have a drink when I'm going to fly, so this wine is such a treat. I'm just back from the fascinating trip. I was in Tokyo and had a seat to come back as a passenger on a commercial flight, but luckily for me, someone asked if I could act as co-pilot on a leg to Cork. It was such a coincidence and I jumped at it, as I was coming here anyway, for this wedding.

H, you wouldn't have believed this jet; huge and painted matt black, so most distinctive. It was like being on Air Force One! I heard that the owner is a Chinese billionaire. We touched down at Dubai where some man got on for a meeting. The pilot knew that his boss often changed or delayed plans, so we had a spare flight crew on board, in case he ran out of hours, but he was still fed up because the meeting went on so long that we missed several take-off slots. Once we'd landed at Cork, I couldn't resist having a good look around. The interior was incredible."

H would have liked to ask if she'd known any more about who Quan was meeting on the plane, but decided it would sound suspicious. Instead, he smiled and said, "I love hearing about the high-life. Tell me more."

After describing the luxurious cabin in detail, she said, "there was a bedroom at the back, just like a film set. I trod on something and when I bent to pick it up, you'll never believe what it was." She stopped and burst out laughing. "It was a pair of handcuffs... lined with pink mink!"

"You're having me on."

"No, truly, that's what they were. I didn't know what to do with them, so I kicked them under the bed and decided not to look any further."

"Wise move," H said with a grin. "Will you be flying with them again?"

"I doubt it," she said, recklessly embarking on her third glass of wine. "As the passengers were disembarking, the cockpit door was ajar and I heard one of them mentioning a big golf competition at Fort Rufus, on the south coast. I gathered that's where they were going."

H paid the bill and drove her back to their hotel, satisfied that he'd got the information he needed.

The wedding party had taken over the whole hotel, so H had dinner in his room. Plans for tomorrow were formulating in his mind. It was the middle of the night in Tokyo, so he emailed Tanaka with his thoughts.

The sounds of revelry from downstairs wafted up and he was sorry he wasn't downstairs dancing with Orla. At 3.30 he woke up to hear a light tap on his door.

"The party was just no *fun* without you, H," Orla said softly, as he got up and opened the door. She was standing in the passage, holding an open bottle of champagne and two glasses.

H smiled and drew her into his room. "Let's have our own party in here!"

She giggled and started unzipping her dress.

Chapter 21

Fort Rufus Golf Links - Near Kinsale - County Cork

The day following their arrival at Fort Rufus, Sora was given an unexpected chance to escape.

She was at her wit's end. She was used to feeling in control of her destiny and was now adrift and confused. Her initial feelings of panic and terror had subsided somewhat, but she didn't know how to get herself out of the predicament she found herself in.

Sleeping fitfully, her dreams haunted by nightmares, she had been denied any form of exercise and her mind and body felt sluggish. That night she formulated various plans, only to discard them when she woke up, as being impracticable. Only one might have possibilities, but it would only have a chance of working if Quan was out of the way.

She was in a strange country, with no money or credit cards and no access to a phone or the internet. Although she was allowed to have a massage in the spa, she couldn't communicate privately with the staff, as one of the ubiquitous bodyguards accompanied her even into the treatment room. The idea of putting strangers at risk, by asking for their help was also preying on her mind. In the hopes of being able to use it at some stage, she took a pen and paper when she went to the bathroom and wrote a brief note outlining who she was: that she was being held against her will and asking for help.

At lunch, her ears pricked up when Quan said that she had a meeting in Cork and Sora was to accompany her in an hour's time.

They would be returning the following day, for the start of the golf competition and first of various gala evenings.

"I've got a stomach ache and I've been feeling a little off-colour this morning," Sora said as she picked listlessly at the delicious food. Quan frowned and looked her over, noticing how pale she was. "I hope you're not going to prove unhealthy. I want you to look your best tomorrow night. Stay here and rest. Zheng will come with me, but you'll be well chaperoned by the others."

'The others' were two more female bodyguards who were travelling with them. Quan had never mentioned either by name. They were less threatening than Zheng, but still intimidating. They obeyed orders, but didn't seem particularly intelligent. Sora had mentally nicknamed them Alpha and Omega and had established that neither spoke nor understood English. At least they *could* speak. Quan had told her that Zheng was a mute. What she didn't add was that she had had her tongue cut out deliberately, so she could never betray her mistress's secrets.

Sora waited for an hour after Quan had left, before putting her plan into operation. For it to have any chance of success, she'd need witnesses. As the day was fine and warm, tables had been set out on the terrace overlooking the sea and Sora had noticed several golfers sitting outside having drinks. Frowning and rubbing her midriff, she asked Alpha to get her something for her stomach ache. After taking a couple of pills, she said she needed some fresh air and they nodded and took her onto the terrace. As she passed one of the tables, she deliberately stumbled into one of the drinkers, who'd just stood up. As he steadied her, she apologised and said she felt a little faint. He followed her as she took a couple of unsteady steps, before collapsing artistically into his arms. People gathered round, with Alpha and Omega roughly trying to push them back.

Someone said she needed a doctor, but the bodyguards didn't understand. "I'll call for an ambulance," said the concerned-looking man who'd caught her. Having deposited her in his chair, he took out his mobile and made a call. Alpha and Omega were in a quandary. This was outside their instructions. If she was really ill, they didn't want to be responsible for denying her proper attention. Omega tried to lift her and take her back to the privacy of her room, but was unable to explain what she was doing. Someone put a hand on her shoulder, saying, "that's no job for a lady. Better leave her with some air until the doctor arrives." There were murmurs of approval and Omega, who looked as if she'd have liked to break his arm, subsided, but stayed beside the chair.

Sora tried to sit up, but groaned and clasped her arms around her stomach, hunching over in pain. The concerned group fanned her with their scorecards and menus and offered her glasses of water. Alpha and Omega had lost control of the situation and looked at each other in alarm. At the sound of an ambulance siren, Alpha belatedly took out a mobile to call Madam Quan, but the number was engaged.

Two paramedics appeared and questioned Sora about her symptoms, before deciding that they should take her to the local hospital. Without speaking, Alpha and Omega forced their way inside the ambulance as well and refused to get out. Shrugging, the paramedics closed the doors and drove off.

Quan's mobile was still engaged.

Chapter 22

Ballingarry - County Limerick

After a late breakfast with Orla, they kissed and said goodbye. H returned to his room where he Googled Fort Rufus Golf Links, paying particular attention to the details of the upcoming competition, before ringing them to see if he could get a reservation. The event was a sell-out and he was told that all of the rooms had been booked for months.

After waiting for a few minutes, and using an Irish accent, he rang back pretending to be a driver from a courier service. He said he'd got a package to be delivered to a Mrs. C.L. Quan, to be signed for personally. The receptionist put him on hold and came back to say that although Madam Quan was a guest, she'd left that morning, saying she'd be returning the following afternoon. H said he'd try again the following day, and hung up. Where the hell had she gone, he wondered.

He now had a day to wait, and realised he was going to need some help. Ringing a number from memory he spoke to Liam Callaghan who was an old friend from his Oxford days and knew *everything* going on in the Republic. He was extremely well connected and exactly the man H needed.

Liam came from a wealthy and well respected Anglo-Irish family. He was an inventor who'd made a colossal personal fortune having created – amongst other things – a phenomenally successful lock which needed no key. It had started life as the KYSS Lock or 'Keep Your Secrets Safe' as a children's toy. In its first year, it had gone global as the *must have* Christmas present. On the back of its instant success, he'd gone on to develop the POM lock, 'Peace of Mind', as an adult version for home safes, then one for bicycles and motor bikes, causing a dramatic drop in thefts worldwide. Sales of his latest keyless locks for homes and garages had taken him into the super-rich category.

"Clear your diary, Liam and cancel your plans for tonight – I'll be in Dublin by lunchtime."

"You bastard, H. Jesus, no word from you for years, then you expect me to drop everything," Callaghan said with mock severity, before laughing and continuing, "it'll be grand to see you. I've got the builders in at home, but I'll book you in somewhere nice."

They arranged to meet for a late lunch. As he was paying his bill and Orla's, he noticed Breda walking through the hall carrying a large bowl of sweetly scented hyacinths. H handed John a 50 euro note. "Any chance Breda could take those flowers up to Orla's room?" John smiled and said, "no problem." H said how much he'd enjoyed his brief stay and John wished him a safe trip.

It was a pleasant day for his drive to Dublin and less than three hours later he was pulling up in front of The Merrion Hotel, where a porter ran down the steps and said he'd park H's car. Checking in, he was greeted warmly and told, "you'll find Mr. Callaghan in the drawing room, sir. We've upgraded your room to a suite; Mr Callaghan is a most valued patron." He took his key card and found Liam sitting by a roaring fire, reading the Irish Times and nursing a large tumbler of whisky. He was very tall and thin and dressed beautifully, with a flamboyant, often eccentric style of his own. He had floppy, sandy coloured hair, a pair of good humoured blue eyes, large ears and a wide, full lipped mouth.

The years rolled back as they caught up with each other's news. After an hour they strolled round to Dawson Street, where Liam had booked a table at Fire, a fashionable restaurant nearby. They both enjoyed superb steaks under the high, vaulted ceiling and as they finished the meal, Liam pushed back his chair and grinned at H. His upper class accent suddenly changed to a thick Irish burr.

"Sure but 'tis not for the pleasure of seeing my blue eyes that you're here, boyo. What's up?"

Liam was one of the few people with whom H didn't have to be careful what he said. H trusted him and he knew what H did for a living and was totally discrete.

"I'm working on a case and although it's always great to see you – and your blue eyes – I do need your help. I want to get a room or, better still, a suite at Fort Rufus Golf Links near Kinsale."

"That's easy," Liam said. "The owner, Arthur Lysaght is a friend of mine. I'm a member, but don't get down there as often as I'd like. It's a sensational course. Are you *sure* you're not on holiday?"

H laughed and outlined the cover story he'd decided to use. Liam looked up a number and got through to Lysaght's mobile. Freely embellishing the brief back-story H had given him, he launched into his pitch with all the aplomb of a successful salesman.

"I've just had lunch with a great mate, who's a *fabulously* wealthy entrepreneur and golf fanatic." He winked at H and went on, "he's raised the funds for a new film about women's golf and is looking to find a leading lady and some cast. He's not Irish, but being a man of discernment, turned to old Liam for help. I said you were always full, but that you'd do a favour for an old friend like me and find him a room –or better still, a suite – this week-end."

Liam held the phone away from his ear as a raised voice came through loud and clear, saying it was utterly impossible to find even a bloody broom cupboard; friend or no friend. Liam listened some more and said that next week was no good and hung up after a few more comments.

H thanked him for the glowing write-up. "He's a magician and a good mate," Liam said. "He'll come through. He said to call back later and he'll see what he can do."

It was frustrating, but waiting was something H was well used to. Taking Liam at his word, he said that having arrived from Japan with only a kit bag, he'd need some suitable clothes. They spent the rest of the afternoon buying what H would need. Liam said that it wouldn't do to arrive in an off-the-peg dinner jacket, or cases that looked too new, so he took him home to kit him out, remarking that it was lucky they were almost the identical size.

Liam's parents had a charming, double fronted house off Dartmouth Square, in the exclusive Dublin 6 area of the City. Liam explained that his parents now preferred living in the country and had recently made the house over to him. It was filled with builders who were putting in a new kitchen, but Liam led him upstairs to his dressing room. Once he'd assure himself that the dinner jacket looked as if it could have been made for H, he added a country suit, a blazer, some golf kit and turfed an old Louis Vuitton steamer trunk out of a box room.

Arthur Lysaght rang back with the offer of a cancelled suite. Quite how he'd managed it, they never found out. H was delighted as well as impressed at Liam's powers of persuasion. As Quan was elsewhere, there was nothing he could usefully do until the next day, so – although *not* on holiday – he decided to leave the evening's plans in Liam's capable hands.

Wanting to show H the best of what Dublin had to offer, they kicked-off the evening with cocktails at the Horseshoe Bar in the Shelbourne Hotel, which was always filled with a lively crowd of 'in' people, from film stars to local personalities, before crossing the corner of St. Stephen's Green for dinner. Residence – an exclusive private members' club – was somewhere H had long wanted to visit. They were in no hurry and had an excellent dinner in Restaurant 41, slowly working their way through the seven-course tasting menu and drinking rather too much wine. They finished off the evening by dropping in to House, a nightclub where Liam had entrée to the VIP lounge. They didn't stay for long, as Liam kept bumping into people he knew. For once, he and H decided to pass on the advances of several local beauties, who approached them, wanting dances and vintage champagne.

They walked back together and said goodbye outside the Merrion Hotel. H thanked him for a wonderful evening and for all his help.

"Serious offer, H," Liam said, as he turned to walk home, "if you find you need a wingman or someone to watch your back; give me a call."

Chapter 23

Kinsale - County Cork

On arrival at the hospital, Sora was wheeled into an examination room. A sprightly, middle aged doctor soon appeared, having had a brief word with the paramedics.

Not wanting to waste a second, Sora pointed to Alpha and Omega, saying that they only spoke and understood Cantonese. Alpha took out her mobile, but the doctor told her that they were banned inside the hospital. Sora translated what he'd said, so she left the room, still anxious to speak to her boss.

As he lifted her sweater to examine her abdomen and ask about her symptoms, she tried to marshal her thoughts. "Please pretend that I'm answering your questions. Don't show any emotion, or you'll put us both in danger. I'm so sorry to mislead you, but there's nothing wrong with me."

He looked up at her for a second, nodded and asked, "does it hurt when I press here?" She arched forward and groaned. "I'm being held against my will." He nodded again, keeping calm as he brought out an ophthalmoscope and shone the light into each of her eyes. He went through the motions of checking her temperature, pulse, blood pressure and respiration rate and entering them onto a chart. "How can I help?" he asked, feeling the glands in her neck before looking into her mouth and asking her to say 'aah'.

"I've written an explanation and hidden it under my bra strap. Can you take it without that woman seeing?

"Turn over, please," he asked.

The folded slip of paper she'd concealed had worked its way loose and as he pulled up her sweater, it dropped onto the floor.

The doctor bent quickly to retrieve it, but Omega had seen it fall and with surprising speed, stepped over and just got to it first. Her eyes glittered with suspicion and she stepped towards him, raising her fist. He backed away, horrified at the look on her face. Sora leapt up and tried to catch the woman's arm. Omega backhanded her across the neck, knocking her off the examination table where she crumpled to the floor, struggling to breathe. The doctor used the momentary distraction to pick up a syringe, whilst pushing a trolley between himself and this fearsome woman. He never had a chance. In one, fluid movement, she picked up the heavy examination table and threw it at him. It hit him full in the face and chest. He went down hard and didn't get up.

Cork

Quan had taken a private meeting room at the Maryborough Hotel, just outside Cork's city centre for her meeting. She'd met Sheikh Deeb bin Adwan during a polo tournament in Japan the year before. Having stopped off in Dubai to meet him on her way to Ireland, they'd thrashed out the terms of a huge arms deal. Today they'd finalised the agreement and Quan would be richer by several million dollars.

The Sheikh had excused himself from joining Quan for lunch, saying that he must return to the Middle East and get back to his country without delay. It was rare for her to have time on her hands and as she waited for the food to arrive, she felt in excellent spirits.

Quan kept her two main business interests completely separate. The legitimate and massively successful arms development side, which had brought her international fame and recognition, was her public face. Hidden from the world was her lucrative sideline in human trafficking – the modern day slave trade.

On this visit to Ireland, she'd been able to combine the two. Now that she'd completed the private arms sale so advantageously, she could forget about it; having no interest in knowing whom the arms would be used against, or in the untold deaths and suffering they would cause.

Her carefully chosen menu for two arrived and was set out on the table in front of her. After allowing a bottle of chilled Krug to be opened, she dismissed the two waiters, saying she'd serve herself. Piling food onto her plate, she ate with gusto, whilst working through the champagne.

With the pleasant idea of combining business with pleasure, she looked forward to the rest of her trip. Attending the women's golf tournament would benefit her in several ways. As it was in aid of charity, Quan would get credit and good will, as well as valuable publicity for making a substantial donation. The golf competition had been the brainchild of an old lover, on whom she'd remained on excellent terms. They were useful to each other. Ada Kuchinsky was an American businesswoman and golf fanatic, who owned a prosperous IT company. In the past she'd recruited talented technicians for Quan's arms development business. Kuchinsky was also secretly engaged in the slave trade. She travelled extensively, visiting amateur golf competitions and picking up the prettiest 'promising' young girl golfers, from impoverished backgrounds. Taking huge commissions from friends like Quan, the girls were quietly swept into the sordid whirlpool of bondage and vice.

Quan lifted her glass and swirled it around, watching the bubbles rising and smiled to herself. Thinking of Sora's exquisite beauty, she could hardly wait to show her off that evening, knowing that Ada Kuchinsky would be green with envy when she saw her.

Her pleasurable daydream evaporated when her mobile rang and she listened to what 'Alpha' had to say.

Sora stumbled to her feet, swaying like a poplar in a strong breeze. She backed towards the door and her hand had just found the handle when it opened and she staggered into the arms of the returning Alpha.

Several inquisitive faces had come to see what had caused the crash. Sensing safety in numbers, Sora opened her mouth to shout for help, but could only produce a croak from her bruised larynx. Alpha slid an arm around her neck and pressed deeply into a pressure point, briefly cutting off the blood supply to Sora's brain. She lost consciousness and, for the third time that afternoon, slid towards the floor.

Picking up Sora and barging their way through the ring of startled onlookers, who instinctively gave way, but did nothing to stop them, Alpha and Omega carried her outside and took her back to the golf club.

Quan – who Alpha had finally been able to alert – was there waiting for them in her bedroom. Omega handed her Sora's note. With a face of thunder, she dismissed the two guards, calling them incompetent idiots.

Sora had come round but was hardly aware of what was happening. The traumatic and painful events at the hospital had thoroughly disoriented her.

Arms folded across her chest, Quan watched her through narrowed eyes. "You ungrateful little bitch. I have given you *everything* and how do you repay my generosity? With stupidity, disloyalty and treachery. You have chosen to cross me and will suffer the consequences."

Turning to Zheng, who was standing beside her, she said, in a caressing voice, "Zheng, my dear, *your* loyalty has always been exemplary. You need a little reward."

She looked at her watch, "At 5.00 the hairdresser and make-up artist will be here to help Miss Mori get ready for the opening cocktail party, which starts at 7.30. She will be at my side and must look her very best. You have almost two hours to teach her a lesson about what happens to those who displease me. Make the most of it, but remember that her face and arms must be untouched." She patted Zheng on the cheek as she left the room, saying, "enjoy!"

Zheng locked the door and started to undo her heavy belt.

Chapter 24

Boissy – A Small Town South of Paris

Maurice Duval was pleased to find everything in order when he got back home to *Boulanger et Patissier Maurice.* He'd trained his staff well and had an able second-in-command in Gilles Blanc. The shop looked immaculate and there were several customers being served by two of his assistants, Roger and Marie.

By lunchtime Maurice had unpacked and was fully up to date. He collected a gruyère and tomato galette from the shop and whilst it was warming in the oven, he poured himself a glass of wine and broke open a demi baguette. He took out the piece of paper on which his friend Pascal had written for him and checked the address. He pulled the telephone towards him and started to dial. Instead of Henri Davoust, a woman answered: "Bonjour, Location de Voitures Saint Pierre." He knew that voice! With trembling hands he cut off the call and took a large gulp of wine.

When he'd first become friends with Davoust, Maurice had been hopelessly smitten with his younger sister, Laure. She was the prettiest thing he'd ever seen, with a friendly, cheerful manner and a good brain. For Maurice it had been a *coup de foudre* – a bolt of lightning and love at first sight. There had been only one problem; she was already engaged to be married. He'd tried to put her out of his mind, but had never managed to forget her.

He took a few calming breaths and picked up the phone again, apologising for dropping the phone, he asked if he could speak to Henri.

"Who may I say is calling?" she asked.

"*C'est Maurice Duval*," he mumbled.

There was a pause, "Mon Dieu, Maurice, is that really you? How very nice to hear your voice again after so long. How are you?"

He explained that he was extremely well and that he'd had dinner with Pascal Garnier the night before, who had given him Henri's new contact details. "Henri will be so glad," she said, "I'll put you straight through. It was good to talk to you and… and, for now, goodbye."

Henri came on the line, "Maurice, you old bastard. *Quelle belle surprise.* What are you up to nowadays and when can we get together?" Maurice told him that he lived less than half an hour away. They arranged to meet at the bakery that evening for a beer. Maurice couldn't help smiling as he put the phone down.

Nine empty bottles of Kronenbourg 1664 were lined up on Maurice's kitchen table before he got around to broaching his idea to Henri. As with Pascal, the day before, it was if they still saw each other all the time. They worked their way through a loaf of pain rustique, a pot of rough Pâté de Campagne, with cornichons and pickled mustard seeds, recalling dangerous exploits and risqué anecdotes.

"Something extraordinary happened a few weeks ago" Maurice began, reaching into a bucket of ice for two more beers. "Quite by accident, I was able to save a man's life." He paused to open the bottles and pass one over, as Henri sat up and demanded, "tell me all about it."

They clinked bottles and Maurice took a long pull before embarking on his story.

"I'd finished making a dawn delivery to a local hotel, when I heard gunshots coming from the woods behind the wall of the local château." He selected another cornichon from the platter and put it into his mouth.

"For Christ's sake, get on with it," Henri said; justifiably annoyed at the wait.

"*Naturellement*, I pulled over to investigate."

Henri laughed, "You don't surprise me."

Maurice related the rest of the story. Henri was fascinated and said wryly, "I comprehend that there are large parts of this story which you are witholding."

"*Naturellement!*" Maurice said again with a smile. "I really took to this young man. He reminded me of what we were like in the old days. When he left, he expressed his gratitude, but it was actually *I* who felt indebted to *him*, for making me feel energised again."

"*Que je comprends*," Henri said, slowly, "but I feel there is more to this. What's on your mind?"

"I want you to help me steal a car."

Henri looked startled. "You have my full attention."

"It's not *exactly* stealing. I've found out that this young man – his name was simply H – had arrived at the Château in his very own Bentley. What the exact circumstances were, I have no idea. However, as he was in no position to drive away in it, the ownership is now, shall we say, disputable. I want to get hold of this car and return it to him ... and I would very much like your help. What do you say?"

"I'm shocked that you should ask," Henri replied. "I'm now a staid and respectable businessman. However, if there's a bit of danger and excitement going, count me in."

Maurice was pleased. Henri had always 'had his back' and they'd relied on each other. For this escapade, Henri was the friend whose help he wanted most.

It was getting late, but they talked for another hour before Henri got to his feet. There were now sixteen empty bottles on the table and all the food had disappeared.

"I feel galvanised by the idea of doing a last, crazy job with you, Maurice. Why don't you come over for dinner with us tomorrow night and we can make a plan?"

"Us?" Maurice asked.

"When I inherited the business, a nice house came with it. My sister Laure moved in with me about a year ago. You remember Laure, don't you?"

Maurice smiled and said of course he remembered her well.

"Poor girl," Henri said, sadly, "She's been through a terrible time. She married young and although they never had children, I believe she and Antoine were very happy together. Almost two years ago he was killed in a car accident."

Maurice murmured how sorry he was.

"It gets worse," Henri continued. "She went into nursing and was actually on duty in the hospital, when Antoine's body was brought in. She was devastated and hasn't been back to the hospital since that night.

How dreadfully unfair Maurice thought, that such appalling things and so much unhappiness had happened to the laughing girl of his dreams.

"I think that moving in with me and joining the business has helped, but she's still low. Do come over tomorrow. I'm sure she'll be pleased to see you. She's a wonderful cook and will give us a great meal."

Henri patted Maurice on the shoulder and said goodnight.

Chapter 25

Dublin

After his late evening with Liam Callaghan, H slept for four hours, before pounding the almost deserted Dublin pavements for an hour, to clear his head. There were things he needed to discuss with Tanaka. After a shower and breakfast in his room, he checked his watch. Tokyo was nine hours ahead, so he should easily be able to catch his uncle at HQ.

Tanaka kicked off by saying, "We still can't be 100% sure that Quan is the villain of the piece, who bought Nomura's invention, but we're *almost* certain. Kyuji has been checking all of KIBO's competitors and monitoring internet chatter, but has come up blank. However, General Wu, in his debriefing, has said that Quan is heavily involved with some of the more radical elements in the Chinese military."

"That would make sense," H said thoughtfully. "If she *has* acquired the new technology, she could make fortunes supplying it – as well as other weaponry -to the Chinese. It's diabolical, but it would be in her interest to actively escalate the friction with Japan."

"The new explosive hasn't been used again yet, but it's an alarming scenario," Tanaka said.

"Agent Sun has come up with new information on the tattoos found on Nomura's assassin. The Chinese underworld gang who use these symbols are heavily involved in the slave trade and are known to use some women operatives. We're checking Quan's employee records and Agent Sun hopes to be able to establish a link."

"The police seemed to think Sora Mori's abduction was related to the slave trade," H said. "There's never been a whisper of suspicion, but do you think it conceivable that Quan could be involved in such a business?"

"I've no idea, but it's worth keeping in mind. We need to know more about Quan's relationship with Miss Mori. Is the girl a willing guest, or is she there under duress: is she aware of the probable connection between Quan and her brother; is she in on the whole business and what does she know?"

H said, "We're not sure either if Quan is aware that Sora *is* Jiro Nomura's sister." He continued, "I've located where the two women are staying. They're at a golf club on the south coast, where a charity tournament is taking place. How it ties in to Quan's plans is anyone's guess. I'm on my way there now, to see what I can find out."

Tanaka wished him luck and rang off.

H took his newly acquired wardrobe downstairs and asked for his car to be brought around, whilst he paid his bill. He walked outside and found his Range Rover Sport SVR waiting. He took the key fob and astonished the porter by kicking his foot up under the side of the rear bumper, without touching it, activating a sensor which automatically opened the tailgate.

"That's a grand thing!" the porter said with a wide grin, gratefully pocketing H's generous tip, as he held open the driver's door.

"It's the latest Range Rover gizmo," H said. He climbed in behind the steering wheel, set the GPS and headed west out of the city, before turning south onto the M50 and west onto the N7.

He had a little less than two hundred miles to drive to Kinsale and made excellent time, arriving in time for lunch.

Chapter 26

Fort Rufus Golf Links – Kinsale

The reception that evening was a sparkling affair. Elegant women, glittering with jewels, mixed in glamorous groups, with all of the guests admiring the sensational flower arrangements. Tall glass vases of lime green guelder rose were mixed with sprays of white lilac, amaryllis and ranunculus, with pale orange parrot tulips and freesias: colour coordinated in honour of the National Flag of Ireland. Small baskets, tightly crammed with lily of the valley, filled the rooms with their heavenly scent. All of the major sponsors were staying in the luxurious suites and many of the Club's high profile members had flown in for the Pro/Am and this evening's dinner and charity auction. The champagne flowed as the guests circulated, some of them discussing the day's golf and others working the room, making contacts and doing deals.

H was one of the last to arrive. Accepting a glass from a waiter by the door, he stood, surveying the room, mentally cataloguing every face. As he moved into the party, he noticed several bodyguards, standing behind various moguls, including Zheng, whom he recognised from Kyuji's photographs. Quan was on the far side of the room. H's first impression of her in the flesh was unfavourable. Although her couture outfit must have cost serious money, nothing could disguise her lack of inches and deplorable figure. Wiser councils had not prevailed and he thought she looked faintly ridiculous in a fussy, silk taffeta dress, but then he looked at her face. The eyes were as hard as granite. At her side Sora stood with a blank expression. Quan took hold of her arm and whispered something in her ear. Sora straightened her back, forced a smile and started talking to the man standing next to her. H noticed the imprint of Quan's fingers above Sora's elbow.

He worked his way towards them and made eye contact with Arthur Lysaght.

"Who is the Adonis?" H heard a flame haired woman ask him in an audible aside.

Lysaght laughed, stepped forward and stuck out his hand. "You must be Liam Callaghan's friend. Welcome to Fort Rufus. Now, let me introduce you… " He touched the arm of the woman who'd asked the question, "Lady Lister, this is Hiroshi Suzuki: Sir John Lister, my wife Florence Lysaght, Ada Kuchinsky, Madam Chow Lee Quan and her delightful partner; the supermodel Sora Mori." As H smiled and shook hands all round, Lysaght said, "Ada, I'm sure you'll be able to help Mister Suzuki. He's making a film about women's golf."

From the brief flash of surprise in Sora' eyes, when they'd shaken hands, he knew that she'd recognised him, but she kept silent. H made an idle remark about the party, but his attention was claimed by Sir John Lister, who asked him if he played golf and the conversation became general.

H turned to Quan, "It's a pleasure to meet you. I read the piece about your latest acquisition in the Financial Times recently. What a *tour de force*."

"Indeed," she said, indifferently.

"Well, we're all slaves to our own success, aren't we?" he said, pleasantly.

She gave him a sharp glance before turning back to the Listers.

Shortly afterwards H eased himself out of the group and went to find out what time they'd be sitting down to dinner. A waiter told him that an important guest had been delayed, so they would not be going through to the dining room for at least fifty minutes. H would have time to search Quan's room. Stopping off to collect a miniature camera, thin gloves and a tiny torch from his room, he made his way to her suite. There was no one in sight, so he unlocked the door using Kyuji's specially calibrated universal-key-card. Without turning on the lights he looked around using his Surefire Titan Plus flashlight, noticing that the bed had not yet been turned down and the bathroom towels hadn't been changed, so he'd need to be quick as he might be disturbed.

There was a laptop on the desk. Using another of Kyuji's gismos, which bypassed passwords and hacked computers, he pushed a small memory stick into the USB port and started downloading the files and also inserted a microchip, which would enable Kyuji to monitor future communications.

Whilst he waited for the download to complete, he walked through an intercommunicating door, into Sora's suite. In the bathroom, he found an open tube of burn cream. In the waste bin were some empty wrappings of three, sterile dressings and used antiseptic wipes. There were two bloodstained hand towels in the laundry basket.

Hearing a knock on the door and a female voice calling, "Housekeeping," he'd just made it back into Quan's suite as the lights came on in Sora's bedroom. He stood still for a moment, to make sure he hadn't been noticed. He couldn't risk using the torch, but managed to remove and pocket the memory stick, hoping he'd left everything as he'd found it. Silently opening the door he stepped back into the passage and pulled the door shut behind him. Another maid was pushing a trolley towards him. He smiled and said good evening, pulses thudding a little, before returning to his room, where he sent the data through to Kyuji.

Twenty minutes after leaving the reception, H re-joined the party and was glad to see that his absence seemed to have gone unnoticed. Shortly afterwards he was button-holed by Ada Kuchinsky, who wore a white, man's tuxedo, bow tie and patent evening shoes. It was obvious that Lysaght had given him a glowing write-up and she seemed eager to help with her golfing expertise. When dinner was announced, he offered her his arm and they went to check the board with the place settings.

At a circular table for ten, H found himself seated with Quan on his right and the rather raddled-redhead, Lady Lister on his left. Sora was almost immediately opposite. H noticed that she moved stiffly and sat down carefully, with her back held away from the chair. Throughout the first course, Lady Lister's affected voice chattered and flirted, her heavily be-ringed hand constantly touching his to emphasise her points. H listened politely, but with only one ear. He learned that she was a keen amateur golfer, who played off a handicap of three. She spoke of competitions won and the sporting prowess of her three children. At one stage, when she was pondering what her doting and generous husband might give her for their anniversary, she said, "oh God, I *do* hope Johnnie doesn't give me emeralds *again*!" H laughed, "can a beautiful woman ever have too many emeralds?" he asked. He looked across the table and caught Sora watching him. He smiled at her, but she flicked a nervous glance at Quan, before dropping her eyes.

With the arrival of the Beef Wellington, H turned politely to Quan. She ate enthusiastically, but was unresponsive and offered little in the way of conversation. H persevered; discussing the competition, the excellent facilities of the club and outlining the reason for his visit. It was with relief that, with the clearing of the plates, he saw that the charity auction was about to begin.

The auction took some time and the only item of interest was a lot given by Quan. She had donated a lunch the following day with Sora Mori, the famous Japanese model, whose looks had been much admired during the evening. Bidding was steep amongst the rich male guests and Ada Kuchinsky was enthusiastically waving her menu. H waited until the bidding stalled at 6,500 euros and put up his hand, saying, "10,000." The auctioneer looked around, and seeing no-one willing to top that figure, happily brought down his gavel.

Quan looked over the table and addressed Sora, breaking across several conversations. "I can see that your headache has not improved, my dear. You look a little pale. Zheng will take you back to your room." Sora looked as if she was about to faint and flinched as Zheng pulled out her chair, but she obediently got to her feet; apologised and said goodnight to the men on either side of her. Without making a scene, there was nothing H could do.

The contents of Quan's laptop kept H busy late into the night. After the party ended, he'd gone back to his room and ordered a pot of strong coffee to keep him alert.

Many of the files of business facts, figures and spreadsheets he skimmed through, knowing that it would be Kyuji's job to make sense of them. Details of Quan's meeting with Sheikh Deeb bin Adwan the day before raised his eyebrows, as he looked at the itemised list of the huge weapons order. It was enough to start a small war, he saw, making a mental note to discuss this with Tanaka.

There was also a file with pages of photographs of young, Asian girls. Various emails between Quan and Ada Kuchinsky left no doubt that both were heavily engaged in the slave trade. 'Sales' were listed beside some of them, at astonishing prices. The final picture was of Sora. This had a question mark beside it. H looked at it with a frown, feeling sickened, before closing the file and opening one entitled 'Itinerary'.

In two days, at the end of the golf competition, Quan would be leaving Ireland aboard her yacht, the *Sappho,* which was moored nearby. Monaco was listed as the destination. Apart from Quan and her ubiquitous female bodyguards, Sora's name appeared, plus those of three other VIP guests from the golf. There was an agenda of parties and gambling listed for the six day Monaco stop, where other well-known guests would be joining Quan's party on the *Sappho.* Quan's jet was booked to take her back to Tokyo the following week. Sora's name did not appear as a passenger.

Chapter 27

When H went down for breakfast, the Clubhouse was already bustling with people. Many of the guests had decided to walk the course to watch the semi-final round of the Pro-Am. The dining room was packed, but Lady Lister beckoned him to a spare seat at her table.

Quan and Sora had finished eating and as they passed, Sir John Lister stood up to say good morning and asked if they were up for the walk.

Quan said, "I have work to do."

Sir John turned to Sora with a smile. "How about you, Miss Mori?"

Lady Lister said, "Oh *do* come; it'll be *such* fun."

Sora hesitated and Quan said, "why not? The fresh air will do you good." As she turned to leave the restaurant she nodded to H and thanked him for his generous bid at the auction.

"Your money has gone to such an admirable cause. I asked for it to be included as one of the charities for this event. LGBTQ has done much worthy work in the lesbian, gay, bisexual, and transgender communities. Enjoy your lunch. A table has been booked for you both here at one thirty."

H felt that Tanaka might take issue with the money he'd spent supporting this 'admirable cause'.

It was a beautiful spring morning. The course looked spectacular and the crowds were anticipating a wonderful days' golf. H watched from his window until he saw the Listers appear with Sora. As he'd expected, one of the female bodyguards followed closely. H knew it was going to be hard to get Sora on her own and unless he put his foot down, one of the bodyguards would no doubt try to join them for lunch.

He put on a light jacket – with many useful pockets – before walking outside to join the spectators. He'd studied the course layout and had decided that the seventh fairway was the place to make his move. He joined them as they walked up to the third green. The marshals had roped-off the area and they stood, waiting for the players to approach the green.

Lady Lister waved him over, saying, "isn't this just too much fun!"

H agreed and turned to Sora. "Does your dog bite?"

Sora couldn't help smiling, but replied seriously, "yes, very much so. She doesn't speak or understand English," she said pointedly, glancing at H to make sure he'd understood, "but she's incredibly persistent."

"Isn't it too utterly ridiculous, to have security people following one even on a golf course. If *you're* going to walk round with us, we can't *possibly* need extra protection," Lady Lister said archly. "Why don't you send her away, Sora?"

"I'm afraid that's not possible. Madam Quan insists she stays with me at all times."

The Marshal held up a board reading, 'Silence Please.' They stood still and waited for the players to make their putts.

Over the next couple of holes, H tried to detach Sora from the group, but the bodyguard stuck like a burr. He also needed to shake-off the voluble Lady Lister, who was making it impossible to have any private conversation with Sora. The crowds were thick and he gradually slowed his pace, allowing the Listers to move ahead, whilst keeping Sora at his side.

Pointing to the edge of the cliffs, he asked, "do you know that this particular area is famous for sighting sharks and dolphins? Would you care to walk over with me?"

Sora nodded and they turned towards the sea. Omega, the bodyguard, sensing trouble, asked what she was doing and said they must keep with the spectators. H didn't let on that he understood Cantonese and allowed Sora to translate.

"Tell her that you'd love to see the dolphins and that it will only take a few minutes. Say that she can come with us and we'll catch up with the Listers shortly."

Omega was evidently uneasy, but shrugged and agreed.

H, who'd reconnoitered the area before anyone else was up, led the way. The ground sloped down towards the edge of the cliffs and they were soon out of sight.

"Speak naturally and pretend we really are looking at nature," H said, taking her arm to help her over some rough ground. He bent down and pointed to some flowers, pocketing a handful of loose earth and gravel as he stood up again.

"Was it really you I saw outside my brother's flat in Tokyo?" she asked.

"Yes it was. Forgive me, but it's obvious that you're in some kind of trouble. How can I help you?"

Sora pointed out to sea, continuing the charade. "If only you could, but it's impossible. Can't you see that? I'm a prisoner."

"Nothing is impossible. Now, let's see if we can shake off your shadow. What would she do if I were to kiss you?"

"What?" she said, caught off balance. "Please, don't even think of it. She'd tell Madam Quan and I would be...would be in such trouble. You can't even imagine."

H had chosen the site with care. They'd descended from the top of the cliff and were standing on a wide, flat promontory. He stood with his back to the drop, with the two women facing him. He smiled at Sora reassuringly. "Trust me," he said, and gathered her into his arms. Omega shouted at him and taking a couple of hasty steps forward, tried to pull Sora away.

"Get back up the slope and stay there," H told Sora, pushing her sideways. He kept his eyes on Omega and waited until Sora was out of the way. Omega looked murderous and pulling out a flick knife, moved to attack him. H stripped off his jacket, wrapped it once round his wrist and rapidly whirled it in a figure of eight movement, trying to entangle the blade. She advanced, stabbing upwards, trying to get in under his ribcage, whilst also trying to force him nearer to the precipice. H took a step sideways and she followed. The knife glinted in the sunshine as she tried again and again to get within striking range, distracted and infuriated by the flapping jacket. As she charged in again, he allowed her to come closer, then threw his handful of grit straight in her face. She howled with rage and pain, blinded as she took a final lunge at where he'd been standing. Her impetus carried her onto the edge of the drop. Her arms windmilled as she tried to steady herself, but she overbalanced and took a disastrous step forward. The ground gave way under her feet and with a shrill cry, she disappeared onto the rocks below.

Chapter 28

It was almost impossible that Omega could have survived the fall, but to make sure, H found a safer place where he could look down over the drop. He saw her body had bounced off the rocks and was floating, face down in the sea.

This unexpected development left H with a problem. As he rubbed his hands on his trousers, to get rid of the grit and pushed his hair back off his face, he was thinking about how to handle the situation. The first thing was to remove Sora from the scene. He looked around and made sure that there had been no witnesses. Apart from some raucous seabirds, they had been unobserved. The noisy, red-billed choughs had also masked Omega's scream as she fell.

He picked his jacket up off the ground and hearing the sound of falling stones, he looked up to see Sora slithering down the slope. She ran into his arms, shivering with shock, so he wrapped the jacket around her. Seeing that she could hardly stand, he took a small flask of sloe gin out of a pocket, unscrewed the lid and held it to her lips. When the colour started coming back into her cheeks he said, "Let's get you out of here."

As the clubhouse windows overlooked some of the course, H led Sora by a circuitous route, emerging into the car park. He clicked the remote, which unlocked the Range Rover's doors and turned on the engine. "We don't want to be seen leaving together, so lie down on the back seat and put this rug over you. I'll let you up when we are clear of the gates."

"Where are you taking me?"

"Somewhere safe, where we can talk," H said reassuringly.

He drove into the nearby town of Kinsale and left the Range Rover in an anonymous car park near the harbour. He avoided the more well-known and larger hotels, knowing that they'd be full during the golf competition. In a side street he found a B and B, painted in a cheerful yellow, with riotous hanging baskets and window boxes. There was a small supermarket next door. H went inside and bought some filled rolls, sweet biscuits, a couple of apples and drinks. He checked them into the B and B for one night and once the door to their bedroom was locked, Sora sank onto the small double bed.

"What do we do now?" she asked.

"First, tell me what's happened to you and how you come to be travelling with Madam Quan."

Sora sighed and said, "I hardly know where to start. It's such a bizarre story that I'm not sure you'll believe me."

There was a teasmade beside the bed. H filled the kettle and put it on to boil. "I'll believe you," he said, handing her a cup and the biscuits.

Her story took some time. H felt anger as well as pity for what she'd gone through. Once or twice she hesitated, as if it was too hard to articulate some of the things Quan had subjected her to. She cried, remembering the other girls who'd been abducted with her and was horrified about what might have happened to them. H was touched that, with all her problems she still worried about them.

When she'd finished explaining, she looked at him with tears spangling her eyelashes. "I don't know how to thank you. I can't believe you've saved me." She gave a shaky laugh. "I'm not usually so pathetic, but I can't seem to think straight. What am I to do now? She'll come after me. You have no idea how powerful she is and she hates to be beaten. I know she'll try and get me back. I'm in a strange country with no money, no passport and I… I just don't know what to do. I had a great life and suddenly I have nothing."

H couldn't bear her distress. "Please hold me," she begged. "Hold me tight and make me forget." He pulled her into his arms and looked into her eyes, stroking her hair and murmuring endearments. Suddenly she was kissing him and pulling at his clothes. The relief at finding herself safe from the nightmare made her desperate for comfort, in a way that surprised them both.

"Are you sure?" H asked her, between kisses.

"Yes, oh yes."

H dimly understood her need to blot out the degrading and loathsome attentions of Quan. She could hardly wait to wriggle out of her clothes and they made love passionately. Her pent-up emotions took hold of her and it seemed she couldn't get enough of his body. The second time was better. H took his time and was tender and considerate. He'd noticed the frightful burns on her back and beneath her breasts, but she seemed unaware of the pain. Finally she collapsed on his chest.

Within minutes she'd fallen fast asleep, clutching one of his hands to her cheek. H lay still, watching the sun move across the window and sink slowly. When Sora stirred and woke up, she smiled at him. "Wow! Was that good or what?"

H smiled back and twisted a lock of her hair round his fingers. "Time to get up. We need to make plans."

She headed for the shower, picking up her discarded clothes from the floor as she went. H lay back on the bed thinking, and lit an illicit cigarette. Tanaka had asked him to find out certain pieces of information: Firstly, was Sora a willing guest of Quan's, or with her under duress? H now knew that it was the latter. Secondly, was Sora aware of the connection between her brother and Quan? Thirdly, did Sora know about Quan's plans.

As he stubbed out his cigarette, another thought hit him. Did Quan know that Sora was Nomura's brother? He knew that it would have been helpful to have had an insider in Quan's camp, but after what she'd told him, there was no way he could ask or expect her to go back. When he'd got the answer to the rest of Tanaka's questions, he'd work out what to do next.

Sora came out of the bathroom drying her hair on a towel. She was dressed and H noticed that two buttons were missing from her blouse. She sat on the bed and picked up her shoes from the floor, together with a heavy locket on a chain. H's photographic memory kicked-in and jolted him in the ribs with a Eureka moment. It rarely let him down, but when he'd seen Jiro Nomura's body for the second time, he'd known that something was missing, but hadn't been able to pinpoint it. Suddenly, here it was; the necklace Sora was putting over her head, he'd glimpsed before, under Jiro's shirt.

"Have you any family who might be able to help you, Sora?"

"No. My parents are both dead. I only have one brother, but he's . . . ," she stopped, with a look of consternation and put her hand to her mouth and burst into tears.

"Tell me," he said gently.

"He's dead. He'd done something so terrible . . . he was considering suicide . . . someone killed him." Half sentences came spilling out in a disjointed mass.

"Slow down, Sora," he said, putting his handkerchief into her hands, Wipe your eyes, take three deep breaths and start again."

She slowly composed herself and began by outlining what she knew about her brother's work and how his ambition and dissatisfaction had led him into trouble. She disclosed the contents of his letter to her, ending with her finding his body the following morning. In shock, and needing time to process what had happened, she'd gone ahead with her planned visit to the women's shelter, where she'd been kidnapped. "Everything happened so quickly, one shock after another," she said, "that I never got the chance to think, or understand what had happened to Jiro. I don't know who could have killed him." Her tears started again and H put his arms around her and let her cry.

The story filled in most of the blanks for H, but there was another vital question. When she was calm again, he asked, "do you know who your brother took his invention to?"

Sora looked blank. "No, he never mentioned the name of the company in his letter."

H took her hands in his. "He took it to Armstec – to Madam Quan."

Chapter 29

Tallois - South of Paris

Maurice Duval and Pascal Garnier spent an enjoyable evening with Henri Davoust and his sister Laure. They admired the house he'd inherited and complimented Henri on his good fortune. Laure had cooked them a delicious cassoulet and when they'd finished eating and the table had been cleared, Maurice unveiled his plans. Laure would have left them to it, but Maurice asked her to stay.

He'd prepared a rough sketch of the Château and grounds, including the outbuildings and stable block. They all gathered round as he unrolled it on the table, weighing down the corners with glasses.

"We can't be sure where the Bentley is now, but the stable block, or possibly here," Maurice indicated a double garage next to the Château kitchens, "seem the most likely places."

"Do you know how many of the staff still live on the premises?" Pascal asked.

"Not yet," Maurice replied. "We'll need to do some research. Once we've found out, we'll need to go in one night and have a look around."

"Do you know what state the car is in? Is it driveable?" Henri asked thoughtfully,

"Hopefully we *will* be able to drive it away," Maurice said, "but if it's a wreck, we may need to borrow your low-loader, Henri. We also need to find out what sort of security they have there."

Their enthusiasm grew as they discussed several ways of entering the grounds after dark and searching for the car. They talked about clothes, equipment and means of communication.

"Isn't that château up for sale?" Laure asked, speaking for the first time. "Might it not be simpler to make an appointment to view?"

"That's an excellent idea," Maurice said warmly.

"It's a bit tame and doesn't sound nearly as much fun," Henri said. The men nodded and Laure smiled.

It was decided that each of them would visit Boissy and do some discrete asking around in the town. They made lists of what they'd need for the recce night. Some money would need to be spent and they agreed to keep receipts and settle-up later. Having discussed the necessity of night vision goggles, Henri suggested that they should be able to save money by hiring, rather than buying them. He also recommended getting some brand new Bragi's, the latest in-ear smart wireless comms system. They'd all kept their old camouflage jackets and would wear knitted watch caps, dark trousers and boots.

Pascal offered to find the name of the selling agents and said he'd be happy to approach them and ask for a brochure, which would give them further details of the property and probably some photographs.

Laure had listened with interest, but had kept in the background, content to leave the decision making to the others, but on seeing their excitement kindling, decided to put forward a suggestion of her own, which she thought would appeal to them.

"Do you think it might be a good idea for you all to wear camouflage paint on your faces and hands?" Laure asked.

They all liked the idea and she offered to source some on the internet.

They gave themselves to the end of that weekend to get prepared and arranged to meet at Maurice's the following Monday evening.

When the evening broke up, they all knew what they had to do, and were in a state of pleasurable anticipation.

Chapter 30

Fort Rufus Golf Club

Quan positively disliked fresh air and even though it was a beautiful day, she chose to stay indoors. She was in a foul mood and even Zheng had the sense to keep out of her way. Her plans had stalled when she found that the data on Nomura's laptop had been scrubbed and she loathed not being in control. She paced up and down her suite, with her hands clasped behind her back, thinking of the telephone conversation she had to make.

A colossal amount of money – even by her standards – was at stake. The Chinese generals with whom she was plotting had been delighted when she brought them news that she'd acquired a new weapon and they'd been extremely impressed with the demonstration. They fully realised its potential and had discussed escalating their plans to destabilise Japan. With a small amount of spin, it should also have been possible to blame the outcome of their plans on the Japanese themselves. Undreamed of quantities of weapons would be needed in the ensuing war she'd planned and the Generals had assured her that the contract would go to Armstec.

Through the utter incompetence of her underlings, Nomura was dead and her bargaining chip with the Generals was lost. She sat down at a desk and made the connection to the conference call on her secure phone. The conversation was highly acrimonious and she was forced to lie and say that there was simply a delay in their obtaining the invention. The Generals said that their arranged meeting on board her yacht, in Monte Carlo the following week, would go ahead as planned; when they expected her to be in a position to hand over the data. No threats were issued. They were implicit. She was left with a monumental problem and less than a week in which to solve it.

She stood up and with a violent gesture, swept everything on the desk onto the floor. A coffee tray, a set of antique Belleek figurines, a large glass lamp and various other items scattered to the ground, spilling coffee, milk and sugar cubes over the carpet. Kicking the lampshade out of her path she poured herself a stiff drink. It wasn't only the dilemma with the Generals that displeased her. Ada Kuchinsky had tried to take advantage of their friendship. Ada had recruited five, highly skilled IT technicians in California to join Quan's operations in Japan. They'd concluded a sale of seventeen girls and money had changed hands, but Ada had insisted on a freebie. She wanted Sora included in the deal.

Quan ground her teeth. No way was *that* going to happen. She's enjoyed grooming Sora and had liked showing her off. When she tired of her she had every intention of getting rid of her, but that Ada had dared to pressure her was infuriating and could not be tolerated.

There was a quiet knock on the door. "Go away," she shouted. The door opened and she pulled back her arm to hurl her glass at whoever was disturbing her. Alpha cleared her throat. "It's the police, Madam."

A youngish Garda inspector and a female sergeant entered the room on Alpha's heels. Quan promptly lowered her arm and took a sip of her drink.

"You wish to see *me*?"

"I'm Inspector Kearney and this is Sergeant Dillon. I'm sorry to disturb you, Madam, but we're making inquiries and hope you may be able to help us."

"What do you want?" she asked.

The inspector's brows lifted as he looked at the mess on the carpet. "I apologise if it's an inconvenient time, but unfortunately, this can't wait. A woman's body has just been taken out of the sea under the cliffs here. She has the appearance of a... a Chinese or Eastern person. The Club Secretary suggested I talk to you, before speaking to the other guests."

Quan turned to Alpha and spoke in rapid Cantonese. "Check the staff and find out if Miss Mori and whoever accompanied her have returned from the golf course. Now!"

"It may take some time to check if all of my staff is accounted for. Does it appear that this woman fell from the cliffs? Were there any witnesses to this accident?"

"It's too early to say," Inspector Kearney said repressively.

She managed to get rid of the officers after the Inspector said they'd continue with their inquiries and return later. They left with backward glances at the debris on the floor.

Alpha got a tongue-lashing for allowing the police into her suite, but Quan's heart wasn't in it. "Get out. Send Zheng to me."

Zheng must have been waiting and came in immediately.

"Did you activate the tracking daemon I told you to upload to Miss Mori's Apple watch?"

Zheng nodded.

"Check the triangulation data we are receiving now and tell me exactly where the girl is," she demanded.

Zheng nodded and left the room. She returned almost immediately and passed over her phone with the tracking app running. Quan looked disbelievingly at the blinking blue dot, which was accurate to 10 cm.

"Get a team together. Use local help if you need to. Go there now, and *do not* return without the girl."

Chapter 31

Kinsale - County Cork

"It's not *possible*," Sora said, looking at H and hoping she'd misheard. "Jiro took his invention to Quan?"

"He did just that," H told her. "However, I think that your abduction was simply an extraordinary coincidence."

She sat for a moment, thinking. "You must be right. She's unaware of the connection between me and Jiro." She went quiet and then asked, "do you think Quan had anything to do with his murder?"

"Yes, I do. He double-crossed her. Killing him was an enormous mistake because she still doesn't have the right data."

She looked into the distance, thinking of Jiro.

"Sora," he said, recapturing her attention. "At the end of your brother's letter, he said you'd know where to look, if anything happened to him. Well, *do* you know?"

Her eyes widened and her hand went to her locket. "Yes," she breathed, "I think it's in here." She pulled the chain over her head and inserted a finger nail into a groove on the locket. It opened to reveal a slim memory stick.

"Wow! Well done, Sora," H said respectfully.

"What shall we do with it?" she asked.

"Can you trust me with it?"

She nodded and handed it to him without hesitation. H slipped it into an inside, zipped pocket, deciding that it was time to tell her a little about who he was and why he'd been sent to recover this data. When he'd finished, she looked at him.

"So *that's* why you saved me," she said forlornly.

"I won't lie to you. My government sent me here to do a job, but getting you away from that monstrous woman has been a bonus and a pleasure. Anything I can do to help you, I will."

H took a quick shower and as he was pulling on his clothes, he said, "I need to get you somewhere safer, whilst I get this information to my superiors. We can't go anywhere near the golf club, but we should leave now."

They went downstairs and as H was paying the bill, Sora opened the street door and stepped outside.

"Sora, no; *wait*!" H said urgently.

He was too late.

CHAPTER 32

For a split second the tableau in front of H was imprinted on his brain, as he stepped outside. Zheng stood waiting. She'd caught Sora in a bear hug. From the benches on either side of the door four men stood up on either side of him, holding glasses of Guinness. They were not Chinese, they looked like tough, local fisherman from the harbour. Apart from the group surrounding him, the quiet street was temporarily empty.

The picture dissolved into real time. As H took a step forward, assessing the opposition, several things happened at once. A car appeared and drew into the kerb. Alpha got out of the passenger's seat. Zheng saw H and smiled. The four heavies closed in and tried to bundle her into the car. With a shout of despair, Sora tore herself out of Zheng's hold and fled into the roadway.

What the driver had meant to do was unclear. The car leapt forward and tore into Sora. She was knocked into the air, landed on the car's windscreen and hit the road on the far side. H smashed an elbow into the face of the nearest attacker, catching him by the front of his jersey and pulled him into the path of the man behind him. They both stumbled and went down. H pivoted to face the other two. He heard a smash as one of them broke his pint glass on the table and came for him, slashing with a jagged shard. H stepped back out of range and jumped up, catching a beam overhanging the door. He swung forward, kicking out with both feet and catching the man in the face. Three down, one man, plus Zheng and Alpha still to deal with.

H never got the chance. He was grabbed from behind, momentarily pinning his arms. He looked up and saw Zheng only a few feet away, now holding a Taser X26 in both hands. H was about to break the hold and hardly had time to register the infrared beam pointed at his chest when two simultaneous thumps of the barbed electrodes hit him in the neck and chest. The force of 50,000 volts highjacked his central nervous system and knocked him backwards, his legs kicking with uncontrolled spasms. An involuntary groan burst from his lips. He was totally incapacitated. His body felt like jelly and his muscles throbbed with pain.

His brain swam, and as his vision stabilised, he looked down and saw two thin wires projected from the wounds. He gasped as Zheng walked up to him and brutally ripped the barbs out of his body. He never saw the blow coming. The last thing he heard was a rough, Irish voice murmur in his ear, "this'll learn you to keep your fecking nose out of other people's business." The Irishman took a cosh out of his pocket and hit H behind his left ear.

Chapter 33

Château Trompette Des Anges - South of Paris

Maurice Duval and his friends Henri and Pascal were ready for their recce of the Château.

Their fact-finding visits to the local town of Boissy had turned up several useful pieces of information. Most of the large staff who'd lived on site when the owner was in residence had been given notice. Now there was only a single caretaker who lived in the Château, a gardener and one security guard who inhabited rooms in the old stable block. It was believed – but not confirmed – that the guard kept two Doberman Pinschers.

They'd chosen this particular evening after ascertaining that both the gardener and the security guard went out for dinner to a local bistro every Saturday night and usually stayed late, drinking.

The three men stood in Maurice's kitchen. Wearing their old camouflage jackets and watch caps, they looked at each other with a feeling of *déjà vu*. They were all in high spirits, thinking about the evening ahead.

During the week they'd found a perfect spot – somewhere out of sight – where they'd leave the car. They didn't want to risk getting stopped wearing their war paint, so they decided to put it on when they arrived at the Château. Laure had ordered some ACU Camo Face Paint sticks, in Olive Green, Loam, Tan, Green Slate, Brown and Black, which she felt should be more than enough.

They made sure their NVGs were in working order and having checked the charge on their wireless system, they were 'good to go'.

There had been some heavy rain over the last few days, but it had cleared during the morning. Dark, scudding clouds obscured the moon for much of the time and a gusting wind brought the autumn leaves tumbling down like confetti.

Once they'd used the camouflage paint sticks on their faces and hands, they clambered over the boundary wall. They stood in a belt of woodland, waiting for a clear patch of sky to be obscured by clouds again, before breaking cover and setting out to cross the open ground in front of the Château. The old moves came back to them as they dropped into crouching runs, zigzagging as they went. Maurice – the least fit of the three – was wheezing a little when they reached the shadows of the bridge, which spanned the old moat.

There were no lights behind any of the windows at the front. They circled the huge structure to begin their prearranged sweep of the outbuildings. They started by checking two garages and a storeroom in a large service yard, all of which were unlocked. Pascal kept watch as Maurice and Henri looked inside. They came up blank in the storeroom and first garage, which was empty, except for a moped, which presumably belonged to the caretaker. As they were about to go back outside to check the second garage, Pascal suddenly held up his hand. They froze.

A light had come on inside the kitchen, followed by the opening of a back door. A large ginger cat slipped through the aperture and scampered out of the circle of light. A man stepped outside, wearing a thick, plaid dressing gown and sheepskin slippers. He lit a cigarette and stood smoking, while looking idly around.

Trapped in the garage, Pascal had quickly pulled the door to. The three men waited in the darkness to see what the caretaker would do. Would he notice that the garage door wasn't shut properly?

It started to rain again. The caretaker looked at the sky, took a last puff of his cigarette, dropped the butt on the ground and ground it out with his slipper. He called to the cat, which reappeared from the darkness. They went inside together and the door was shut and locked. Through a lighted kitchen window, the caretaker could be seen heating up a nightcap, before eventually leaving the room and switching off the light.

Nerves jangling, Maurice and his friends waited for ten long minutes before moving. There was no sign of the Bentley in the second garage. It was time to widen the search.

The large stable block was next on their agenda, but they never got to start their exploration. A square courtyard was surrounded on all sides by buildings and was approached by arched entrance set over the driveway. In days gone by there had been stabling here for over fifty horses. A large coach-house took up one side of the quadrangle and the loose boxes, a saddle room, tack room and hay store took up the other three sides.

Henri was the first through the archway, but as he stepped into the courtyard a blaze of lights came on. He ducked back into the shadows under the arch.

They heard the sound of a window being thrown open and an angry voice shouted, "*Qui est là?*" followed by the sound of barking dogs.

Henri, Pascal and Maurice stood waiting, furious about the dud information they'd received about the two inhabitants always being out on Saturday nights. The rain became a deluge and they heard the man saying, "merde," as he slammed the window shut.

After five minutes of not daring to move, the lights went out and they were in darkness again. The security guard was lax and didn't bother to let the dogs out, although they were still sounding unsettled.

Thoroughly dispirited, they decided to make their way back to where they'd left the car. The rain was incessant and the ground was turning into a quagmire. They were less than thirty yards from the stables when the accident happened. Pascal had reached the driveway, when he slipped and put his foot into a storm drain. He fell heavily, with a hastily smothered yelp. Maurice and Henri hit the deck and lay still, waiting to see if they'd been heard. They could hear Pascal swearing quietly, a few yards away.

This was becoming a farce, Maurice thought as he wriggled forward until he was beside Pascal. "Are you ok?" he asked anxiously.

After more swearing, it emerged that Pascal's left foot was stuck in the grille over the drain. It took both Maurice and Henri several minutes to free him. They couldn't see what they were doing in the torrential rain and didn't dare use torches. Maurice belatedly remembered his night vision goggles and with their green light – once he could see what he was doing – he managed to free Pascal's foot.

With his arms over Maurice and Henri's shoulders, Pascal was half carried back to the car.

When they'd gently loaded him onto the back seat, Maurice turned to Henri.

"Ok, so what was Plan B again?"

Chapter 34

Dublin and Kinsale

Liam Callaghan lit another cigarette, deep in thought. He was wondering how H was getting on in Kinsale. He couldn't pinpoint the cause, but he felt worried. He kicked himself that he hadn't asked H for his mobile number, so he rang the golf club. Mister Suzuki, he was told, was not in the Clubhouse, so he left a message. He drummed his fingers on his desk, his feeling of unease persisted and his antennae prickled, making it impossible to settle to the work on his desk. He set in motion a Newton's Cradle ball clicker and mindlessly watched it for a few moments. It didn't help. Sighing, he called his PA and asked him to book him a room at Fort Rufus and to cancel all his meetings for the next couple of days.

Having made the decision, he went home, packed a bag, grabbed his golf gear and drove to Kinsale.

On arrival he checked-in and asked the staff for H, but nobody knew where he was. He'd noticed a Garda car parked outside. It seemed strange that H had dropped off the radar. Feeling increasingly concerned, he went in search of the owner, Arthur Lysaght.

They went into the bar together and ordered drinks, chatting about how the golf competition was going. After a few minutes, Liam said, "I've come down to join my friend Hiroshi Suzuki, but he's not in his room. Have you seen him around?"

"I can't say that I have. Let me ask at reception." Lysaght got up and went out into the hall. He was away for several minutes. "It appears that no-one's seen him since this morning. The restaurant manager says he wasn't here for lunch, even though a table had been booked."

"Thanks," Liam said, "I expect he'll turn up. By the way, what's going on with the Garda? I saw a car outside."

Lysaght looked grave. "Someone who was staying here fell off the cliffs this morning and was killed. The Gardai are looking into it."

"God, how awful. A man or a woman?"

Lysaght's attention was diverted as he saw Inspector Kearney come into the bar and make his way towards them. "Here's someone who's good at finding people," he said, jokingly.

Liam, knowing that trouble followed H around like a comet's tail, kept his mouth shut.

"Just the man we need!" Lysaght said, standing up and shaking hands. "This is Bill Kearney, our local Garda Inspector – Bill, this is Liam Callaghan. Any chance you could park your police car round the back, Bill? You're frightening the paying customers."

Kearney laughed. The few other people in the bar were certainly riveted to their conversation. "It will be done. We're about finished here and should be out of your hair soon. Just to let you know, we've temporarily cordoned-off a section at the top of the cliffs." A waiter stood at his elbow and he ordered an orange juice and sat down.

"You haven't come across a Hiroshi Suzuki have you?" Lysaght asked.

"How much?"

Lysaght repeated the name. "We seem to have mislaid him." He explained the situation and Kearney looked surprised.

"Curiouser and curiouser," he said, as he was fond of quoting Lewis Carroll. "This is normally a fairly quiet time of year, but we have this dead woman on our hands, plus a hit-and-run fatality and now I've been told that the local hospital has had a man brought in, unconscious – carrying no identification."

He finished his orange juice and stood up. "Thanks for the drink, Arthur. The mortuary is filling fast and I'd better get back to work."

"Inspector," Liam said, "before you go, the hit-and-run victim and the unconscious man – do you have a description?"

"Oh yes, your missing friend. I know that the hit-and-run was a woman in her twenties. I haven't seen the man yet, but I'm on my way to the hospital to see if he's regained consciousness. The World's gone mad. Apparently he was mugged in broad daylight in Kinsale. No witnesses." As an afterthought, he turned and said, "come with me, if you like. It may even clear up one of today's problems for me."

Leaving Lysaght to his drink, Liam thanked him and said he'd follow the Inspector in his own car.

When they arrived at the hospital they were led to a small private room. H lay under the sheets, his head bandaged, still unconscious. Liam was shocked, but positively identified H, which pleased Inspector Kearney.

Kearney introduced Liam to Doctor Ryan and a Garda constable, who'd been detailed to take notes if the patient woke up.

Doctor Ryan explained to the Inspector, "We've given him a cardiograph and checked his vital signs. He received a heavy blow behind his left ear, requiring three sutures. An unusual feature is that he also appears to have been Tasered. Not something one would expect in Ireland." He pulled down the sheet and exposed the small puncture wounds on H's neck and chest. "We'll be keeping a close eye on him and he seems to be surfacing, albeit slowly."

Liam asked if he could stay with H and was given permission. Kearney had a few words with his subordinate, telling him he'd be relieved at midnight. He turned to say goodbye to Liam, saying, "we don't know what provoked this attack, so it seemed sensible to leave a man here to watch him. Can you give this Garda officer some details about your friend? We need to find out why he was attacked and by whom. I don't suppose you have any ideas?" Liam shook his head. Kearney went out, muttering, "I don't like this sort of thing happening on my patch."

After returning to his car to collect his Kindle, Liam pulled up a chair and sat down for what might be a long wait.

CHAPTER 35

There was no light. H felt as if he were weighed down under black, heavy blankets. There were voices, but the sound seemed far away. He tried to open his eyes, but couldn't summon the energy. He sighed and let the darkness cover him again.

Time passed and he swam slowly up through layers of fog, still incapable of coherent thought. Something seemed to be wrong with his head, as if a steel band was being tightened around his forehead and needles were being hammered into his temples. The voices seemed to exacerbate his headache. "Please – shut up – go away," he said, but he hadn't made a sound.

Two men were speaking in low tones. One he'd never heard before, but the other voice seemed vaguely familiar. He tried to remember who it was, but it was too much effort. It was the stranger who did most of the talking.

"It really is a fascinating gadget. I've been reading up on it. When a Taser X26 is fired, it emits an initial charge of up to 50,000 volts, but by the time it comes in contact with a body, its power is usually diminished to about 1,800 volts. It – by that I mean electricity – I think. Anyway, it sends signals to the central nervous system, which causes pain and muscle contractions. The two probes attach themselves to the body, which creates an electrical circuit, which totally disrupts voluntary control of the muscles." The voice droned on and on.

H was becoming more aware. The voices seemed closer and more distinct. H tried to block them out, when something was said which made the muscles on his scalp contract.

"…. paperwork to see to. A poor woman was brought in earlier – killed outright in a hit and run. I'll look in again shortly."

"What?" H said surfacing back into the world in a rush. His eyes fluttered open.

"So, you're awake again, are you?" H focused slowly and a bearded face swam into view.

"I'm Doctor Ryan. Look at my finger, and keep looking at it." The finger moved slowly from side to side, with H tracking it, wincing as he inadvertently turned his head to the left.

"There's no need to move your head. Good," Ryan said, taking out an opthalmoscope to examine H's eyes. He checked for levels of consciousness and responses before looking into both ears with an auroscope for signs of a ruptured eardrum or any bleeding.

"Now, can you remember what happened to you?" he asked, after taking H's pulse and adding some notes onto a chart.

H shut his eyes and a frown creased his forehead. "No," he said after a pause.

"That's ok. What's your name?" This time the pause was much longer.

"You've had a bang on the head. Don't try and force your memory." He looked down at the chart. "I see you were given a CT scan when you arrived and it looks ok. A nurse will come in and check on you every hour. In the meantime, try to rest." The advice seemed good and H closed his eyes.

It was early morning when he finally came to his senses. He took a couple of deep breaths and looked around. Dimmed lights showed him that he was in a strange room, thin cotton curtains were drawn across the windows and two men dozed in uncomfortable looking chairs. Something nagged at the back of H's mind. It was something about a woman. He tried to catch hold of the thought, but it eluded him.

He struggled to sit up and the slight noise woke the two men, who both stood up and came to stand by the bed. One was dressed in a blue Garda uniform, the other – a tall, sandy haired man smiled down at him, "Not dead yet, then? My God, you gave us a fright."

"Are you a doctor?" H asked.

The man's smile faded. "H, it's me – Liam."

Quan's temper had not improved. Her call to the Generals had infuriated her and Zheng still hadn't returned with Sora. She had been interrupted again by two members of the Club staff, who came to clean up the mess she'd created and replace the broken items; even a section of the carpet was hastily re-laid. After ordering herself a substantial meal, she paced the room. Now, she thought angrily, she had to concern herself with matters she considered beneath her notice.

Captain Féng had brought her yacht the *Sappho* into Castlepark Marina at Kinsale that morning. On receiving Alpha's call, he made haste to the Golf Club and his employer's suite.

Without greeting and after a preamble, briefly outlining the situation, Quan said, "this is now your problem. The local Inspector will be returning shortly. Your command of the English language is valuable. Explain to him that I am unavailable and that I am leaving the matter in your hands. Say that one of my security staff *does* appear to be missing and that the rest of my people are out looking for her. The body will need to be identified; that will be your job. You have met the woman, her name was Bo Huáng. Get details of her next of kin from my office and tell the Inspector anything else he needs to know. He will, no doubt, wish to get statements and will organise a translator. Make sure my staff co-operate and are available. See to it. I do not wish to be disturbed any further on this matter. It needs to be handled speedily, as we leave for Monaco tomorrow, as planned."

Captain Féng was used to dealing with the super-rich, and so he phrased his comments with caution. "Certainly, Madam Quan. However, if the Inspector *does* wish to see you again … ."

"I don't give a shit," she cut in. "Just *sort* it."

He left the room, metaphorically mopping his brow and almost colliding at the door with a room-service waiter, wheeling in a laden trolley.

As she started her meal, Quan rang Alpha, to see if Zheng and the search party had found and detained Sora. Her hand clenched on the receiver as she listened to a lengthy report. For the second time that day, the contents of her tray were hurled onto the floor. Her bill for damages was going to be substantial.

CHAPTER 36

H looked up into his friend's concerned face and smiled. "Liam, what happened? I'm a bit confused. What are you doing here?"

Liam grinned in relief. "It's good to see you, H. You've been … "

The young Garda broke in, "excuse me sir, but I need to ask a few questions first. If you feel up to it?"

H said, "sure."

The Garda pulled his chair close to the bed and took out a notebook and pencil. "Can you tell me your name?" H did so. "Do you know what day of the week it is?" This time H frowned and said no. "Can you recall what happened to you?" H searched his memory and came up blank. "I don't remember." The Garda looked at him and asked, "just go back in your mind and tell me the last thing you *do* remember doing."

H struggled to get some sort of order into his sluggish brain. "I remember having dinner in Dublin with Liam, here. Can you tell me where I am now?"

The Garda chewed the end of his pencil. "I think we'll leave it for the moment. I'll call Doctor Ryan to come and have another look at you." He pressed a call bell and asked a nurse to see if the doctor was still in the building. Liam gave H a drink of water and they waited in silence.

Doctor Ryan appeared a few minutes later and had a few quiet words with the Garda, before approaching the bed. He checked H's vital signs again and added further notes to H's chart.

"How does your head feel?"

"It feels as though someone's working on it with a pile-driver," H replied.

"I'm not surprised. You had a hefty thump behind your left ear. I'll give you something for the pain." He made another note on his chart. "Short term memory loss is not at all uncommon in these cases. Don't try and force it and hopefully you'll be able to fill in the pieces before too long."

"Thanks, doctor. When can I leave?" H asked.

"I'd like to keep you under observation for the moment. Give it a couple of days and then we'll see."

The Garda said, "I've spoken to my Inspector and he says that I can return to the station. If, I mean when you remember more, we'd be grateful if you could drop into the station and give a full statement, before you leave the area." H nodded and thanked him. Liam said he'd spend the rest of the night in H's room and the Doctor and Garda left together.

The nurse returned and gave H a combination of Naproxen and Paracetamol. Liam suggested H lie back down and try to sleep, but as soon as the door swung shut behind the nurse, H threw back the covers and slid his legs over the side of the bed. Liam looked horrified. "What are you doing, you madman? Stay where you are."

H, whose head was swimming, reluctantly agreed.

"It's driving me crazy, not knowing what happened. It's coming back in fragments and I do remember going to the Golf Club and the big dinner last night, but after that, I've no idea what I did today. Look, can you go through the pockets of my clothes and see what's there?"

Liam took everything out of the locker and put a few items on the bed. H's encrypted mobile was there, plus his wallet, the Range Rover key fob, cigarettes and a lighter, a clean handkerchief and an ornate locket. H picked up the locket and turned it over in his hands. "Don't say anything. I know this, but I need to concentrate." His finger nail found the hidden catch and onto the bedclothes fell a tiny memory stick.

"That's it! Look, I can't tell you everything, Liam, but I've remembered something. I know where I've seen this before."

A few more pieces of the puzzle slotted into place and H remembered Sora and her giving him the necklace, saying that her brother had given it to her for safekeeping. It was just a snapshot, as if a curtain had been briefly opened, allowing him to see through, before it closed again. It was maddening, but he couldn't see any further. His mind raced around in circles and stopped when he thought of Sora. Where was she now?

"Liam," he said, "I was only half listening earlier on, but someone mentioned there are two women's bodies in the morgue here. I need to know who they are."

Liam, seeing H was about to get out of bed again, pushed him back down. "Stay where you are. I can do it for you." Liam walked swiftly out of the room. Twenty minutes passed with agonising slowness for H. Why did he think that Sora might be in the morgue?

Liam returned, saying, "I had to sweet talk an orderly into letting me in. Here's what you wanted." He handed H his mobile phone.

The first photograph was of a young woman. He felt no flicker of recognition. The other woman had only half a head and face left. It was a gruesome image. From what he could see she was obviously Chinese. Suddenly he had another flash and saw her snarling and coming for him with a knife in her hand. Then the image collapsed and he saw nothing more.

"Thanks, Liam," he said with relief. "I think, I hope, that the girl I'm trying to remember may still be alive."

Liam was scanning H's medical notes. "That doctor gave you a sleeping pill as well as some painkillers."

He looked up, but H was fast asleep.

Chapter 37

Château Trompette Des Anges – South of Paris

Plan B proved more of a success for Maurice, Pascal, Henri and Laure.

Over a post-mortem breakfast meeting the day after the abortive recce, they laid new plans and thrashed out the details. It was decided that they'd go with Laure's original suggestion to view the Château as prospective buyers. Pascal, with his injured ankle wouldn't be able to take an active role, but he telephoned the Estate Agents and arranged an appointment for the following afternoon. Henri and Laure would pose as a wealthy married couple from Paris and Maurice would act as their chauffeur.

They had to look convincing. A stately 1964 Rolls-Royce Silver Cloud III had been part of Henri's legacy from his uncle and which he now hired out for wedding parties. It would be perfect, but to be on the safe side, he'd change the number plates for this occasion. Henri then looked out a chauffeur's cap, which Maurice tried on, but they were all slightly concerned that one of the remaining staff at the Château might recognise him from his nearby bakery shop. After some heart-searching and with serious reluctance, Maurice agreed to shave off his cherished moustache, which completely changed his appearance.

They arrived in state, to find the agent, Monsieur Legrand, waiting outside the front doors of the Château. Maurice hopped out and held the door open for Laure and Henri. Laure loved historic buildings and found much to admire. The grand Baroque hall with a vaulted *trompe l'oeil* ceiling and magnificent double staircase were just the start of their tour.

Laure went out of her way to charm the agent. Henri's interest in architecture was tepid, but as they looked around, he managed to drop several hints into the conversation, as to their considerable wealth.

"I've been in banking all my life. We like to travel and have various homes and properties around the world. We love to entertain and this place looks perfect. I want to give my wife something extra special for her birthday." The agent looked impressed and stepped-up his sales patter. He smiled and smiled.

Laure backed Henri up. "I've been looking for some time for somewhere to keep my horses. I've read the brochure, but would like to have a close look at the stable block."

The agent suggested they go there immediately. Maurice drove them over and Laure explained, "I've got some promising show jumpers and I've always wanted somewhere to start my own equestrian centre. I do hope that this will prove suitable." They discussed the available land, paddocks, water systems and the possibility of an indoor school.

The tour of the stables started in the old coach house. As they stepped inside they saw two cars. One was a muddy and well used Renault Scenic. Behind it was a far larger, gunmetal grey car.

They'd found H's Bentley!

There it was, dusty and neglected. On the driver's side, the door was battered and dented and the main window was broken, with a spider's web of cracked glass. Without showing any interest, Laure managed to continue round the entire stable block, asking questions and taking photographs as she went.

Henri dropped back and wandered around on his own. He took another look around the coach house and noticed a small metal wall-mounted box near the entrance. He flicked the door open. To his surprise and delight, there were two sets of keys inside on hooks. Beside the Renault keys hung the chunky Bentley key fob. Call yourself a security guard? he said to himself in disgust. This fellow has *no* idea of security.

He strolled back outside, where he saw the gardener driving a Cushman into the courtyard, filled with fallen leaves. The man introduced himself as Clement Morel. They shook hands. Morel was interested in the visitors and started by mentioning the car they'd arrived in.

"When the old boss was alive, sir, I was one of the two chauffeurs here. No call for that anymore, so now I tip around doing gardening instead. There used to be five looking after the grounds, but now it's just me." Henri let him waffle on and when he managed to edge in a word, he said, "talking about cars, I noticed a beautiful one in the coach house."

"Terrible waste, that," Morel said. "It was in a crash up by the bridge. We managed to drive it back here. It's a wonderful machine and it's a crying shame to see it left like this. No one to give the orders now, you see."

The security guard arrived back from walking his two Dobermans and came over to join them. Both men were anxious to retain their jobs at the Château and wanted to make a good impression.

Laure and the agent returned and she said, "Henri, Monsieur Legrand has to get back to his office. He kindly says we may stay a little longer."

The agent left with profuse apologies and Henri said he'd be in touch within the next couple of days.

Henri turned to the guard and Clement Morel. "Look messieurs, I don't want to keep you from your work, but we *are* interested in this place and would like to hear more about it. As you know it so well, perhaps we might be able to get together again?"

"We are both free this evening," Morel said.

Henri turned to Laure. "Why don't we take them out for dinner? It would save us another trip from Paris. What do you think?"

"*Pourquoi pas*?" Laure said. "That seems sensible, but *do* let's make it early. Don't forget we're off to New York tomorrow." Morel mentioned a local restaurant and they all arranged to meet there at 7.00.

The coast would be clear.

Chapter 38

In the morning H felt well on the mend. The thumping, pounding headache of the night before was still with him, but far less severe. His dreams had been vivid and disturbing and he tried to unravel his subconscious thoughts from reality. Liam was also awake early, after an uncomfortable night dozing in the chair. They were both offered breakfast and H felt up to making some plans.

"The first thing I must do is to contact my boss."

Liam took the hint that this would need to be private. "I'll go back to the Golf Club and have a bath and a shave. I'll pick up some fresh clothes for you and be back as quickly as I can."

"Thanks," H said as Liam headed for the door. "Please could you bring my laptop as well? Keep an ear out for any gossip about what happened yesterday."

H's conversation with Tanaka took some time. He glossed over his injuries and explained that he was still in a local hospital and had no recollection of what had happened to him. Tanaka was obviously worried, but hid his concern. H gave him the one piece of good news; that he had possession of the memory stick, which should, he hoped, contain all of Jiro Nomura's work.

"That's excellent," Tanaka said. So presumably Madam Quan does *not* have this information. Do you have the facilities to send it through to Kyuji?"

H said he should be able to send it within the next couple of hours. He explained the welcome help he was getting from Liam Callaghan and Tanaka said he remembered him well and asked H to send him his regards. They finished the call with Tanaka saying they'd talk again as soon as Kyuji had checked the data.

When Liam got back to the hospital he found H trying to persuade Doctor Ryan to discharge him.

H immediately broke off what he was saying and delved into the bag Liam had brought. He pulled out his laptop and powered it up. He pushed in the memory stick, tapped a few keys and sent the information flying through the ether, to Japan.

"Can you talk some sense into your friend?" Doctor Ryan asked Liam.

"Probably not!" Liam replied. "He's got a mind of his own and I have to say that his recuperative powers are pretty amazing. I'll keep a close eye on him if you discharge him."

Doctor Ryan accepted defeat. "Just try and take it easy for a few days at least. I'll give you some Naproxen for your head. They are pretty strong, but believe me, you *will* need them."

"On my own head be it!" H said. "No pun intended and thanks for looking after me doctor."

He accepted the prescription Doctor Ryan wrote out and they said goodbye.

Whilst Liam had been out, H had taken a shower and was now emptying his overnight bag and starting to get dressed. "Thanks for bringing my stuff, Liam. What news from the Club?"

Liam was looking closely at H, who'd taken off the dressings on his neck and chest, revealing angry-looking ripped skin from the Taser barbs. There was also a large, darkening bruise on his neck. H was frowning as he bent down to put on his shoes. Liam sighed, knowing it was useless to try and get H to stay where he was.

"I think I've found out who the Chinese woman in the morgue is. Most of the people staying for the tournament have left. Those who are still there are all talking about a fatal accident, which happened during the final round. Apparently some woman fell off the cliffs. The Gardai are looking into it."

"Do they think it was an accident, or what?"

"Nobody seems to know, but – as you can imagine – the Club grapevine is buzzing with wild speculation. The woman worked as a security guard for a Madam Chow Lee Quan, who is still at the Club, but leaving today on her yacht, for Monte Carlo. Does any of this ring any bells?"

H's head appeared through the top of his sweater and he cautiously shrugged himself into a jacket. "I *do* remember Quan *and* how she fits into why I'm here, but I wish to God I could remember more about yesterday. Until everything comes back, I may trip myself up. I never underestimate the opposition and it's hard not knowing what *they* know, if you understand. I feel I'll be fighting in the dark."

Liam nodded sympathetically. "Look, why don't you ring your uncle and see what he suggests?" Liam had met Tanaka on a couple of occasions, during his student days at Oxford with H.

"Good idea. I spoke to him earlier and he's calling back when he's seen the information I've sent through. In the meantime, let's get out of here. I need some fresh air and I've had enough of hospitals." He stuffed his clothes from the day before back into the holdall. The shirt – marked with blood on the chest and collar – went into the rubbish bin.

Liam was leading the way out to the car park, when H suddenly stopped in mid stride. "My car," he said, putting a hand to his forehead. "Where the hell did I leave my car?"

Liam said thoughtfully, "I was talking to the Garda and he said you were attacked in Kinsale. It was outside a B&B down near the harbour. Why don't we go and look for it? Unless ... might you have left it at Fort Rufus?"

"I simply don't know," H said. He sorted through his pockets and came out with the key fob to the Range Rover. "Let's try the harbour first," he said.

They climbed into Liam's latest extravagance; a brand new, deep blue Maserati Levante SUV. H adored cars and his mood improved as soon as he saw it. "This is great," he said, settling into the passenger seat and admiring the red leather interior. "I didn't know this was on the market yet."

"I was staying in Dubai recently, at the Desert Palm Retreat," Liam said. "Maserati was sponsoring a Polo Tournament there. I saw this and ordered one straight away. It's perfect for the Irish roads."

He parked in the town and was still discussing the car and its capabilities as they walked around the gaily decorated streets. H breathed in the salty air and felt stronger with every step. They were lucky; within ten minutes they heard the answering beep when H clicked his key fob for the tenth time. The car was as he'd left it. H stood beside it and did a slow 360 degree turn, trying to work out which way he might have walked. Stubbornly, his memory didn't bring up the answer.

H checked his watch. "It's almost lunchtime. Do you feel hungry, Liam? I'm starving. Let's go and find somewhere to eat." A smartly dressed woman was passing them on the pavement and H asked if she could recommend somewhere good, nearby. She gave them directions to Fishy Fish; a pleasant looking restaurant on Crowleys Quay. They both chose the Seafood Chowder and Grilled Organic Salmon. The food was delicious and as H had no other plans until he heard back from Tanaka, they were able to take their time.

Liam suggested they take their coffee outside onto the terrace and shortly afterwards, H's phone rang. Liam stood up and tactfully said he'd go and find a pharmacy and get H's prescription. H put the phone to his ear.

"Hiroshi," Tanaka said. "Here's what I want you to do."

Chapter 39

Time seemed to pass slowly for Quan, as she waited for Zheng to return with Sora. Anger boiled through her like acid and she felt physically sick. What had happened on the cliffs and how had Sora managed to get into Kinsale?

When she finally heard sounds of arrival, she threw open the door. Zheng walked in carrying Sora and was followed by Alpha. In the rear, Quan recognised her personal physician from the *Sappho*; a dour looking woman in a white coat.

"She's not badly hurt," the woman began, in a strong Australian accent, "but your people wanted me to check her over, so they brought her to the yacht. In my opinion, the girl will not require hospital treatment."

Zheng carried Sora through into the bedroom and laid her down on the bed.

"What are her injuries?" Quan asked.

"The only cause for concern was her right hip. I gather that the car which hit her – although accelerating – was not moving at any great speed. The fender caught her on the right side and she was thrown over the car. The impact caused a significant hematoma. I've given her a light sedative, as she was in considerable pain. Apart from some minor bumps and grazes, she got off lightly. When she wakes up – probably in about an hour – she'll be stiff and sore for a few days, but otherwise, she should recover quickly."

"Thank you, Doctor Armstrong. Why was she brought back here? As we are leaving this evening it would have been far more sensible to have left her on board. None of you uses any common sense. It seems I'm surrounded by incompetents."

Doctor Armstrong and Alpha both glanced at Zheng, but neither of them spoke. Quan flicked a hand dismissively and they left the room. She walked over to the bed and looked down at Sora. The girl was breathing heavily and her face was blanched and pale. Quan's anger drained out of her and, for once, she felt some emotion stir in her chest. It was compassion. Such feelings startled her as they seemed to come out of nowhere. This girl actually meant something to her; she was special. Quan sat down on the bed and smoothed Sora's hair back from her face. She took her hand and patted it. She was still there when Sora started to stir.

Sora's eyes fluttered open and Quan bent down and gently kissed her on the lips. "Welcome back, my dear. Don't try and talk. Here, have a drink." She raised Sora's shoulders and held a glass of water to her mouth. Sora realised she was desperately thirsty and drank until the glass was empty. Quan lowered her back onto the pillows, saying, "rest now and we can talk when you're feeling better."

Sora was drowsy from the after effects of the sedative. There was nothing to wake up for and she felt she'd like to sleep for a month. Her life seemed to have been put on hold. The brief elation and excitement she'd felt in escaping from Quan and the hour she'd spent in Hiroshi's arms had given her new hope and optimism. Now, lethargy and the wretchedness of her situation submerged her.

Then she thought of H. What had happened to him after she'd been hit by the car? Maybe he'd somehow managed to escape. He'd seemed so strong; so capable and confident. Anything was possible. Maybe – even now – he was on his way to rescue her again. She hugged the thought to herself, suddenly feeling a spark of confidence.

She pulled herself up and helped herself to another long drink of water from the carafe on the bedside table. If H did come, she needed to be up, dressed and ready to go.

Her thoughts were interrupted by a light tap on the door. "Come in," she said. One of the chambermaids who cleaned her room looked in, and seeing she was awake, and alone, came over to the bedside.

"I have a message for you from a Mister H." Sora's eyes widened and she caught hold of the woman's hand. "Quickly," she said urgently. "Please, tell me quickly. Madam Quan may come back at any minute."

Chapter 40

Tanaka came straight to the point. "Are you fit to continue, Hiroshi, or should I send over another agent?

H never bullshitted his uncle, so he answered truthfully. "Yes, sir. Physically I'm fit to continue. I'm getting headaches, but they're being kept under control with some good pills from the Doctor. Bits and pieces of my memory keep coming back, but there are still some blanks."

"Understood, Tanaka said. "Now, from the information you sent us, we know that Quan is going on to Monaco. Getting her itinerary from her laptop was most useful. She's planning to do a lot of entertaining on board her yacht, but I'm sure that's a smokescreen. She's blotted out a whole afternoon for a meeting, but it's frustrating that she doesn't mention *whom* she's meeting. Follow her there as quickly as you can and try and find out what she's up to."

"I've discussed Monaco with Liam," H said. "He's been planning to go there on business in the near future and has kindly brought it forward. He's getting his jet to fly down to Cork, from Dublin and we'll fly to Nice together, either later this evening, or tomorrow morning. He's booking us rooms at the Hermitage."

"He's a good friend to have and I'm relieved that you'll have his company until you get there. I'm despatching Kyuji and a team to rendezvous with you there. I'll get Mai-Li to book them into the Hermitage as well. It's a good choice; central and near the harbour. Now, tell me the status of Miss Mori. Is she still 'in play'?"

"Yes, I believe so. I assume that she's still alive and that Zheng has taken her back to Quan. I don't know how bad her injuries may have been in Kinsale, but for a time I was worried that it might have been her in the mortuary. However, the body which Liam photographed there was that of a stranger who'd been involved in a hit-and-run. It was simply a coincidental accident, which had nothing to do with us."

"I see," Tanaka said. "Ask your friend Liam if he can find out anything from the Club. You mentioned he knows the owner, which might help. Supposing, for the moment, that she is fit enough, do you think she'd want to help us? It may be too dangerous for her, but Kyuji has come up with an intriguing idea, but it would only work with her assistance."

"Presupposing she's ok, I think she'd *definitely* want to help in any way she can."

"This idea is not without significant risk," Tanaka said. "If it backfires, the consequences could be dire. I've already discussed it – in principle – with the Prime Minister. He understands the wider implications without having to have everything spelled out for him and has given consent for us to go ahead.

We know that Quan is deliberately out to foment and promote trouble between Japan and China. This is a fact. It's not too much to say that this might even lead to war. If she is now aware that the data sold to her by Nomura is inaccurate, she'll try and cause mayhem some other way. We have a unique opportunity here, Hiroshi, which must not be wasted. Are you sure that the data on the memory stick in your possession is 100% accurate?"

"Yes, sir."

"We have a real chance to catch Quan red-handed and to put her away for good. Kyuji has come up with a plan. He's called-in the Army's top explosives expert and they've been working together since you sent it through. With his input, they are confident that by making some minor adjustments, Kyuji can reconfigure the data. Quan will believe it is perfect and use it. They've almost completed their computations, but it's a hell of a risk, as he's only 99% sure that it will be effective."

"My God, what if he's wrong?" H said.

"It doesn't bear thinking of," Tanaka said soberly. "I don't believe he would ever have suggested it, if he didn't think they could make it work. I trust him and have never known him to promise what he can't deliver."

"I agree, but it's the 1% that's terrifying.

"I have decided that it is worth the risk." Both men were silent, thinking about the consequences if Kyuji was wrong.

Tanaka made his decision. "Here are your specific instructions. Once Kyuji sends you the new data, upload it to the memory stick and get it to Miss Mori immediately, explaining what we've done to make it safe. She is to give it to Quan, stressing that her brother entrusted the final version of his invention to her, as a back-up. How she does it will be up to her. We know how unpredictable Quan is and what she's capable of. She may decide to get rid of the girl or even kill her for running away, but I think it's quite possible that giving her what she's wanted so desperately (and thought she'd lost) could actually save the girl's life."

There was a pause and Tanaka concluded, "it all hinges on Miss Mori; let's hope she's up to it."

Chapter 41

H finished his call to Tanaka and sat for a moment with the phone still in his hand. He punched in the number for the Club and asked if Madam Quan was still there. The Receptionist had been trained not to give out personal information, but knowing that he was friendly with the owner, she told him that Madam Quan and her party had cars organised for 6.30 that evening. H thanked her and rang off.

It was breezy on the terrace. He brushed the hair back from his forehead and looked up to see Liam walking towards him. Liam sat down and handed him the packet of Naproxen. H thanked him and swallowed one with a glass of water. He checked his watch and saw that it was almost 4 o'clock.

H looked across the table, thanking God for such a good friend. "Are you game for doing a job for me, Liam? It could be dangerous"

"I told you in Dublin that if you needed a wingman, or someone to watch your back, that you should call me."

"That's just it," H said, "I *didn't* call you; but you'll never know just how pleased I was when you turned up at the hospital."

Liam looked embarrassed, "You're too damn self-sufficient, that's your trouble. Always were – always will be. What do you want done?"

"I've found out when Quan is leaving for the yacht. We only have a couple of hours. For obvious reasons, I can't do this myself, but if you'd do it for me, it's … ." he paused, then went on, "look, you know I can't tell you everything; I wish I could, but you don't have any security clearance and anyway, you'll be safer *not* knowing the details. Seriously Liam, just believe me that this is something vitally important.

H pulled the locket out of his pocket and sat twisting it in his hand for a moment, pulling the slim silver chain backwards and forwards through his fingers. Liam looked at it curiously, but said nothing.

"I need you to go back to the Club and get this to Sora Mori, *without* Quan knowing. It won't be easy, but I'm sure you'll find a way. Tell Sora I want her to give this locket to Quan. She'll think I've gone mad, but tell her it's been made safe. It's important that she understands that. It's a bargaining chip. If she plays her cards right and Quan believes her, it may keep Sora alive."

H handed over the chain and locket. Liam slipped it into an inner pocket of his jacket. He repeated his instructions. "Well, I'd better get moving. What are you going to be doing?"

H debated for a moment and answered, "I'll go and nose around the bars in the harbour. I may get lucky and find someone from Quan's yacht. It's amazing what you can find out, if you ask the right questions." He checked his watch again. "When I'm finished, I'll go back to my car. Let's meet there."

"Fine," Liam said.

"Talking about cars, we have two between us. If we take mine to Cork Airport, I can drop it off there. What about your Maserati?

"No problem," Liam said. "I'll call my office and have someone pick it up from the Club tomorrow."

The two men stood up. "Thanks, Liam," H said, clapping him on the shoulder.

"No problem," Liam replied.

They both spoke together. "Take care." They laughed and parted company.

Liam drove back to Fort Rufus as fast as the narrow roads would allow. Tall banks, covered with gorse bushes and wild fuchsias edged much of the twisting lanes, where occasional gaps showed glimpses of ruined cottages and flashes of the sea. When he arrived, he walked slowly down the corridor towards Quan's and Sora's suites, thinking about how to handle H's request. One of the female bodyguards was standing outside the doors. He said a polite good afternoon to her as he passed, but after a hard stare, she totally blanked him. Well, she'll know me if she sees me again, he thought. He took out his key-card and continued on to his room.

He glanced at himself in a large wall mirror, straightened his jacket and smoothed his hair into shape. Having assured himself that he was his usual, pristine self, he sat down on the bed and pulled the internal phone towards him. After checking down the list of options, he pressed the button for Housekeeping and asked for someone to come as soon as possible. Whilst he waited, he pulled open the French windows and stepped out onto the terrace. A stiff breeze blew salty air into the room, whipping his hair into a tangle again. He lent his arms on the railing and looked out over the golf course, towards the sea.

A knock on the door heralded the arrival of a cheerful-looking and smartly dressed girl in her late twenties. "I'm Sinead," she said. "What can I do for you, sir?"

"Tell me Sinead, are you a discrete girl?"

"Close as the grave, sir," she replied promptly.

"I could tell just by looking at you, that you were a woman after my own heart," he said with a grin.

She giggled, watching as he took a bill-fold out of his back pocket and peeled off two 50 Euro notes.

He handed them over, saying, "Now, Sinead, my dear, here's what I'd like you to do."

Chapter 42

Château Trompette Des Anges - Near Boissy

This time everything worked according to plan. On their way to meet the gardener Clement Morel and the security guard for dinner, Henri and Laure dropped Maurice off in sight of the Château gates. Once he'd seen the two men drive out in the Renault Scenic, Maurice gave them a twenty minute head-start, before making his way to the stable block. As it was still early evening and broad daylight, he kept to the trees wherever he could, but knew that the caretaker should be the only person on the property – apart from himself – and the chances of being seen were remote.

He walked cautiously under the archway and stopped to listen before going on into the courtyard. The silence was absolute. The fact that the Dobermans *didn't* start barking, worried rather than relieved him. Perhaps they were allowed to roam freely when their owner was out. Maurice shuddered at the thought of them appearing and attacking him. The sooner he got into the car, the safer he'd feel. He went inside the coach house and found the metal key box on the wall, exactly where Henri had told him it would be.

Noticing that the car had its bonnet close to the wall, Maurice saw he'd need to reverse out, so he walked over to the entrance and pulled open the wide double doors, to allow himself room to manoeuvre. He used the Bentley keyfob, which unlocked the car with a satisfactory and distinctive thunk. The driver's door was so badly damaged that he got in through the passenger side and slid across into the driver's seat. Maurice pushed aside the airbags which must have deployed during the crash. Henri had warned him that he might have to use jump-leads to start the car, as the battery probably hadn't been turned over for quite some time, but he needn't have worried. Maurice pushed the start button and the engine roared into life.

Maurice found that his heart was thudding. If that noise hadn't brought the dogs out; nothing would. He checked the rear view mirror and reversed carefully into the yard. After putting the car in park mode, he got out to close the double doors, keeping a wary eye out for the dogs. The fact that they were shut would help to delay the moment when the Bentley's loss was discovered.

As he eased the car along the back drive, he wondered whom they'd tell and whether they'd inform the police as well. It was something he hadn't got round to discussing with the others, so he made a mental note to do so later. Resisting the temptation to put his foot down, he nursed the big car gently towards Henri's garage in Tallois.

The dreadful weather of the last few days had been replaced by a sunny, autumn evening. After a while the adrenalin rush started to subside and his heartbeat returned to normal. He began to enjoy driving the Bentley, which was a far cry from his old Citroën.

When the idea of had first occurred to him, he hadn't realised quite how much entertainment and excitement it would give him or how much he'd enjoy being reunited with his old friends – and Laure. The planning, the organisation and the execution of his plan had been such a change from the norm. He suddenly felt pumped-up again, with an astonishing sense of achievement. In a rich baritone he began to sing the stirring lyrics of La Marseillaise, beating time on the steering wheel.

He did feel conspicuous driving a car with a smashed side window and damaged door panel, so he felt relieved when he saw Henri's showroom ahead. He turned off the road and took the Bentley round to the workshop at the back – out of sight.

He'd done it!

Chapter 43

One of the reasons that Quan was so successful was that she never allowed herself to waste time. She decided that it would be a little while before Sora was up to talking, so one of her many personal assistants had been sent over from the *Sappho* and she'd gone through some mundane paperwork. She understood that hard work and attention to detail was what kept a good business strong. Wherever she was, she took daily reports and briefings from the CEO's of her various companies around the world. Meetings needed to be scheduled, new contacts followed up, sales figures checked, appointments made, and staff promoted or fired.

Once she'd finished the paperwork and the PA had left, Quan went to the wall safe and keyed-in her code. Inside was a large, crocodile skin box, which she took out and placed on the desk, under a lamp. She lifted the lid and a glittering array of jewellery sparkled in the light. Emeralds, rubies, sapphires and diamonds made a kaleidoscope of scintillating colours. One by one, she took the pieces out and examined them. Finally, she made her choice; an elegant diamond and ruby bracelet, fit for a queen. From a drawer at the bottom of the jewel case, she took out a long shagreen box, lined with black velvet and arranged the bracelet inside. Satisfied, she locked the box away in the safe and slid the bracelet into one of her wide pockets.

It was time to see if Sora was fully awake. They needed to talk. She opened the intercommunicating doors and walked through. Sora was sitting up in bed talking to a young member of the housekeeping team. They both looked up, startled, as Quan entered the room. Sora's face was flushed.

"And what's going on in here?" Quan demanded suspiciously.

Under the covers, Sora surreptitiously pushed the locket under the pillow and slipped a twisted silver ring off her finger. She held it up, saying, "Sinead, here has just been returning this ring to me. It must have dropped off somewhere and was handed in to the reception desk."

"I'd noticed it before, on Miss's dressing table, so I knew it was hers," Sinead added. "If there's nothing else you need, Miss, I'll be getting back to work."

"That's fine," Sora said, smiling warmly at the girl. "Thank you again for your help." Quan stood unspeaking as the girl sidled out of the room, quietly closing the door behind her.

Sora's flush had died down and she was now as pale as a lily. She hid her trembling fingers under the covers and waited, holding her breath, to see what Quan had to say.

"Why did you go with that man and why did you run away?" Quan's mild tone surprised Sora, who'd expected a more violent outburst.

Taking a deep breath and trying to keep her voice level, Sora said, "I wasn't trying to run away."

"What then? Explain it to me, Sora."

Since waking up, she'd been thinking furiously of what she should tell Quan. She knew she'd have to force herself to speak slowly, or she might make a slip. Her mind was still slightly fuzzy and her train of thought had been broken by the news Sinead had brought her. On one hand she was elated that H was still alive and that he'd found a way of contacting her. Thankfully, Sinead had been bright enough to follow her lead, and Quan had seemed to accept their story. On the other hand, she'd had no time to factor in the new information from H. One wrong step and the plan might easily fall apart. What to say and what to leave out? All these thoughts jostled together and she fervently wished her mind felt sharper and that she had more time.

Start with the simple bits, Sora told herself. "It's rather a long story. As you know, I went out to watch the golf. Omega – I'm sorry, that's a nickname I gave her – I mean Bo Huáng your bodyguard was with me. We walked round with Sir John and Lady Lister and a few others. Lady Lister saw Mister Suzuki and called him over. After a while he started talking to me and the Listers had moved further on. Mister Suzuki said he knew my brother. As I hadn't seen him for a while, I asked for news of him. I'd had enough of the golf by then and he suggested driving into Kinsale. Knowing that he'd made the successful bid for a lunch with me, at the auction, I thought it would be ok. I'm sorry. I should have asked you first."

Quan frowned. "And where was Bo Huáng, whilst you were planning to go off gallivanting in Kinsale with a stranger?"

Sora hesitated. "There was such a crowd that we'd become separated. I looked around for her, but couldn't see her anywhere."

Quan was still frowning and looked sceptical. "That seems extraordinary. It was her job to stay with you."

"I thought it was strange too. I did look for her, but she seemed to have vanished. In the end, I just gave up. I simply didn't think, and I'm sorry if I upset you."

Quan's face softened. "Naturally I was worried about you. *Don't* do such a thing again." She tapped Sora on her cheek. "I'm sorry you got hurt by that car. I can't think how it could have happened." Her eyes narrowed and her voice sharpened, "but I will find out, and punish whoever was responsible."

Sora shivered and Quan suddenly smiled. "Silly girl. I'm happy you are back with me. Now, you need to get ready; we're leaving for the *Sappho* shortly. We'll be on board in time for dinner." She reached into her pocket. "To welcome you back, I have a little present for you, which I hope you'll like."

Sora opened the box and gasped as she saw the bracelet. It was a magnificent peace offering and truly lovely. She lifted it out and forced herself to smile at Quan. "Is it really for me? It's wonderful."

Quan bent forward and clipped it round Sora's wrist, where it twinkled as she moved her hand. Sora forced herself to accept Quan's kiss, as she thanked her.

To distract her, Sora said, "I'm worried about my brother. May I ask for your advice?"

Quan stood up. "Later, my dear. We can talk about it later."

Chapter 44

After almost an hour of searching the waterfront bars of Kinsale, and keeping away from the tourist-filled centre of the town, H had had no success in finding any of the crew from the *Sappho.* He'd felt obliged to drink a couple of beers and knew that they didn't mix well with the Naproxen. He walked along the harbour, watching the boats rocking gently at their moorings.

He lent against a bollard, watching the world go by. The flickering lights of the sun on the water warned him of his headache returning. He closed his eyes and dozed for a few minutes, listening to the mewing of the herring gulls. He was disturbed by the sound of men's voices, raised in argument a little further along the quay. He tried to block them out and hoped they'd move away and leave him in peace. One of the men said, "keep your *fecking* nose *out* of my business."

H's eyes snapped open. He'd heard that voice say almost the exact same words to him. In an instant, his memory clicked back and he remembered. He shook his head to clear the mass of information suddenly flooding back into his brain. Looking to his left, he saw the two men. One had gripped the other by the front of his jersey and pushed him away roughly. The second man stumbled and turned away, saying, "ok, ok, Dermot. I get the picture." He strode away down along the quay. The first man picked up a heavy coil of rope and started down some steps towards the water.

H stood up and stepped forward to look over the railings. He saw the man on a small concrete platform below, beside a small boat tied to a stanchion. He gauged the distance and swung himself over the railings, dropping down between the man and the boat. Dermot looked up in surprise and his eyes widened as he recognised H. Without giving him a chance to react, H punched him hard in the solar plexus. Dermot was driven backwards. He doubled-up, took a step and tripped over the rope. "What do you want?" he gasped. H pulled him upright and slammed him against the wall. "Information, Dermot. Why did you and your friends attack me?"

A startled look crossed the man's face. He glanced around, but nobody could see them and H was still between him and his boat. He was wheezing and the words came out with difficulty. "How do you know my name?"

"Never mind that. Answer the question."

A sly look crossed Dermot's coarse face. "It'll cost you, lad," he said, his confidence and bravado trickling back.

"You're in *no* position to bargain, but if you tell me what I want to know, you may save yourself a ducking. I owe you for that cosh." Unconsciously H's hand rubbed the back of his head.

"Hurt did it?" Dermot said, watching H with satisfaction. "That Taser didn't look much fun either! You must be one tough bastard to be out of bed so soon. I'll say that for you."

"Enough of the compliments," H said, moving forward again.

"Ok, ok. Weren't we approached by a couple of foreign women? The money was good and all they wanted was a bit of muscle. Me and the boys were happy to oblige." He hesitated. "Satisfied? Then I'll be on me way."

Dermot straightened off the wall, balled his fists and came on fast, his right arm swinging, but he'd made the mistake of underestimating H, who sidestepped and chopped the outside of his hand down hard on Dermot's exposed neck. The outcome was inevitable. Dermot's momentum took him forward and he took a step into thin air, cursing as he went over the edge and down into the water.

H watched him rise, spluttering to the surface, desperately struggling to get out of his gumboots, which were threatening to drag him under again.

H gave him a wave and walked up the steps and set off for the car park.

When Liam returned to the car, he found H fast asleep behind the wheel, with the seat racked back. H came fully awake the instant he heard Liam tap on the window, and unlocked the door. Liam slid in beside him and gave him a thumbs-up.

"Well done – good initiative!" H said, after Liam had explained everything. "You're wasted making gadgets. Have you ever considered joining us spooks?"

Liam laughed. "I'm happy as I am, thanks, but I found I quite enjoyed a bit of the cloak-and-dagger stuff. How did you get on?"

"You won't believe it, but my memory's come back!"

Liam looked delighted. "What, all of it?"

H filled him in on what had happened. "In one second – hearing that voice – the missing bits just fell back into place," he concluded.

"That's brilliant. I didn't like the idea of you charging off to Monte Carlo with some of your brain shut down."

"I wasn't thrilled with the idea either," H said wryly. Switching the subject he said, "Do you want to fly to Nice tonight or tomorrow? If Quan's going by sea, we've got a bit of leeway. Whichever you decide is fine by me."

Liam turned in his seat and looked at H. He knew he'd deny that he was still feeling the after effects of the last two days, so he said, diplomatically, "I think we'd be better off staying at the Club tonight and heading off tomorrow. I'm not used to all this rushing around and excitement. I could do with an early night."

H saw straight through Liam's story and laughed. H wasn't used to having someone else looking out for him and was touched by his friend's consideration. He sat up, pulled the seat upright and started the Range Rover.

"Right, you're the boss… until we get to Monte Carlo."

Once back at the Club, they had an early dinner and went to say goodbye to Arthur Lysaght. They found him in the bar and he invited them to join him for a drink.

When they'd been served, Lysaght turned to H. "That Chinese woman, Madam Quan – she had an awful lot of questions about you."

"What did she want to know? H asked.

"All the usual things: who you were, what you did for a living, where you were going next. How well did I know you and stuff like that."

"What did you tell her?" H asked curiously.

"I did my professional oyster act. I said that I'd never met you before, but you were a friend-of-a-friend (not mentioning Liam's name). She looked most unsatisfied, so I threw her a small bone. I said I'd heard you were in the film business and that your next stop was Monaco. Was that ok?

"Perfect," H said, raising his glass with a smile.

Chapter 45

There was no opportunity for Sora to speak privately to Quan that evening. After they'd gone on board the *Sappho,* she'd been shown to a luxurious cabin, where a uniformed stewardess was unpacking her clothes. A bath had already been run, but she spent a few minutes discussing the clothes she wanted to wear that evening. To please Quan, she chose one of her favourite Bruce Oldfield pieces: a blood-red velvet cocktail dress, with a matching velvet wrap which would go perfectly with her new bracelet. Gold Jimmy Choo heels and a small gold clutch bag from Judith Leiber completed her outfit.

Her hip was stiff and her body ached, so she swallowed a couple of painkillers and made a mental note not to drink any alcohol. She lay for a long time, soaking in steaming hot water, which made her feel a little better. When she was dressed, she knocked lightly on the intercommunicating door and was told to come in. Quan was seated at a dressing table, wearing a startlingly colourful silk dressing gown, covered with writhing dragons. A beautician in a white outfit was making up her face and a manicurist sat beside her, painting her talon-like nails. She pulled a hand away and twisted round to look at Sora.

"You look charming, my dear" she said, "utterly charming." She raised a hand and made a circling motion with her index finger and Sora obediently turned in a full circle. "Yes, you've chosen well and I'm pleased to see you wearing my gift." She turned back to the mirror. "Hurry up Sasha, you're taking far too long. I could do it myself in half the time." The poor woman held out a lipstick for her approval. "Not that one you imbecile. It's completely the wrong shade. Use a coral one; to match my nails."

Sora sat down carefully, realising that now was not a good time.

Quan said over her shoulder, "I'm going to be late. Go along to the Saloon and look after the others and check the seating plan. I haven't had a moment to do it. There are only ten of us. Make sure you put Giles Trelawny next to me, with Abe Schwartz on my left. I want those boring Patels as far away from me as possible." She turned back to the mirror and Sora realised she was dismissed.

Dinner passed in a haze. She felt exhausted and it was an effort to make small talk to the guests. Two of the couples had come with them from Fort Rufus and one single man and one other couple had joined them that evening, having flown down together from Dublin.

After the coffee had been served, Sora found she couldn't remember a single word of the conversations she'd had during the meal. The combined scents of the tuberoses and lilies, which were massed on the table was overpowering and she started to feel a little giddy. The fact that all of the flower arrangements had been sprayed with black florist paint, added to her feeling of oppression. She took a gulp of iced water, gripping her glass and waiting for the room to steady.

Quan was seated opposite her and Sora hesitated until there was a gap in the conversation before asking, "would you mind if I retire?"

Words of refusal rose instinctively to Quan's lips, but then she looked carefully at Sora, remembering what had happened to her earlier. The girl's eyes were ringed with dark smudges and she looked worn out.

"Of course, my dear," she said graciously. "You must be tired."

Sora said her goodnights thankfully and slipped away, trying not to limp. She got ready for bed, switched off the lamps and lay in the darkness, hoping that she'd be able to get Quan on her own the following day, and in the right frame of mind to listen to what Sora had to tell her. The yacht had left Castlepark Marina and was making way. The motion was barely discernible, but it was peaceful. She was still working out what she was going to say, when she fell asleep.

Chapter 46

Henri Davoust's Garage - Tallois - South of Paris

When Laure and Henri returned from their dinner, they found Maurice and Pascal drinking coffee in the kitchen.

"Well?" Laure asked, "did everything go according to plan? Where is it?"

Maurice gave a broad grin. "Let's go and see, shall we?"

They all trooped out to the workshop. "It's really here," Henri said unnecessarily. "Outstanding!"

Henri walked all round the Bentley, assessing the exterior damage. "Tomorrow I'll have a proper look at the engine and then I'll have a better idea of what parts are going to be needed and how long it's going to take to repair."

"Won't it cost a fortune to put right?" Pascal asked.

"Well, not a fortune, but a fair bit. I'll do a rough estimate of the costs tomorrow. To give you some idea, you can see from the outside that it'll need a replacement window, body-shop repairs to the door panels and a paint rework." He opened the passenger door and peered inside. "The two airbags which deployed have caused the usual damage, so I'm afraid that the driver's seat will need replacing. I'll check all the wheels and tyres and we'll definitely need to do a chassis alignment when we've finished. Apart from that, we'll know better tomorrow."

"Would you be able to do everything here?" Maurice asked hopefully.

"Ideally, of course it should be sent back to the Bentley Service Centre in Paris. However, it'll cost substantially less if we can do the repairs and refurbishments here. George, my head mechanic is a wonderful old guy. He trained at Bentley in Paris and knows all there is to know. We'll ask his advice."

Laure was getting bored of the technicalities. "Let's go back into the house. I think a celebration is in order. I didn't want to tempt fate, but I bought a bottle of good champagne and put it in the fridge yesterday. Let's go and drink it."

When Henri had opened the bottle and poured their drinks, Maurice tapped his glass. "A toast to you all! Thank you for helping me in this adventure. I give you, *the Bentley*!" he said with a little bow.

"*The Bentley*," they all chorused as they lifted their glasses.

"Maurice, do tell us what happened at the Château," Laure said.

He smiled at her. "Well, to begin with, I couldn't believe how lax their security is. They seem to leave all the gates and doors unlocked, even when they're out. They wouldn't last five minutes in any job where they were supervised."

He re-told the events of the evening, with one humorous anecdote. "Because of the damage to the car, I was keeping a good look out for *les flics*. Not five minutes after I got onto the main road, one of their cars passed me, with the sirens blaring. I nearly had a heart failure, but they flashed past me and continued going."

They all laughed and Laure poured out refills. They congratulated Maurice again and he asked them how their dinner had gone.

"We found out more information about the Château than we ever needed to know," Henri told them. "The evening was fine and they both fancied Laure like mad, which was a good thing, because we wanted to keep them out of your way for as long as possible."

Pascal laughed, but Maurice looked at Laure, who seemed a bit embarrassed. "I feel a bit bad about leading them on." Maurice raised an eyebrow. "I mean," she went on, "that they believe we want to buy the Château and now they think their jobs will be safe."

"Save your sympathy, Laure," Henri said. He turned to the others. "Talking about their lousy security, can you believe that those *cretins* actually came out for dinner with those guard dogs and left them in the back of the car!"

Pascal started on a rather long and involved story about a lazy guard dog. Henri tuned-out. He couldn't stop thinking about the Bentley and the challenges of renovating it. He got up and left the room for a few minutes – he simply couldn't resist going to have another look at the car.

When he came back, he looked excited. "You won't *believe* what I've found. We definitely won't be able to take that car anywhere near the Bentley dealers – they'd have a fit. There are bullet holes in the boot! It's packed with some serious kit, hidden away inside, even some sort of machine gun. It's like something from a film. God knows who put them in, or why, but they're giving me some strange ideas about your friend, Maurice. What can you tell us about him?"

"Practically nothing, I'm afraid," Maurice said, slowly shaking his head. He'd promised Aristide de Lamerie that he'd keep H's occupation confidential and would honour his word. They all pressed him, but he wouldn't say any more.

To change the subject, he started talking about the Bentley. "I've never driven such a fabulous car and only wish I could have put my foot down. The interior was incredibly luxurious and the seat was so comfortable that I could have slept in it."

Henri joined in. "I totally agree. Old George has been telling me some great stories. If you'd be interested…?

They all agreed. They were lingering contentedly over their drinks and nobody was ready to break up the party.

"I've learnt a lot about Bentley and their history from him. He was telling me recently how Mulliner – Bentley's coach building arm – came about.

In England, way back in 1559 the Mulliner family had a company producing saddles. In the 1700s they were granted a royal warrant for carriage making, as well as building and maintaining carriages for the Royal Mail. Fast forward to 1900, when they spotted the potential in the infant automobile industry and branched out into coachbuilding. Since then, they've gone from strength to strength."

His enthusiasm was infectious and he could see that they were all interested.

"Mulliner has created many special projects including the State Limousine for Queen Elizabeth II in 2002. Their association with Bentley started back in 1923 when they made a bespoke 3-litre, two-seater Bentley for the Olympia Show and in 1959 they cemented their partnership with Bentley by becoming a part of the business."

"I'd never heard any of that," Maurice said. "What a fascinating story."

By that time they'd finished the bottle and everyone was starting to feel tired. Maurice stood up and stretched, clapped Pascal on the back and said, "*en avant, mon vieux*." He'd invited Pascal to stay with him, so they said goodnight and went back to Boissy.

It had been a thoroughly satisfactory day.

Part Three

Chapter 47

Monte-Carlo

H and Liam left Ireland together the following morning, flying from Cork in Liam's elegant Cessna Citation Latitude. H loved the jet and told Liam that his business must be doing even better than he'd thought. Liam had made all of the arrangements and H was delighted to sit back and enjoy the ride. They touched down at Nice Côte d'Azur International Airport and took the helicopter shuttle, which landed seven minutes later at the Héliport de Monaco. Liam had also organised a car, which took them to the Hôtel Hermitage in the centre of Monte-Carlo.

When they checked-in, H found two messages waiting for him. They went up to their rooms, agreeing to meet downstairs for lunch in half an hour. Their bags had already been brought up and after tipping the porter, H unpacked and hung up his clothes before opening the French windows and stepping out onto a private balcony. He put on his Ray-Bans, breathed in the salty air and looked with pleasure over the panoramic view of Port Hercule below. The weather in Cork had been a cool, breezy 11 degrees. Here the sun was pouring down and the temperature was 21 degrees. H revelled in the warmth and turned his face up to the sun. He felt better already.

He opened the first of his messages, which was written on the Hotel notepaper. '*Welcome to Monaco,*' he read. '*I'm dining with an old friend of yours this evening and if you are free to join us, please give me a call on this number.*' It was signed Aristide de Lamerie.

The short note was intriguing. H had met de Lamerie, the head of the DCRI – the French Internal Intelligence Service – the year before, when he was working on a case in France. The two men got on well together and had mutual respect. H brought up a mental picture of de Lamerie: urbane, elegant, charming and shrewd. H would very much enjoy seeing him again and as there was no chance of Madam Quan and the *Sappho* arriving that day, he decided to ring and accept. He'd check what Liam's plans were, over lunch.

Suddenly feeling hungry, H checked his watch and opened the other envelope. It contained only four lines, which brought a broad smile to his face. *'If you are free, please join me downstairs in the foyer at 6 p.m. as I have something to show you, which I think will make you happy.'* This note was signed Maurice Duval.

When H walked onto the terrace, he found Liam already sipping a glass of champagne and discussing the menu with the Maître d'. As usual, he was flamboyantly dressed, in a sky blue linen jacket, with pale pink golf trousers and bright blue suede Tods on his bare feet. By comparison, H looked positively conservative in his navy blazer, white cotton oxford shirt and chinos, with an old pair of Wildsmith loafers. The restaurant was buzzing and most of the tables were already taken. As they were in the playground of the rich and famous, H recognised several faces from the world of show-business and Liam's table was next to a group of well-known tennis players.

As usual, there were lots of pretty girls on show and Liam noticed – with a wry smile – that it was H whose good looks were attracting most of their attention. Following a train of thought, he said, "H, when this job or mission or assignment, or whatever you call these things is over, I'd really like to come and see you in Tokyo. I hardly know that part of the world at all and would like to have a look around. It would also be useful to check out the competition on the locks, keys and toys front. I've always been attracted to the gorgeous Japanese girls too!"

H laughed and said he'd be delighted. He took a quick glance at the menu and after they'd ordered, he mentioned his two messages and asked if Liam was free for dinner.

"I'd love to. I've spoken to my business associates and I'm not meeting them until tomorrow morning."

With the air of a conjuror producing a rabbit from a hat, Liam flourished a pair of tickets in the air.

"Did you know that the Monte-Carlo Rolex Masters tennis competition is on? I got talking to some Americans who were checking out. They were bemoaning the fact that they had to leave unexpectedly, so I bought their tickets."

"That's great," H said, deciding that tomorrow would be early enough to start exercising again. After all, Doctor Ryan had advised him to take it easy for a few days. For once, H was able, and happy to comply.

They decided to spend an hour lying in the sun before going down to the Country Club to watch some tennis. They thoroughly enjoyed a leisurely meal in the aptly named L'Hirondelle Restaurant, where swallows swooped and dived, performing their graceful aerial acrobatics in the air above.

Chapter 48

In the Mediterranean

The weather got appreciably warmer as the *Sappho* made its way through the Straits of Gibraltar, moving from the Atlantic Ocean into the Mediterranean Sea and turning north east towards Monaco. The guests lay around on the Sundeck, basking in the sunshine and enjoying the luxury of being waited on by the meticulously trained staff. Every whim could be indulged and they took advantage of everything that was on offer.

One or two of the more perceptive guests thought it strange that their hostess should have chosen this cruise, instead of the quicker mode of flying to their destination. Quan had her reasons and could have enlightened them, but chose not to. She used people as chess pieces; moving them around in complicated and intricate games. Each one suited her purposes for a time and when they'd outlived their usefulness, they were discarded without a second thought.

On a lower deck, Quan kept a fully staffed office with all the latest technology to keep her abreast of World events and news, as well as her varied business empire and those of her competitors. Finishing a long morning of calls and paperwork, she dismissed her secretary and one of her PAs. Once she was alone she sat back for a moment and closed her eyes.

A question on her mind was Mister Hiroshi Suzuki and whether he posed a threat to her. She had set her team of investigators on him after he'd taken Sora away from the Golf Club. There had been something about him that had caused her antenna to tingle. The story of why he'd attended the Golf Tournament was reasonable, but he seemed too confident, too charming and she felt uneasy about him, without knowing quite why. The reports, which had reached her that morning, had been unhelpful. They had turned up eleven Hiroshi Suzuki's of the same sort of age and general description. She had ordered copies of every picture taken by a professional photographer at the competition, but he had not appeared in any of them. He'd mentioned he was going on to Monte-Carlo. It would be easy to find out where he was staying, as well as whom he met and where he went. A copy of his passport – if she could get hold of it – might also prove helpful. A honey-trap was another option. Information could be gleaned from so many different sources. She rang Mister Johnson, the head of her investigations team and gave him a set of explicit instructions.

Quan decided that she deserved a short break before lunch and reached for the intercom. "Send my stewardess to my stateroom, then find Miss Mori and have her join me immediately."

Having changed into a voluminous beach robe, Quan walked out onto her personal balcony. Sora was already waiting for her, leaning on the rail and looking out over the sea towards the Spanish coast. The stiff breeze caught her hair and her floral dress blew sideways, making a lovely picture, as though she was posing for a promotional yacht photo shoot.

Quan's hard expression softened as she looked at Sora. "How are you feeling this morning?" she enquired.

"Much better, thank you."

"Come and sit down and entertain me."

The girl looked alright, Quan thought dispassionately. Her interest in Sora's health was tepid and as long as it didn't impinge on her own plans, it could be safely ignored.

A steward appeared and served them drinks, before disappearing inside. Quan discussed the previous night's dinner party and made a few disparaging remarks about her guests' manners, clothes and eating habits. Sora kept quiet and waited for a convenient opening.

"I wanted to ask your advice about something, if you wouldn't mind?" Sora began. "You have so much knowledge and experience and I'd really appreciate your help." Sora wondered if she'd laid it on too thick, but Quan was not impervious to flattery. Her interest in any other person's personal problems was almost non-existent, but she was prepared to humour Sora.

"Any guidance I can give you my dear, would be a pleasure."

Sora had had long enough to consider exactly what she wanted to say. However, it needed to look unrehearsed and natural. As if choosing her words with care, she said, "my parents both died a long time ago and for years, my only family has been my brother. We are very close, but I'm really worried about him."

Quan checked her watch and hoped this wouldn't take too long.

"I saw him for lunch in Tokyo, but the restaurant was attacked by gunmen and Jiro disappeared. I haven't heard from him since."

Quan's ears pricked up. Jiro was not an uncommon name, but coupled with the mention of the restaurant shooting, it interested her. She'd read about the attack at the time and had wondered what was behind it.

"How frightening for you; I'd no idea you were there. Tell me more about your brother."

"He has all the brains of the family. He's an inventor and totally brilliant."

"What line of work is Mister Mori in?"

Sora laughed, "Oh, Mori is only a modelling name, thought up by my agent. Our family name is Nomura."

Chapter 49

Monte-Carlo

H stood on the first floor balcony of the Jardin d'Hiver Lobby, resting his hands on the rail of the ornate white and gilded ironwork, looking down into the lobby, to see if Maurice was there. He looked up to appreciate the stained glass cupola of the airy atrium, designed by the famous Monsieur Gustave Eiffel, and then ran lightly down the steps on one side of the sweeping double staircase. His nose twitched as he sniffed the air, trying to pinpoint a faint but characteristic smell, particular to the Hermitage. The closest he could get was that it reminded him of a Bulgari cologne, but the name eluded him.

The treads were covered in a thick red and gold carpet and H didn't realise that someone was following him down. At the foot of the stairs, he paused to admire some attractive large blue and white pots, filled with ferns, white orchids and a tall ficus tree, still thinking about the elusive aroma. He was startled by a woman's voice saying, "*Oh là là,*" as she bumped into him. He spun round and saw an opulently endowed, but conservatively dressed woman, of a certain age. Her capacious handbag flew out of her hand, spilling some of the contents. "*Je suis vraiment désolé, Madame,*" he said as he picked up a riding whip which landed at his feet. He handed it back to her with a bow and a wicked smile and kissed her hand, noting that she didn't seem in the least embarrassed. She gave him a crooked grin in return. Over her shoulder he saw Maurice hovering at the entrance to the lobby, with a broad grin on his face. "I must go, Madame. It was nice to have almost met you," he said, as he moved away.

"You rascal and breaker of hearts," Maurice said, throwing his arms around H and kissing him soundly on both cheeks with Gallic fervour. "That lovely woman looked most disappointed." He held H at arm's length. "Let me look at you," he said. "Yes, a definite improvement on the last time I saw you."

H laughed, looking with affection into Maurice's creased, well lived-in face. "It's so good to see you again, but how on earth did you know I was here?"

Maurice took his arm and steered him towards the exit. "Later, later, all will be revealed, but first I have something to show you." He led H into the main lobby, across the white marble floor and out though the doors onto the street. He nodded to the doorman, who put a hand in the air and beckoned. A large, gunmetal grey car edged out of a parking bay and pulled to a stop beside them.

It took a lot to shock H, but he stood rooted to the spot, hardly able to believe his eyes. In front of him was his treasured Bentley GT. It was in pristine condition – perfection on wheels.

He was recalled to the present by a testy voice saying, "*s'il vous plaît, Monsieur, s'il vous plaît.* You are blocking my way."

H apologised and stepped aside. He saw that Maurice was beaming like a proud parent who'd produced a prodigy. Maurice slid a tip into the waiting hand of the young porter who'd got out of the driving seat and was holding the door open. Maurice waved H to the passenger side and slid in behind the wheel and pulled out into the road.

"I have surprised you, *n'est – ce pas*?"

H found his voice, "That's the understatement of the year! However did you do it?"

"*C'est une merveilleuse histoire,*" Maurice said gaily.

He drove the short distance to the Café de Paris, where parking places are as rare as hen's teeth. As he approached, a car pulled away from the kerb, almost outside the entrance. The driver flashed his lights and gave a salute before driving away. H raised an eyebrow at Maurice, who said: "my army training led me to ensure we wasted no time on mundane matters. That was a friend of mine. He'll join us for dinner later – when he finally finds another place for his car."

"My compliments on your staff-work," H said sincerely as they got out of the car. He walked around, smoothing a hand over the perfect paintwork and admiring every detail. "Maurice, *c'est incroyable.* I never thought I'd see my pride and joy again. I can't wait to hear the story."

Satisfied with H's reaction, Maurice ushered him into the Bar des Jeux of the Café de Paris.

Once their drinks had been placed in front of them, Maurice took a long sip of his cocktail, brushing the froth carefully off his moustache. "I wanted to have you to myself for a while, before we join the others for dinner. I have *so* much to tell you and the fact that you are pleased makes me more than glad."

H sat enthralled at the story Maurice related. When he'd finished, H signalled the barman and ordered another round of drinks. He lifted his glass to Maurice. "Not only are you a Good Samaritan, but you're a miracle worker too. Maurice, I salute you. Thank you for everything."

H insisted on paying the bill and they strolled out into the evening sunshine. "We're going to Cipriani's for dinner," Maurice told him. "Your host is another old friend. Perhaps you know who it is?" H asked how Maurice had come into contact with Aristide de Lamerie and Maurice related how they'd met at Monique Lavalle's funeral and had later become friends.

They were both silent for a while, thinking about Monique. Maurice sighed and then continued, "I told Aristide my plans for your Bentley. He was pleased to approve! He promised to let me know when he heard you'd be in France again. *Et viola* – here we are!"

Chapter 50

Somewhere in the Mediterranean

There was a stunned pause as Quan took in what Sora had just told her. How was it *possible* that she hadn't known Jiro Nomura was Sora's brother? The world was full of coincidences, but this was ridiculous. Quan's brain buzzed with speculation as to how she could turn this new knowledge to her advantage. She played for time by adding some more ice to her drink, but Sora hadn't missed the flash of shock in Quan's eyes.

Quan decided to allow Sora to continue talking and see what she could learn. It was obvious that the girl had no idea that she already knew a great deal about Nomura, or that she'd ever heard his name.

"Normally we keep in constant contact, but, as you know, that hasn't been possible recently." Sora paused, but Quan understood exactly what she meant. "This morning, I, er…I borrowed an iPhone from one of your guest's and checked my emails. There was nothing from Jiro. I tried to call his mobile too, but it was switched off." She expected an outburst from Quan, but when none came, Sora went on, "that man at the Club, Mister Suzuki, he told me that he knew my brother. That's one of the reasons I went with him to Kinsale; to find out if he'd seen him recently, or had any news."

"And had he?" Quan asked.

Sora bit her lip. She hadn't meant to mention H. She needed to calm down and keep to her prepared script. "Sadly not," she said, feeling her way. "He just mentioned that he knew of our relationship and wondered if I had news of Jiro myself. It was most disappointing." It sounded lame even to her ears.

Quan was also feeling her way. She didn't want to scare Sora and kept her tone casual, "did he say *how* he came to know your brother?"

"No," she said slowly, as if trying to remember, "I don't believe he did."

Quan looked sceptical, so Sora continued, "anyway, that's not really important. What I wanted to ask your advice about was something completely different."

Quan was about to say that *she* should be the one to decide what was or was not important, but she held back.

"Tell me, what's on your mind, my dear," she said gently.

Sora knew that her moment had come to reel Quan in. If she played her cards right she'd be a step closer to punishing Quan for what she'd done to Jiro and also helping H as well. H hadn't confided in her as to exactly what Quan was planning or how he meant to stop her. Sora only knew that this was the one way in which she could be of real use. She fingered the locket around her neck, holding it tightly in her hand and drawing strength from the cold metal.

She took a deep breath, "Jiro trusts me. As children, we shared everything and had no secrets from each other, but recently he's changed. At that last lunch – before the shooting started – I could tell he was worried. He said he wanted to tell me something important."

Sora's mouth felt dry. After taking a drink, she took the chain from around her neck.

"He never got the chance to tell me, but he did give me this," she said, holding up the necklace.

Quan's eyes were riveted on the swinging chain in Sora's hand.

"I've looked inside. It contains a computer memory stick. I think that it has information on it, which must have been important to Jiro. I feel he knew it would be safe with me."

How wrong you are, you little idiot, Quan thought to herself. Her rising excitement was hard to conceal. If it did contain what she fervently hoped it would, her plans could go ahead and the Generals would eat humble pie. Her plan would be back on track and no one could stop her. She realised that Sora was looking at her strangely.

"Would you like me to get my technicians to have a look at it? Then you'll know what it was your brother wanted you to keep for him."

Quan held out her hand for the locket.

"I suppose so," Sora said. "That's what I wanted to ask your advice about. Do you think I should find out what's on it, or perhaps Jiro would wish me to keep safe it until he asks for it back again. I just don't know what to do for the best."

Quan was in no doubt at all. "I think it's better to know. Surely, if your brother had not wanted it seen – whatever it is – he would have told you so."

"Thank you. You are right. I knew you'd be able to advise me."

Sora put the locket into Quan's outstretched hand.

Chapter 51

Monte-Carlo

Six men from widely different walks of life sat down to dinner together at Cipriani Monte-Carlo: the French Secret Service supremo, a master baker, a designer of toys and gadgets, a provincial bank manager, the owner of a car hire firm and an Anglo-Japanese Secret Service operative. Sitting on the Cipriani signature brown leather chairs and drinking Bellinis, they were surrounded by shining mahogany walls, covered with mirrors and classic film posters.

Aristide de Lamerie was an excellent host and on his recommendation, everyone chose the superlative homemade baked green tagliolini with veal ragù. Liam knew only H; the bank manager and the car hire owner knew only Maurice; Aristide knew H and Maurice. However, the evening could not have been a greater success. They had common bonds: their love of good food and wine, excitement and danger, as well as a growing fondness for Hiroshi Suzuki.

Maurice, Pascal and Henri were still flushed with the success of their car-jacking enterprise and could hardly wait to fill-in H and the others on exactly how they'd pulled it off. As the idea had been Maurice's brainchild, he was allowed to begin the story, which lost nothing in the telling. He was a natural raconteur and made the most of his moment. Henri and Pascal chipped-in with personal, hilarious additions, capping each other's stories. By the time they'd finished their homemade vanilla ice cream *à la minute* – a speciality of the house – it was if they'd all been friends for years.

When the party broke up, Maurice said that he was going for a long walk to enjoy the sights of Monte-Carlo. Liam offered to drive back to the Hermitage in the Bentley and to drop the others off on his way.

Aristide and H sat down again and ordered a final drink. The death of Monique Lavalle, who'd worked for Aristide and been a girlfriend of H's, linked them together. They spoke of her fondly and toasted her memory. H thanked him for getting him in touch with Maurice again. "He wouldn't have taken no for an answer," Aristide laughed. "I much enjoyed this evening. By the way, you should try and co-opt Liam into our line of work; he's got all the makings of a good agent." H described what Liam had done for him in Ireland. Aristide said he'd been in contact with Tanaka, who'd filled him in on Madam Quan and H's current mission.

They left the restaurant together. Aristide had a car and a security detail waiting outside and offered him a lift, but H said goodnight and thanked him for dinner, saying he'd enjoy a walk. As he got into his car, Aristide said, "here in Monaco, we're outside my jurisdiction, but I do have good contacts in the Principality. Please do call on me if I can be of any assistance. You have good friends here, but you may find you need some professional help."

Chapter 52

Somewhere in the Mediterranean

The leisurely lunch party had drawn to a close and Quan retired to her personal balcony, where she would not be disturbed. She'd spent a couple of hours 'pressing the flesh' and was satisfied that the guests she'd invited would prove financially beneficial. Having softened them up, it was good to be able to get away from them and contemplate her plans for Monte-Carlo in peace.

She was in two minds as to what to do with the technology which had so unexpectedly fallen back into her hands. The idea of presenting it to the Generals was exciting and more than tempting. Their joint plans could be executed in the very near future. She rubbed her hands together, anticipating their reactions and savouring the fact that she would be back in control. The meeting played over in her mind's eye. They would be impressed and grateful. One of the oldest and most senior of the Generals had always given her trouble. He'd tried to undermine her authority and belittle her contributions. The idea of having to attend the meeting empty handed and having him gloat over her failure to produce the plans on time had been preying on her mind. Now, *now* he would be forced to eat humble pie.

Ideally, she would have liked to have organised another trial run, but to delay their plans would be unnecessary and senseless. She finally decided that she would go ahead, without mentioning how she'd retrieved the data. What could go wrong? The first demonstration had been an unqualified success. Nomura had duplicated his data and left it with his sister as a back-up. Quan could appreciate and applaud his precaution. She would have done the same, but she would have hidden it more securely than the inventor had done.

Having made her decision, she rang a bell and ordered a selection of light snacks.

Chapter 53

On Board the Sappho

The deafening throb of helicopter blades brought all conversation to a halt on the Bar Deck. Everyone looked up as a black Sikorsky S-76 descended towards the *Sappho.*

Quan hadn't mentioned that she was expecting anyone and Sora wondered who was arriving. In a way, she felt a little bored. The other guests were pleasant enough, but she'd had more than enough of their company and of being cooped-up on the *Sappho.* The only person she'd struck up a mild friendship with was Purna Patel, a rich, but unhappy woman from Lahore. Sora had listened and sympathised with Purna, who'd confided in her. After an arranged marriage, she'd fallen madly in love with her husband, Javinda, only to find that his affections had already been engaged by a much older and far more sophisticated mistress. They had been married for two years and Purna was still not pregnant. Javinda had got the beautiful, trophy wife he'd wanted, but he made it clear that he expected a wife who'd provide him with sons. Sora had not shared any confidences in return. Purna wasn't in any position to help her, so she decided against discussing her own problems.

Sora's mind drifted to H. He'd told her he'd be in Monte-Carlo and she laughed at herself, thinking she must be an old fashioned girl to go weak at the knees at the very thought of him. His reassuring presence gave her the belief that she might escape from Quan and get her old life back.

As the helicopter engine shut down, the sounds of the rotors gradually faded and conversations resumed. Sora got up and moved until she could see who was arriving. She saw a middle-aged man, in a crumpled suit climb down onto the Helideck. He clutched a briefcase under one arm and his free hand went instinctively to his head, in a vain attempt to hold his comb-over in place. The newcomer looked thoroughly disgruntled. He waited until the wash of air had died away, before putting his briefcase down and using both hands to smooth his hair back into place. He was met by one of the junior officers, who shook his hand and led him towards the lift. They'd only walked a few steps before a strong gust of sea breeze lifted his hair again like a cock's comb, exposing his bald pate. He looked totally ridiculous and for the first time in days, Sora laughed out loud.

Half an hour later, Quan looked at the man standing in front of her. "You may sit," she said, belatedly noticing that he was still on his feet, after giving her his report. Although he was a hardened investigator, after one look at Quan's forbidding expression, he hadn't liked to take the liberty of sitting down before being invited to do so.

"I have never quibbled at the exorbitant fees you charge for your investigations, Mister Johnson, but would you not agree that this report of yours leaves something to be desired? I wanted answers to my specific questions."

She fanned-out some photographs on the desk in front of her and looked up at him. He felt suddenly like a moth, about to be impaled on a board by a lepidopterist.

Feeling flustered and in a desire to gain some control of the meeting, he began to speak too fast. "The subject *seems* to lead a normal, if privileged life. In my experienced opinion, the details I have uncovered seem to be a fabrication. It's just a feeling, but his persona seems to have been cleverly mapped out. His affluent family life, schooldays and subsequent career are there to be found – if one digs deep enough – but I'm not convinced that they are anything more than a clever and painstakingly tissue of lies. I simply don't buy it. My gut tells me that everything I've discovered is a fraud and … ."

"You are becoming repetitive," Quan cut in. "*Facts* are what I pay you for." She tapped a long fingernail on the nearest photographs. It was a group shot of six men, standing on the pavement outside a restaurant. "Tell me more about these people."

Johnson went to stand behind her shoulder. Zheng, standing silently by the door, moved forwards, but was waved back by Quan.

"These surveillance shots show all of the men the subject has been meeting with. This one," he said, pointing to the second shot, showing H outside the distinctive portals of the Hermitage Hotel, laughing with Maurice and climbing into a Bentley, "is Maurice Duval. He spent some years in the French Foreign Legion and currently owns a successful, provincial bakery business, started by his Father. They seem on friendly terms," he added unnecessarily. "These two," he continued, circling the faces of Henri and Pascal, "also served in the army in the same unit as Duval. As far as I can discover, none of the three has any previous association with the subject." He shuffled the photographs and put another on top. "This is Liam Callaghan – a successful, Irish entrepreneur. At this stage I can find no connection between him and the subject either. I suppose it's possible that he plans to use them in some way, with the golf film he's purporting to be making, but it seems a stretch."

Quan looked sceptical and Johnson hurried on. "This chap looks like a film star himself." He indicated a shot of a bronzed, well-dressed man, who looked as if he'd just stepped from the pages of a glossy magazine. "However, he's by far the most intriguing of the lot. His name is de Lamerie and he's the head of the French counter-terrorist unit."

Quan looked up swiftly and caught his look of smugness at having surprised her. She frowned and said, "please tell me that here, at least, you have actually found a connection."

He muttered something about further investigations being needed.

"Further expenses, you mean," she replied. "Did you do any better with the honey-trap I suggested you set up?

Johnson looked crestfallen and had to admit defeat. "Unfortunately, the subject did not follow up the contact my woman Cheryl made with him. I must say I was surprised. In the past she has been most successful in … "

Quan sighed, "*Another* failure Mister Johnson. Really, if you wish to be retained by me in the future, you are going to have to do far better than this." She sorted through the photographs again. After a pause, she pointed to the one of Maurice. "You have one more chance to redeem yourself. This one," she said. "Bring him to me."

Chapter 54

Monte-Carlo

When H got back to his room, he found an email from Kyuji, saying that he and a team of three other agents would be arriving at the Hermitage early the following morning. H replied, arranging to meet them in his room and then hung a card on his door, ordering breakfast for five people at 8.00.

He slept soundly and woke to the sound of birdsong. Although he'd been to Monaco twice before, he'd never had any time to explore. He dressed in running clothes, left the hotel and set off through the almost silent streets. He headed uphill towards Monaco-Ville, the old part of the town known as The Rock, climbing the Rampe Major staircase and on to the 13th century medieval fort perched up on the cliffs. The air was fresh and cool and the panoramic views over the port and the sea were breathtaking. Everywhere he looked, there was something to enjoy. The Principality was filled with beauty: sculptures, public gardens, elegant churches, the Palace, grand buildings and boulevards as well as ancient, narrow cobblestoned alleyways. Palm trees rustled in the gentle breeze and enormous pots of mature fruit trees scented the air with their blossom.

Eventually he turned back towards the hotel. It was almost six a.m. and in the heart of the town, the stallholders in the Marché de la Condamine on Place d'Armes were getting ready to open for the day, setting out their wares and erecting bright red and yellow striped awnings. The large esplanade was filled with colour and the enticing, heady scents of flowers, fruits and spices. H sat down outside a café in a shaded arcade and ordered an iced green tea and opened a local newspaper.

Out of nowhere, the hairs on the back of his neck rose and he felt that he was being watched. As far as he was aware, no-one knew where he was, so it seemed probable that he'd picked up the tail when he left the hotel. Without appearing to do so, he checked the area for signs of surveillance, his Ray-Bans covering his search. He spotted three possible marks. A young man, his rump perched on the bonnet of a parked car, was consulting a tourist guide; a priest, in conversation with an elderly woman by a market stall, who glanced his way and then turned around, and a middle aged man with a bad comb-over and very white legs, which protruded from a pair of ancient, drill shorts, who sat idly on a moped, watching the world go by. He memorised their faces and clothes, before getting up and walking into the back of the café, where he spent a couple of minutes in the Gents, wishing he had some form of weapon. He palmed a steak knife off a service trolley as he returned outside to his table

He sat down and signalled a waiter for his bill. In the few minutes he'd been inside, the scene outside had moved on, with many more people out to do their early marketing. The delivery vans had all gone and been replaced by people. The youth who'd been reading the tourist guide was no longer in sight. The priest was still there, but was now chatting to one of the stall-holders. H had to search to find the middle aged man who'd moved and was now on the far side of the esplanade, looking into a shop window; his moped parked at the kerb, near the corner of a street behind him. H did another sweep, but didn't spot any other likely contenders. The tail, he thought, must have had quite a time keeping up with him on his run, which probably ruled out the priest, who would have been too conspicuous, running through the town. He certainly hadn't heard the constant sound of a moped.

H finished his drink. Glancing at the bill, he left some euros on the table and smiled his thanks to the waiter. He walked directly towards the most likely candidate. He saw that the man was so positioned that he could see H approaching, reflected in the glass of the window. Dropping all pretence at his interest in the wares on display, the man jumped onto his moped, fired it up and disappeared from H's sight. H ran towards the corner, but when he got there, the man had gone. Traffic was starting to build up and H realised there was little chance of spotting the man again. As he walked back to the Hermitage, he wondered who'd been tailing him and why. On his way he discretely replaced the steak knife he'd borrowed from the café.

Back in his room, he showered and dressed as he waited for Kyuji and the others. They arrived promptly and over breakfast, he updated them and discussed his plans.

Kyuji handed him a pack of cigarillos, telling him that it contained six genuine cigarillos, but also provided another function, which he explained. Out of a pocket, he produced a pair of Ray-Bans, identical to H's own. "I've added a refinement to these," he said. "It does make them a little heavier, but I think you'll find them useful. If you press this," he said, indicating a tiny button on the outside of the shaft, "it will start a video feed, which beams directly back to us. The battery should keep a live uplink going for six hours. When it's turned on, what you see, we'll see."

Thanks, Kyuji," H said, trying them on. "I wish I'd had them earlier this morning." He explained the tail he'd picked up and what had happened.

H answered a knock on the door and a hotel porter handed him an envelope. He ripped it open and read the typed message. *'Madam Chow Lee Quan hopes that you will be able to join her on her yacht, the Sappho, for a short cruise and lunch party tomorrow at 11 a.m. If you have any special dietary requirements, please let me know.* There was a name and telephone number. H showed it to Kyuji, who whistled in surprise, before handing it back, saying, "An excellent and unexpected opportunity." H agreed and rang to accept.

As he put the telephone down, it rang again under his hand.

Without greeting, Aristide de Lamerie's voice said tersely, "H, I think we may have a problem. I'm downstairs with Henri and Pascal. May we come up? Maurice has disappeared."

Chapter 55

Maurice had enjoyed a splendid evening. It had been extremely generous of Aristide to invite everyone to such an exclusive restaurant, and the food had been memorable. Maurice felt a proprietorial concern about H's wellbeing and was relieved to know that someone like Aristide was obviously taking an interest in the young man and keeping an eye on him and his career. It also pleased him to find that H had such a good and loyal friend in Liam Callaghan.

It had been a wonderful adventure, now ended to everyone's complete satisfaction. Tomorrow, he thought, he'd return to the bakery, but tonight he'd take the opportunity of having a good look around this wonderful place. He walked slowly around the harbour and enjoyed seeing the magnificent yachts, moving along the streets filled with exclusive shops and hotels, passing groups of late night pedestrians and restaurants with seats still filled with chattering, beautiful people, all enjoying themselves. He admired the way so many roads were decorated with flowering trees and shrubs and decided that it would be possible to recreate the idea – on a smaller scale – outside the bakery. There were also plenty of parked cars to enjoy. While he was happy with his own battered old Citroën Deux-Chevaux Azu, he loved a good looking car and had never seen so many expensive and fabulous machines everywhere he looked.

After a couple of hours he decided that he'd seen enough and that it was time for him to go to bed. His sense of direction was good and without much trouble, found his way back to the street where his small hotel was situated. He felt content and whistled an old tune as he walked. Ahead of him he saw a young boy with a dog. The

Principality was considered one of the safest places on earth and he'd read somewhere that it had the world's largest police force for its population and size. Even so, thought Maurice, it's far too late for such a young lad to be out of bed and walking the streets unaccompanied. However, it was none of his business, so he merely smiled and said a friendly *bonsoir* to the boy and patted his pockets for his room key.

The attack was so unexpected that he was hardly aware of what was happening to him, until it was too late. He was grabbed by three men, who'd suddenly materialised. One punched him in the stomach, knocking the wind out of him and another clamped a hand over his mouth from behind. Maurice kicked back hard, catching the man on the shin and trying to free himself, but he was out of condition and the heavy dinner he'd eaten, as well as a considerable amount of alcohol slowed him down. Within seconds he was hustled into a malodorous alley, where a beating started in earnest. Two of the men held his arms, whilst the other laid into him with his fists and when they let him slump to the ground, the first man used his boot. This is a bit much for a mugging, Maurice thought as he tried to protect his head. A final kick, harder than the rest knocked him out and his final thought was for the eighty euros he had in his pocket.

Michel Bonnard was a lonely child. His Mother had run off with a travelling salesman when he was six years old and his Father had remarried within a year and had produced two children within a short space of time. Monsieur Bonnard owned a small butcher's shop and was wrapped up with his new family and demanding second wife and had little time to spare for Michel. His second wife was jealous of the boy and contrived to make his life a misery. Michel's only solace was Copain, a mongrel dog he'd saved from some bullies who were tormenting it. As it cost nothing to keep – there being plenty of scraps of meat from the shop – he was grudgingly allowed to keep it.

That evening, he'd been in trouble again with his stepmother. As usual it was over some trivial fault and he'd been locked in his room which was a tiny storeroom behind the shop. Wriggling out of the window, he tied a length of string to the cotton bandana, which served as Copain's collar and they set off looking for adventure. They roamed the familiar streets of Monte-Carlo and Michel lost track of time. He wasn't worried that he'd be in further trouble. No one would check on him until his door was unlocked in the morning.

He'd never owned a watch, but knew that it must be getting very late. He wandered aimlessly, pondering on the unfairness of life and wishing something exciting could happen to him. A small, ginger cat ran across the road and Copain leapt after it, pulling the string out of Michel's slack fingers. Three men were rounding the street corner as Copain plunged between their legs, startling them. The cat had found refuge in a tree and glared down from a safe height. The largest of the three men had tripped, but not fallen over the trailing lead. "Bloody fucking bastard mongrel," he swore, lashing out with a boot and catching Copain in the side. In hot pursuit, Michel arrived just in time to witness the kick and heard Copain's howl of pain. Michel ran forward, shouting. The man's two companions pulled him away, telling him not to be a fool and they continued down the street.

After checking that his dog was not seriously hurt, he re-attached the string lead and decided to call it a night. He was only a short walk from his home, which was in the same direction the men had taken, so he followed them slowly. He passed a small alley-way, with foul smelling dumpsters from an adjoining restaurant. The men ahead stopped and disappeared into the porch of a small, unpretentious hotel. Michel was close enough to hear them talking and decided to wait in the alleyway until they'd gone. A middle-aged man walked towards him, whistling a tune. The man smiled and wished him a cheery goodnight.

Michel walked down the alley, hoping to be able to get out at the far end, but when he saw that it was a cul-de-sac, he retraced his steps. He heard the sounds of a scuffle ahead and ducked behind a dumpster, dragging Copain with him. The only light came from a single, dim bulb over the back door of a restaurant kitchen. Michel peered cautiously out of his hiding place and saw the whistling man had been set upon by the other three. He heard the sound of several blows, then one man saying, "that's enough Jean, you cretin. Let's get him out of here."

Michel waited, wondering what to do. When he looked again, the alley was empty. He came out of his hiding place and peered into the street. Two of the men were carrying the man Jean had knocked out. Michel decided to follow them. He kept back, being careful not to be seen.

The men went a short distance before stopping outside a small garage and the third man unlocked a door and they disappeared inside. Michel crouched down behind a concrete container of shrubs and watched. No lights came on inside and in less than five minutes the three men came out again, locked the door behind them and walked away, talking in low voices.

Here was an adventure! It was chance to get even with Jean for kicking Copain and to try and save the whistling man. He walked over to the front of the garage and peered through a grimy window and into the small office. He could see the man tied to a chair, with a gag in his mouth. He was not moving and his eyes were shut. Michel stood back to look at the garage and noticed a small window on the first floor was open at the bottom. Copain was going to be a problem, as he'd certainly start barking if he was left on his own. Michel set off home as fast as he could and let Copain in through the window, closing it behind him. He rushed the short distance back to the garage. All was quiet.

Reaching the upstairs window was not too difficult for an agile boy. He pushed the sash up quietly and wriggled inside. He stopped to listen and, reassured by the silence, found his way downstairs and into the office. The injured man was coming round and he watched Michel as he slid into the room. Michel quickly untied the gag and went to work on the knots behind the chair with his penknife.

"*Monsieur*, I have come to rescue you, but we need to be very quiet. I saw what happened to you and followed you here. We need to escape before those men come back."

When he'd cut through the ropes, he put an arm under the man's elbow and helped him to his feet.

"You wait here," Michel said. "I'll go and see if there's another way out; I think it would be safer." He disappeared and was back in less than a minute. "Can you walk?" he asked anxiously. The man nodded. "Come this way, *Monsieur*. I can take you to my home. It's very close."

The man looked shaky and sick, but he pulled himself together. "Thank you *mon ami*. Let's get out of here." He pulled Michel to his chest and clapped him on the back. "My name is Maurice Duval and I am very much in your debt."

Chapter 56

Mister Johnson, the private investigator, had been confident that this job of Madam Quan's would be easy. He'd briefed Jean, his best employee and two other men he'd used in the past and provided them with a photograph of Maurice Duval and the address of the hotel where he was staying. His instructions were to snatch him off the street, and deliver him to the *Sappho* without attracting attention.

It was after midnight, but he'd waited up, having told Jean to report to him as soon as he'd done his job.

"What went wrong?" he asked, after one look at Jean's sullen expression. He realised that he'd been over confident and too sanguine in their abilities. He felt heartburn flooding acid up his throat and fumbled in the breast pocket of his shirt for the antacid pills he always kept on him.

"We did like you said and got him off the street easy. He was a tough old bird and tried to make a fight of it. We didn't want the police to come nosing round, so I gave him a couple of taps to soften him up, but he passed out. I took him to Emile's garage round the corner. He keeps his car there and I thought we'd drive the chap down to the port later. Stupid, effing bastard couldn't find his fucking keys, so we left your man tied up and went to get my wheels."

"Then what?"

"Honest to God, I don't know how he did it. We weren't away above half an hour, but when we got back, the bastard had gone. I know what you're thinking, but you're wrong. Tied him up myself *and* did a proper job. The rope was cut through. I don't know how, but that's what happened. Not a good night," Jean finished gloomily.

"Get out, you useless bastard. Don't look to me for payment. You've landed me in a pile of shit." Jean got the message and left.

The antacid pills didn't seem to be working. Johnson was sweating and felt sick. Madam Quan had been one of his most lucrative employers and he couldn't see her wanting to use him again. He took a long swig from a tepid bottle of water, wondering how he could explain himself.

It was hard to look intimidating when lying topless on a sun-lounger; but Quan managed it easily. She made no effort to cover herself, or even sit up when Johnson was brought to her by Zheng.

"Can I not have even five minutes of peace?" she said angrily, throwing a file onto the deck. "Where is the man Duval?"

Johnson, after one appalled glance, looked at a point just above Quan's head. He mopped his face with a handkerchief, stumbled through his explanation and waited for the axe to fall.

Quan verbally tore him to shreds and told him that his services would never be required again. She spoke in a quiet voice, which frightened him more than if she'd screamed at him. He had no arguments to defend himself with, being well aware that – on this occasion – he'd provided an unacceptably poor service. When she finally waved him away, he backed out feeling limp and as if he'd survived a hurricane.

Thinking back over her long association with Johnson and the jobs he'd done for her, Quan came to a decision. He knew too much. She pressed the intercom and called for Zheng.

Chapter 57

H introduced his colleagues to de Lamerie, Henri and Pascal and ordered coffee for everyone as they listened with dismay to what de Lamerie had to say.

"Henri rang me earlier. He and Pascal had arranged to meet Maurice for breakfast at eight o'clock, but he didn't turn up. By nine o'clock they went looking for him. After knocking on his door and getting no response, they asked a chambermaid to open the door with her pass-key. The room was empty, everything was tidy and the bed was made. From the state of the room, it looked as if Maurice had not been back last night. They asked the concierge downstairs if she'd seen him come in, during the evening, but she couldn't remember having done so. Henri rang me and, well, here we are."

H rang the Princess Grace hospital to enquire if anyone matching Maurice's description had been admitted, but the answer was negative. Pascal reminded them that Maurice had left them after dinner, for a walk around Monte-Carlo. He hadn't been seen since.

There was a loud knocking on the door and they all stopped talking. H walked over and opened it. Maurice stood there with a beaming grin on his battered face. The group burst into a round of applause. Maurice bowed and then embraced H, kissing him on both cheeks.

"Were you worried about me?" he asked innocently. "Excuse me, but I forget my manners and must introduce you to my gallant saviour." He turned to the open doorway, where Michel stood smiling shyly, holding Copain on his string lead. Following Maurice's actions, he also bowed and was given a cheer.

"This young man is Michel. Without his help, I'd probably be dead."

H put his arm around Maurice and Michel's shoulders, pulled them into the room and sat them down. He rang down for two, chilled bottles of champagne and a large Coca-Cola.

H inspected the tired face with its black eye, swollen, split lip and grazed chin.

"What does the rest of you look like?" he asked Maurice,

"I haven't dared to look," Maurice replied.

The champagne arrived swiftly. "To Maurice and Michel," H said, and they all raised their glasses.

"To Copain," Maurice said. "He also played a part in our adventure."

Kyuji went into the bathroom and returned with a bowl of water, which he set down in a corner for the dog, who trotted over with a wagging tail and started to drink.

H was due on board the *Sappho* at mid-day. He surreptitiously checked his watch and was surprised to find that it was only just after ten, so he had plenty of time to hear the details.

The story took some time. Maurice sighed with pleasure as he sipped his champagne and started to relax. He explained what had happened.

"It was like something you see on the television," Michel added. "It was frightening, but we were lucky. We'd only just got out of the back door of the garage, when we heard a car coming, so we hid. It was them! The three men had come back for Monsieur Duval. We didn't wait for them to come looking, but Monsieur couldn't move very fast," he said with an apologetic look at Maurice. "We could hear them shouting inside. They were furious. I couldn't think of anything else to do, so I took him home with me for the rest of the night."

Maurice took up the story. "When I woke up, I didn't want to go back to my hotel, even for a shower and a change of clothes. I did try to ring Henri and Pascal, but they were out, so we came here." He looked a little embarrassed, but H smiled understandingly.

"Very sensible of you," de Lamerie said, approvingly.

Henri and Pascal both spoke at the same time, asking, "but who were these men and why did they attack you?"

"I have no idea," Maurice said.

"Did you overhear anything?" H asked.

"Two of them were French and the other sounded English. He spoke like someone from the East End of London. I was busy trying to fight them off and didn't hear anything useful."

"I did," Michel piped up.

They all looked at him in surprise. "I heard one of them said he wasn't going to carry the ... er, bastard was what he said, all the way down to the boat." H exchanged glances with Kyuji and de Lamerie, as Michel added, "the one who kicked Copain said they'd go and get his car to drive him down to the ... " he closed his eyes, trying to remember the words. "He said, 'to the Saffer,' or a word which sounded like that. Does that help," he asked hopefully.

"Indeed it does. Well done, Michel," H said.

Most of the men looked blank, but H and de Lamerie understood.

"Have you reported this to the police?" H asked.

"We did discuss it," Maurice said, "But, knowing your, er, your line of work, I decided that we should discuss it with you first, in case you thought it might have anything to do with something you are working on."

"I'm afraid that you are right. I can only apologise for getting you into this. It's not something we can discuss now," he said, glancing meaningfully at Michel, who looked mystified.

Kyuji stood up and told H they'd be in their rooms, which were adjoining, if he needed them. He set down his glass and the four agents left the room.

Maurice was talking to his two friends. He turned to H and said, "Henri and Pascal will take me back to our hotel, so that I can wash and change into some clean clothes. Then I'm going to take Michel out for an enormous, celebration lunch. We'll stop on the way and choose a proper collar and lead for Copain, before I take him back home."

"Pascal and I will go with them. Safety in numbers," Henri said.

H said thoughtfully, "Good idea, but I don't think you'll be in any more danger, Maurice. They won't try the same trick twice. I'd like to see you again before you all go home, but I have to go out shortly to an appointment, which I can't miss."

They all shook hands and Michel thanked H for his Coke as they left the room.

"What do you make of it?" H asked de Lamerie.

"I think someone wanted information about you and that you must have been under surveillance. Maurice seemed to be an easy mark."

"Look, Aristide, I don't want to impose on you too much, but I need to let Tanaka know what's happening. I'd like your input, if you can spare the time?" de Lamerie nodded and H called his uncle. He started by saying that de Lamerie was in on the call and the two men exchanged greetings. When H had finished, Tanaka said, "I'm glad to hear that Mister Duval managed to escape. It seems certain that Madam Quan is desperate to find out more about you. Something in your cover story must have triggered her suspicions. That needs looking into. Go to the lunch party and let me know what transpires. Kyuji will have given you a couple of his gizmos to take with you. If there's any chance of hearing any information on what Quan's plans for the explosives are, it could crack the case wide open. Aristide, I appreciate your assistance in this matter and Hiroshi will put you in the picture; it's possible that he may need to call on you for further help."

When he'd rung off, H answered various questions de Lamerie had about Quan and her plans and thanked him for agreeing to help. As de Lamerie got up to leave, he turned to H, touching his forehead and said, "I almost forgot to mention this. I hope you'll forgive my presumption, but I've made some arrangements concerning your Bentley, which I hope you'll agree is fair. The damage to your car was due – in great part – to a fault of the French authorities failing to provide you with the back-up they'd promised." H sensed what was coming and started to protest, but de Lamerie held up his hand. "No, H, let me finish. I feel strongly that this is a debt of honour, which I must redeem. I've had a quiet word with Henri Davoust and asked what it cost to repair the Bentley in his workshop. He was reticent and tried to brush me off, but I managed to persuade him and he finally worked out a figure for the parts, but flatly refused to accept anything for the labour. Henri, Maurice and Pascal would – I feel – never have taken anything from you. *Alors*, the affair is now settled most amicably and there is no more to say." He stood up and clapped H on both shoulders.

H was relieved, as well as grateful. He'd been wondering how to broach the subject with Maurice, without hurting his pride.

When he'd thanked de Lamerie and seen him out, H changed into appropriate lunch party clothes, checked his handgun and stuck it into the back of his waistband. He also made sure that his new sunglasses were working and his cigarillos were in his pocket before leaving his room to walk down to the T-Jetty in the Port.

Chapter 58

As he walked, H checked for signs of surveillance, but saw nothing suspicious. If it was Quan who'd been having him followed that morning, at least she'd know where he'd be now. Satisfied that he was 'clean', he decided to call Liam. His mobile rang as he was pulling it out of his pocket. He looked at the caller I.D. and saw that it was a case of thought transference. H asked how the business meetings had gone, before telling him what had happened to Maurice. Liam was horrified and asked H to wish Maurice well.

"My main meeting this morning went incredibly well," Liam said. "I've landed a huge, new deal, but it's thrown-up a mass of work and contracts to get signed and sorted out with the lawyers. That's why I was ringing. I really ought to get back to Dublin this afternoon."

H explained that his assignment was moving ahead and told him about the party on Quan's yacht. "I'll keep in touch and let you know how things go. It's been like old times, spending time together again and you know, without my telling you, just how much I appreciated your backing me up and for ... well, thanks Liam."

H was smiling as Liam told him not to be an idiot and rang off.

There was no difficulty in finding the *Sappho*, as all of the largest yachts were to be found in the T-Jetty, otherwise known as the Swimming Pool Dock. As he approached he could hear that the party was well underway. With so many yachts in such close proximity in the harbour, it was considered the height of bad manners to inflict loud noise – of any kind – on other people. Quan completely ignored this unwritten rule, although Captain Féng had mentioned it to her.

Several people stood at the foot of a wide passerelle, waiting to go on board. H had his name checked-off by a smiling Chinese girl, who was dressed in a jaunty sailor suit, and joined the throng. He accepted a glass of champagne and pushed the bridge of his sunglasses up his nose – in a manner somewhat reminiscent of Clark Kent – and in doing so initiated the live video uplink. He went over to pay his respects to Madam Quan, who was still greeting guests and holding court by the bar. She watched him approach and shook his outstretched hand. "I'm pleased you could find the time to join us, Mister Suzuki."

"It was kind of you to invite me to your delightful party," H replied.

She lifted the corner of her lip in what passed for a smile. "You'll find some of our friends from Ireland here and Sora will be around somewhere."

"I'll be pleased to see them all again," H said, moving back to allow her to greet some late arrivals.

The Monte-Carlo season was in full swing and although the tennis Masters had just finished, the Principality was already gearing-up for the Monaco Grand Prix, in a few weeks' time; preceded by the Cannes Film Festival along the coast. Each spring and summer, the South of France is a mecca for attracting hoards of the wealthy, famous and glamorous people who attend fashionable events. There is always much rivalry as to who could throw the most sensational and unusual parties, to appeal to the jaded tastes of the glitterati. It was an 'A' list party and H recognised many faces from the world of film, music and entertainment. There was also a sprinkling of sporting personalities, television celebrities, as well as several high profile politicians from around the world. The business world was also well represented, but these movers and shakers of high finance were less easily recognisable, unless one was tuned-in to the financial journals.

The decibel count was rising by the minute. A group of rumbustious young men had already stripped down to swimsuits and were engaging in frolicking games in the swimming pool, with shrieks and much laughter from bikini clad girls. An excellent Caribbean steel band, wearing colourful shirts, was belting out popular West Indian tunes on their steel drums. The music was infectious and many of the partygoers couldn't resist moving to the music, with glasses of tropical cocktails trailing from their fingers as they swayed to the beat. H judged that there must be almost a hundred guests, who were already hitting the drink and getting into the party spirit. Casual chic was the order of the day, with the men in linen suits, navy blazers or open necked shirts and many of the women were also opting for linen or floating silks and cotton voiles from Ralph Lauren, Prada, Tom Ford and Peter Pilotto. H was interested to see that several of the women were wearing fashionable Aquazzura stiletto heels – usually high heels were banned on the wooden decks. Quan must be one of the new breed of super-rich hostesses who didn't worry about the expensive repairs which would be necessary.

A long table had been set up under an awning and was covered with canapés. Every imaginable delicacy was laid out on platters lined with banana leaves and set onto bowls of crushed ice. H spotted Sora in the centre of an admiring group of young men. As if aware of his glance, she looked up and saw him. Her face broke into such a revealing smile that H hoped Quan hadn't been watching them. He quickly checked to see, but she was facing the other way, deep in conversation.

Making his way towards Sora, he was waylaid by a hand on his arm. He looked round into the over made-up face of Lady Lister. "*Darling* Mister Suzuki. How *heavenly* to see you again. Come and dance with me." He had no choice, as she grasped his hand and led him into the gyrating bodies. He raised his eyebrows at Sora and saw that she was laughing. He escaped after a long rendition of 'Don't Worry, Be Happy,' and looked around again for Sora.

She'd been waiting for him to be free, but hadn't noticed that Zheng was also lurking nearby. As Sora moved towards him, H said, "Miss Zheng, how delightful to see you again." Sora paused in mid step, looking swiftly over her shoulder, in time to see Zheng bow curtly.

"Miss Mori, I hoped I'd see you here today. How are you?" He put out his hand and Sora followed his lead. Ignoring Zheng, H put a hand under Sora's elbow and steered her over to the rail.

"You *have* to get me away from here," Sora said, in an urgent whisper. "Please, H, I can't stand this much more. You said you'd help me."

H could see that she was on the verge of hysteria and glanced around before replying.

"Why else do you think I'm here?" he said gently. "You've been incredibly brave. For now, keep calm and leave it to me. By tomorrow, I'll have you off the yacht and safe."

Sora straightened her back and lifted her chin. "Can we at least have one dance?" she asked. H nodded and as he led her onto the dance floor he asked, "who were the other guests on the yacht?" Sora gave him the names and thumbnail sketches of the guests who'd travelled with her from Ireland. None of them rang any bells, but H knew that Kyuji would have been following the conversation and would be checking them out. Sora also mentioned the man with the comb-over, who'd visited the *Sappho* and that he'd arrived on Quan's helicopter, but she hadn't heard his name.

At the end of a lively rendition of 'Brown Eyed Girl', H told Sora that they were still under observation and should split up. He assured her that he'd be keeping an eye on her. She longed to ask for details of his plan, but trusted that he'd somehow make good his word, so she nodded and allowed him to leave her with a group of young people at the bar.

H mingled with the partygoers, observing the staff and guests, as he made a slow circuit of the deck. He spent several minutes talking to Sir John Lister, who was momentarily on his own and beckoned H over to talk about golf. They stood not far from the gangplank, sipping their drinks. Over Sir John's shoulder H noticed something going on. He excused himself and found somewhere unobtrusive to watch. Quan – with Zheng in attendance – was moving purposefully to greet some late arrivals

These were obviously no ordinary party guests. A convoy of three cars; two, black SUVs with a stretch limousine in between them had pulled up at the foot of the gangplank and several bodyguards spilled out onto the walkway. After doing a 360 degree sweep, they opened the back doors of the limousine. Three men stepped out and walked swiftly across the passerelle and came aboard, followed by two underlings. Although they all wore dark suits, H recognised their military bearing. By the respectful way in which Quan greeted them, they were obviously here for the important meeting. She shook hands with the first three and ushered them into her private lift. H's eyes narrowed as he took in the implications and he hoped that Kyuji would be able to identify them from the photo feed from his sunglasses.

The men were all Chinese. Things were starting to move.

Chapter 59

The lift came to a halt in the bowels of the *Sappho*. The meeting room was a secret space and rarely used. Quan had ordered the yacht builders to create a glass bottom to the floor. Specially designed lighting illuminated the seabed. As they were moored in the harbour, an artificial scene had been recreated and what the visitors actually saw was a video of white coral reefs and astonishingly coloured tropical fish, which also played on wall mounted screens. The effect was mesmerising.

They took their seats at a unique and incredibly beautiful table of various coloured marble inlays, depicting starfish, seahorses and shells, for which Quan had paid an obscene amount of money. It had originally been commissioned by an English naval captain, who'd made his fortune in the days of 'Good Queen Bess,' capturing Spanish galleons filled with treasure.

Quan settled herself in her chair and waited for the others to seat themselves. "Welcome, gentlemen and thank you for coming such a long way for our meeting today."

As she'd expected, the first person to speak was General Weisheng, her constant detractor and critic. The name Weisheng means 'greatness is born' and she knew that the General firmly believed that this was true in his case.

"We *hope* that our valuable time has not been wasted," he said smoothly. Certainly he wished for their monumental plans to succeed, but it galled him that they had to rely on Quan. The very thought of the immense amount of money she would make from the ensuing arms deal made him feel physically sick. While he'd made it clear at the outset that her inclusion offended him, he was a realist. For the greater glory of China, he would listen to what she had to say.

Quan knew that she held them in the palm of her hand and wanted to savour the moment. Whilst they helped themselves to drinks she said, "It is fortunate that we were able to schedule our meeting to co-ordinate with the International Air Show being held near Genoa this week, so there will be no raised eyebrows at your presence in the area." She asked after their journey and made small talk for a few moments. General Weisheng was getting restive and fidgeted in his chair. She looked at each man in turn and then got down to business.

"You will remember that I said I would bring the data to our meeting today." She watched their serious faces and cautious nods. A small, gold box rested on the table in front of her and, with a sense of the dramatic, she slowly opened it and brought out Jiro Nomura's memory stick.

"This, gentlemen, is what I promised you. All the data for constructing the new weapon is contained in this tiny, but priceless object. I am returning to my main Armstec factory outside Tokyo tomorrow, and – with your agreement – I have arranged for my most senior explosive expert to get to work on it." She paused as General Peng, the most senior of the elite group rose to his feet and began to clap his hands. The others followed suit, with General Weisheng being the last man to stand.

General Peng said, "I believe I speak for us all when I congratulate you, Madam Quan. This is excellent news. I must admit that we were… concerned when you mentioned a possible delay, but you have – as they say – delivered the goods and restored our faith in your capabilities."

"Thank you," Quan said. "Now, as time is of the essence, perhaps you would like to open our discussions on the time frame and plan of action?"

The General rose to his feet. "It goes without saying that secrecy is paramount here. *No* notes will be taken and *no* record of our meeting will ever appear in printed form. Ostensibly, my friends and I have accepted your hospitality for a party on your lovely yacht, on a social basis, whilst awaiting the start of the Air Show tomorrow. What could be more natural or open?" He received a murmur of agreement and they settled down to thrash out the details, which would – if successful – have a cataclysmic global impact.

Chapter 60

H drifted casually, glass in hand, towards the lift doors, which had closed behind Quan and the Chinese. A burly bodyguard, dressed as a crew member, stepped forward and gave H a hard stare. Burying his nose in his glass, H looked up and asked the man where he could find the cloakrooms. The man pointed to a staircase to his left. H nodded his thanks and sauntered off in the indicated direction.

During his breakfast meeting earlier that morning, Kyuji had shown H a plan of the *Sappho*. With his near photographic memory H knew roughly where to start his search. Quan's private lift had stops on several of the six decks. Deciding that the lowest was the most likely, H made his way downwards to the Tank Deck. Feeling conspicuous, the first place he headed for was a crew cabin, where he changed into the deck shoes, white cotton drill shorts and white polo shirt, which constituted the crew's uniform for that day.

It took him some time to locate where the meeting was being held. When he spotted a bodyguard waiting outside a particular door, he knew he'd found the right place. Without showing himself he worked his way around this central block, searching for a place where he could listen-in. Always on the lookout for the slightest anomaly, he noticed a map hanging on an otherwise blank wall. He felt carefully around the frame. It slid sideways and H found one of Quan's many hidden spy-holes. He made sure there was nobody around, before taking a look into the meeting room behind. His view showed the back of Quan's head and the men seated opposite her. The meeting had started and they were deep in discussion.

As Kyuji had instructed, H pressed pack of cigarillos behind the map. The top of multiple labels adhered to the wall, leaving others underneath. The audio bug was a paper thin device, which would be undetectable. He made sure that it was securely attached and checked that the audio feed was working and relaying the sound back to Kyuji. He hoped that the forty minutes running time would be enough to get the information they needed. Without someone watching his back, H didn't want to be caught unawares. He moved the map back into position and went to find somewhere to wait out the time, before returning later to retrieve the device.

He was seconds too late.

Chapter 61

Zheng – much to her disgust – had been excluded from the meeting room and felt rejected. The Chinese generals were an unknown quantity and she knew there'd been some bad feeling between them and Quan. She was the senior bodyguard and agonised whenever she was not at Quan's side. Having nothing constructive to do, she was conducting a security sweep of the Tank Deck and knowing of the spy-hole, she was also determined to see if she could find out what was going on in the meeting room.

Her soft soled shoes made no sound and as she walked around a corner, where she was brought up short by the sight of one of the crew in front of the hidden spy-hole. For an instant, the man's face was reflected in the glass front of the map and Zheng's eyes gleamed as she recognised H. She had a score to settle with him after Kinsale and the trouble he'd caused her boss. In so far as she was capable of caring for anyone, she felt a devotion to Quan which bordered on obsession and it would be a pleasure to rid Quan of this meddlesome intruder. She was wearing a handgun, but decided not to use it. There would be no swift end for Mister Suzuki, she would enjoy fighting him and giving him pain. He should beg to be put out of his misery, which she intended to prolong and enjoy. She ducked out of sight and waited for her quarry to appear.

H rounded the corner and felt as if the ceiling had fallen in on him. Zheng had clubbed him on the side of the skull; hard enough to make his head swim, but not hard enough to knock him out. Shaking his head to clear it, he instinctively moved back about six to ten feet, out of range, to give himself room to react and manoeuvre.

They both dropped into fighting stances, circling each other warily, looking for openings. Like Zheng, H was also armed, but for different reasons, he too decided against using his gun. Ricochets were a real danger, with the metal walls and H also knew that the sounds of gunfire would speedily bring people to the scene; if that happened, he doubted if he'd get off the *Sappho* alive.

Zheng had gained the advantage of surprise. She was powerfully built and well trained, but, now in her late thirties, she'd allowed her training and fitness to slip somewhat and good living was further slowing her reactions. She had lots of dirty tricks to fall back on and had no hesitation in using them. Moving in confidently, she aimed a rapid kick at H, which he deflected easily. He managed to catch hold of her foot and twisted it hard, bringing her down and followed up the advantage with a double punch to her solar plexus. Rolling out of reach and gasping, she regained her feet, with a look of surprise and anger. Barrelling in again, she threw a series of quick jabs and kicks, but H reacted hard and fast, using multiple techniques. An unexpectedly accurate double palm strike to H's chin found its mark and snapped his head back. Not wanting to be caught off-balance, he spun away and as she came for him again, aiming another punch, he swiped her hand away on his forearm and followed it up with an elbow to her face. Now Zheng was the one off balance. H managed to manoeuvre himself behind her and putting both hands around the side of her head, pulled backwards and then stepped aside. Gravity took over and Zheng crashed to the ground.

Stumbling back to her feet, Zheng looked like an angry bull, literally pawing at the ground and breathing hard through her nose. She put her head down and charged at H, who side-stepped and she hit the door of a cleaning cupboard. The door burst open and in her rage, Zheng tore off the metal handle and threw it at H's face. He ducked, but it caught him a glancing blow above the temple. Blood trickled down his cheek and in that second she managed to get an arm around his throat and started to choke him. Zheng took a moment to slowly lick the blood off his face, smiling as she did so.

Sickened, H instantly reacted by using one of his favourite training techniques and clamped his chin down hard on the pressure point above her elbow. Her eyes widened at the sudden pain, followed by numbness, as her arm fell away.

Zheng was weakened and tiring, but her urge to kill him was strong enough for her to catch his wrist with her free hand and spin him round, charging forward and trying to smash him into the wall.

As H stretched out his left arm to catch himself against the door frame, Zheng kicked him in the back. Whether or not she'd intended to hit that particular spot, the outcome was the same. H's shoulder dislocated with a popping sound as the kick forced the joint into an impossible position.

It was a game-changer. He gasped at the instantaneous and excruciating pain. Time moved into slow motion as sweat broke out all over his body, he felt nauseous and a wave of weakness flooded his system.

Behind him, he sensed Zheng moving in for the kill.

Chapter 62

Hotel Hermitage – Monte-Carlo

With a pair of headphones clamped over his ears, Kyuji listened to Quan's meeting with the Generals from the directional microphone H had hidden. The meeting had concluded and he was listening for the second time to the recording, every so often making small adjustments to dials and controls to maximise the tonal quality. He had had no idea that at the same time, H was fighting for his life only feet away from the listening device.

Quan had been sitting with her back to the microphone, but the voices of the Generals, who were on the opposite side of the table, had come out far clearer.

He was reasonably pleased with the quality, but the hairs on the back of his neck rose as he listened to them calmly discussing the destruction and mayhem they'd planned for his beloved capital city.

There was quite a lot of useful information, but one vital piece of data was missing. The meeting had started before H was able to plant the listening device and the tape started just as they'd evidently finished discussing the exact sites of the bombs they planned to set off. Kyuji sucked his teeth in frustration, but the first recorded words were, ".... Are we all agreed that this is the perfect site for the initial bombings?"

A date was mentioned – eight days ahead – but it was subject to confirmation.

Kyuji made a note of three unknown names which were mentioned and he tasked one of the other agents with the job of delving into their occupations and backgrounds.

Demonstrations were apparently being planned in Tokyo and other major Japanese cities, in the days following the bombings; further destabilising the situation and causing panic among the citizens, the government and the financial markets.

The Emperor's Palace, several key government installations and the offices of the main Bank of Japan were to be targeted by further bombs over the ensuing days. Kyuji was both excited and relieved to hear that these were itemised in detail, which would give Tanaka some time to deploy his forces to have them defused.

Evidently, the first day of bombing was to be the biggest, with the most spectacular damage and loss of life. The Twin Towers in New York were mentioned during the conversation, but the name of the building in Tokyo had already been discussed and remained a mystery.

Those in the meeting considered, at length, the aftermath of their plans and how it would affect China's relations with Japan. They spoke of the quantities of arms, ammunition and ordnance they'd ordered from Quan; going into some detail about their disposition, delivery and payment.

Kyuji took off the headphones and his thick glasses, which were pinching the bridge of his nose. He rubbed a hand over his eyes and face, thinking that he'd have appreciated H's input, but he knew he didn't have the luxury of waiting. The quality of the tape was now as good as he could get it. He checked the time. It was almost four fifteen in the afternoon, which – as Tokyo was seven hours ahead of Monaco – meant it was eleven fifteen in Japan. Using an encrypted phone, he put a call through to Tanaka's direct line, hoping he'd still be in his office.

He was in luck. Tanaka had been waiting for the call and Kyuji gave him the facts. After hearing him without interrupting, Tanaka said he'd listen to the tape, and call back with instructions as soon as he'd heard it through.

Tanaka sat back in his chair, oblivious to the panoramic view of the city spread below him. He worked out what his course of action would be and prioritised the list of what steps should be taken. He rang the Prime Minister on a secure line and after explaining the gravity of the situation, asked for a crisis meeting of the Cabinet and of the National Security forces to be arranged as a matter of urgency, where he could brief all those concerned.

Chapter 63

On Board the *Sappho*

H went instinctively into survival mode. He had to act decisively in the next couple of seconds or it would all be over. He flashed a glance into the open store cupboard, searching for anything he could use as a weapon. In one movement, he scooped up a heavy fire extinguisher with his right hand and swung around in an arc. Zheng should have moved faster, but she hesitated for a split second, savouring the sight of H's agony. Because he'd moved so fast, she was slow to react. The metal canister caught her on the side of the head; breaking her neck and killing her instantly. For a moment she stood staring at him in shock – literally dead on her feet – before she pitched forward onto the floor.

H's legs buckled and he sank to his knees beside her. He touched the fingers of his right hand to her neck, to double-check the carotid artery, but there was no pulse.

Breathing in gasps, H was so lightheaded that he found himself bombarded with a mass of different scraps of information. His memory bank brought up various details from the medical parts of his training and he tried to process them. He knew that muscle, cartilage and other tissue would have been stretched and torn when the humerus was wrenched out of its socket and that the muscles surrounding his shoulder joint would now be going into spasm, making any movements progressively painful; if not impossible. He tried to focus on what he needed to do. He was dangerously incapacitated and at any moment he could be found with Zheng's body.

He realised that he'd have to try and manipulate the joint himself. This was something he'd witnessed once, during his training. It was not for the faint-hearted and carried some significant risks. Astonishingly, he felt a laugh flutter in his throat as he remembered reading, *'medication is advised to sedate and comfort the patient prior to and during the relocation procedure'*. Not going to happen, lad, he told himself; just get on with it.

Kneeling on the floor, H carefully felt for the pulse in his left wrist and elbow with the fingers of his right hand, at the same time testing for sensation to assess the blood and nerve supply. He was relieved to find that his lower arm didn't feel cold or numb and hadn't turned blue, which might have indicated damage to the arteries and nerves.

Cradling his arm, he struggled cautiously to his feet. There were several things he'd need to do, so he moved slowly back to the room where he'd changed his clothes. Fortunately it was empty. He took several deep, steadying breaths. He closed his eyes and allowed his memory bank to pull up the relevant information he'd learned years before. *'Only in a case of significant emergency should one attempt to relocate a shoulder unaided. The main complications related to doing so are the possibility of: further tearing of the tendons, muscles and ligaments; damaging nerves and blood vessels; severe pain that results in loss of consciousness.'*

None of this sounded encouraging, but he had no other option. He'd only get one chance to do it right. He positioned himself beside an angle of the wall, closed his eyes and spent a few moments in mental preparation. After several more deep breaths, he grabbed a hand towel and stuffed it between his teeth, opened his eyes and slammed the injured shoulder against the wall.

After a flash of indescribable and blinding agony, the pain miraculously receded. He'd done it!

The relief was enormous now that his shoulder was successfully back in place. Moving with extreme caution, H re-dressed himself in his own clothes. Looking around the room he noticed a cold drinks cabinet and his eyes lit up as he saw there was an ice dispenser beside it. Ice would help control the swelling and the pain. He gulped half a bottle of water before making himself a makeshift ice-pack and sliding under his shirt. He used his leather belt to fashion a sling, which he knew would help the shoulder muscles surrounding the joint to relax and to support the bones against gravity.

He put his jacket over his shoulders to cover the sling and checked an inside pocket. He always carried a small tin of emergency items and he took out two extremely strong anti-inflammatories and swallowed them with the rest of the water. As an additional back-up, he also took a black pill. The doctor who'd given it to him stressed that it was for 'dire emergency' use only. He hadn't said what it contained, but assured H that it would give him an extra boost for a couple of hours.

A quick look in the mirror over a hand basin showed him that he looked reasonably normal. He splashed some water over his face and raked his fingers back through his hair. He straightened his shoulders before backtracking to the fight scene, where he retrieved the recording device from behind the map on the wall.

Zheng's body lay sprawled on the floor by the open cupboard. Three options flew through H's mind: he could leave the body where it was, hide it in the cupboard to delay its discovery or try and wedge the body, face downwards on a nearby spiral staircase, in the hope that Zheng's death might – at first sight – appear to have been an accidental fall. This would require time and physical effort. Deciding that his main priority was to get off the yacht safely, he left the body where it was and made his way back to the upper deck.

Chapter 64

Recognising how debilitated he felt, H rang Kyuji and, after briefly explaining the situation, asked if he'd send agents Onishi and Murata down to the *Sappho* to accompany him back to the hotel. If Zheng's body was discovered quickly, he realised that he might have trouble leaving. He also asked Kyuji to arrange for the hotel doctor to come and have a look at him.

When he got topside, he found that although the lunch party was winding down, there were still a couple of dozen guests in view. There was no sign of Sora. Quan was still in the meeting and he saw Sir John and Lady Lister, looking around for her and waiting to take their leave. H walked over and joined them as they moved across the deck. Lady Lister went into eulogies about the lunch party and the amusing people she'd met, before launching into a detailed description of her costume for the ball that evening and the character she'd decided to portray.

After a searching glance at H, Sir John asked quietly, "are you feeling quite the thing, old chap?"

"I'm afraid that I may have eaten something which disagreed with me."

Satisfied, Sir John said, "Nasty things these tummy bugs. Foreign food is the devil." He thought briefly and then said, "look, we have a car waiting for us here. Would you care for a lift back to your hotel?"

H thanked him and was about to refuse, when he noticed sudden signs of activity among the crew. Had Zheng's body been found? He looked ashore, but there was no sign of Agents Onishi or Murata on the quay, so he thanked Sir John and, without seeming to hurry, moved them towards the passerelle, eager to leave before one of the crew decided to retain the remaining partygoers. A senior officer was talking earnestly to one of the crew members and was scrutinising everyone left on board.

H disembarked with relief and stepped into the waiting car, where he called Agent Onishi to apologise and explain that he'd got a lift. Ten minutes later he stepped into his suite, where he found de Lamerie waiting with an anxious look on his face. Beside him stood a dapper little man with a small moustache and the competent air of a doctor. Kyuji had taken an executive decision to call on de Lamerie for help, rather than take a chance on the discretion of the hotel doctor.

After a thorough examination, Doctor Monvert gave H a short lecture on the dangers of the dislocation re-occurring and, as a precaution, advised him to visit the Princess Grace Hospital that afternoon, for an MRI scan. He professed horror at the rough and ready way H had dealt with the situation, but applauded his prompt action with the ice-packs and anti-inflammatories. He provided him with a more professional sling, gave him a supply of Diclofenac pills and strongly suggested H use the arm as little as possible for the next few days.

"In a couple of weeks," he said, "when the shoulder has recovered somewhat, you'll need a referral for physiotherapy. There are exercises that strengthen and tighten the joint, so that it's less likely to dislocate in the future and some specific stretches to help you regain full mobility and range of motion in your shoulder. I advise you to take this seriously. Keep using the ice-pack for forty eight hours, continue the anti-inflammatories for a week and wear the sling in the meantime."

As a colleague of de Lamerie's, Doctor Monvert had a good idea of what H did for a living. After asking H if he had any plans for the next few days, he threw up his hands in despair when H started by outlining what he was going to do that evening.

"Go *now* and lie down on your bed for an hour or two. See how you feel then."

H demurred, saying that he felt fine, but was over-ridden by de Lamerie. The Doctor shook his head over a patient who obviously had little intention of following his professional advice. He snapped the catches on his bag shut, stood up and clapped de Lamerie on the arm, before the two men left H alone in the room.

H surprised himself by falling asleep. When he woke up, over two hours later, he felt marginally better. After half an hour of soaking in a bath with steaming hot water up to his chin, matters improved further.

Checking his watch, H saw that he had just over an hour before he needed to get ready for the ball. He was committed to getting Sora off the yacht and away from Quan. He knew that she must be worrying about where he'd gone, but that couldn't be helped; he'd join her as soon as he could. He picked up the intercom and asked Kyuji, Onishi and Murata to come round to his room. As he cut the connection, he dialled the number for Room Service and ordered a large pot of coffee and club sandwiches for four.

H answered a knock on the door and they sat down for a briefing on how Kyuji had got on with the audio feed of Quan's meeting. Murata listened carefully, but didn't contribute much to the conversation. Onishi was one of the rising stars in the department and asked one or two pertinent questions and made a couple of good points. They discussed the tape and its ramifications and decided to call Tanaka with their conclusions, even though it was the middle of the night in Tokyo. Over the sandwiches, H updated them with what had happened and that he'd been left with no option but to kill Zheng. He was already a hero to the younger agents and they listened to him with avid attention.

Tanaka sounded wide awake and was still in his office as he described the arrangements he'd already set in motion and then asked for H's report. After briefly outlining what had happened, H gave a short account of the fight and the possible blow-back when

Zheng's body was found. Knowing from past history that it was impossible to keep anything from Tanaka, he mentioned his injury and ended by explaining what the doctor had advised.

Tanaka complimented Kyuji on his good sense in going through de Lamerie to find a discrete doctor. "In the light of your shoulder not being fully functional, H, I'd like you to take agents Onishi and Murata with you tonight and make your own arrangements as you see fit when you get on board."

"We have a diplomatic minefield to negotiate here. From what we've heard on the tape, we've enough evidence to arrest Quan immediately on conspiracy charges. However, it's not that simple. Firstly, she is a Chinese citizen and second, she's not on our soil. I'm meeting the Cabinet and National Security heads in the morning. I'll strongly advise that we bring Monaco into the picture and, once they've heard the tapes, I hope they'll agree to issue an immediate arrest warrant. H, it's vital that you handle this evening diplomatically. If Quan gets even a whiff of suspicion that we are onto her, she could take the *Sappho* into International Waters, which would then throw up a different set of diplomatic problems."

H agreed to do so and asked about Sora Mori. Tanaka listened to his arguments and ended up by giving H the green light to act as he saw fit and get her off the *Sappho,* if he could do so safely and without attracting attention.

It was almost time for H to leave for the ball, so he thanked his uncle and rang off. As he finished giving some instructions to Onishi and Murata, he dressed in the Zorro outfit, which included a black silk mask and a long cloak that fortunately covered his sling.

Kyuji wished him luck and H made his final arrangement as he walked back downstairs and out of the hotel. He took out his mobile and punched in Liam Callaghan's number in Dublin.

"Liam, might you be willing to take in a house-guest for a few days?"

Chapter 65

The caterers and florists had been anxiously waiting to start preparations for the ball that evening, but there had been a handful of lingering guests still on deck long after the lunch party was supposed to have ended. Sora had looked for H, but hadn't been able to see him leave the yacht. She knew that Madam Quan had been closeted somewhere for an important meeting and had still not reappeared. Sora went down to her stateroom, closed the curtains and turned down the bed. She was feeling keyed-up, which had brought on a headache and she hoped that a nap might relax her and get rid of it. Deciding that she'd been taking far too many pills recently, she sprayed some lavender water on her pillow and dabbed lavender oil on the pulse-points on her wrists and behind her ears. After kicking off her shoes, she lay down, covered herself with a light cashmere rug and closed her eyes.

Her pleasant dreams of leaving the *Sappho* safely and flying off into the sunset with H were interrupted when Quan flung open her door.

"Whatever are you doing down here in the dark?"

Sora explained about her headache.

"Well, you haven't got time to have a headache now. It's time to get up." She took hold of Sora's wrist and pulled her off the bed.

"You need to pack. I have to get back to Tokyo and we'll be leaving shortly. Get some of the stewardesses to help you"

"What about the ball tonight?"

"The *ball*?" Quan asked, as if she'd forgotten about it. Gathering her thoughts, which had been leaping ahead to what she'd need to do when she reached Tokyo, she said, "it's a total irrelevance. If necessary, the ball can take place without us." She checked her watch with a frown. "We may not leave until after I've greeted the guests, so put your costume on now, but I want you ready and packed in one hour. Zheng will come and collect you."

Sora waited until the door closed behind Quan before leaping into action. Before ringing for a stewardess, she wanted to pack a small bag herself. Opening the cupboards, she made a rapid selection of the few essential things she wanted to take with her. There was a holdall on a shelf above her clothes and pulling it down, she swiftly filled it. She left the jewellery, the designer and couture outfits, the shoes and handbags where they were. It might be impossible to take even this small bag with her, but she wanted to be prepared. She put her passport into a Bottega Veneta tote and looked around to see where to stash the two bags out of sight. Stepping through the door onto her balcony, she stuffed them down behind a wicker chair.

Her outfit for the ball was hanging up, ready for her to put on. It was a copy of Audrey Hepburn's little black dress, from 'Breakfast at Tiffany's'. The matching shoes, pearls, diamond hair-clip and a long cigarette holder were laid out beside the dress. After one, final look around, to see if she'd forgotten anything, she called for help with the rest of the packing.

Quan was irritated to find her stateroom filled with steamer trunks, piles of folded clothes and a welter of tissue paper. Three stewardesses stood up politely when she came in, but she ordered them out, telling them to come back later and instructed them to send Zheng to her immediately.

When ten minutes had passed with no sign of Zheng, Quan demanded that some senior person in her security detail come to her instead, but when there was a knock on her door, it was Captain Féng who stood there.

He took off his cap and gave her a small bow before stepping inside.

"Madam Quan, I'm afraid I have some distressing news for you. Zheng is dead. Her body has been discovered on the Tank Deck."

Quan's eyes narrowed as she looked at him. "Dead? How? Was it an accident, illness or foul play?"

"It seems that she died from a broken neck. We have no idea at this time how she sustained the injury. I've had her body taken to the sick-bay, pending further inquiries, which the local authorities will no doubt wish to pursue."

"That is *not* going to happen. This is an internal matter, which will not be conducted by any outside authority. Do I make myself clear?"

The Captain had a great job and didn't wish to jeopardise it. He was careful to keep his personal misgivings to himself.

"Perfectly clear, Madam Quan."

Alpha was in the corridor, waiting for Captain Féng to leave. She'd already heard of Zheng's death and was petrified. As a member of the large security team, she knew her limitations and had never aspired to become Quan's Head of Security. On this particular trip, she'd been third in the rankings, under Zheng and Bo Huáng. At home, she was even lower down the scale. The huge responsibility of the top spot was something she'd never anticipated, even if it was only on a temporary basis. The turnover among Quan's staff was high and she knew that the price of failure would mean she'd be out of a job; quite possibly without a reference.

"Don't just stand there, come in and give me your report. As my new security chief, I'll expect much from you."

With a sinking feeling, Alpha pinned on her most confident face, hoping she'd be able to answer her boss's questions.

CHAPTER 66

Quan's fancy dress ball on the *Sappho* was a spectacular occasion. Following the dinner, there would be dancing and a cabaret. The party was planned to end with a dazzling fireworks display.

In order to fit such a large number of guests on board, they'd moved out of the harbour and anchored a little way along the coast. This allowed them to have the musicians playing from a floating platform, garlanded with flowers and would free-up more space on board. Other small craft plied to and fro, ferrying guests from the harbour.

These arrangements saved Captain Féng from an incipient nervous breakdown. He'd funked the idea of telling Madam Quan that it was impossible to have the party in port, where the noise would have brought down the wrath of all the other boat owners nearby and more than likely a visit from the police. He also had to comply with strict rules regarding the number of people allowed aboard when a vessel was not in port. Health and Safety regulations demanded that there were sufficient life-jackets, craft or lifeboats for the numbers on board. The tenders and smaller boats would standby throughout the duration of the party, which relieved the Captain of another problem. Quan never wished to be bothered by what she considered petty annoyances and expected her captain to sort out any problems which might impact on how she wished her parties to be organised.

During the early part of the evening, a small crowd of tourists and locals gathered on the key, eager to catch a glimpse of the rich and famous, dressed in their fantastic and extravagant costumes.

They were not disappointed. The theme of the party was 'Stars of the Silver Screen' and the guests had really gone to town, trying to outdo everyone else with the flamboyance of their outfits. Some were easily recognisable as: Cleopatra, Snow White, a space-age silver outfit worn in The Bodyguard, a Marilyn Monroe look alike, in the celebrated white, pleated dress. A famous actress wore her own costume from one of the Star Wars films and a gorgeous Ursula Andress lookalike, scantily dressed in the iconic bikini, with a large knife stuck into her belt. Lady Lister had outdone herself in her portrayal of Queen Elizabeth 1st, with an enormously wide brocade dress, a jewel encrusted lace ruff, topped off by a mighty tiara. The men also represented a good cross section of well-known characters from box office hits. There were two Lone Rangers, several pirates (mostly from the Caribbean), a fearsome looking Dracula, a King Arthur, a Ben Hur, a Robin Hood and even a realistic looking Jesus of Nazareth. They were a good-natured group, out for an enjoyable evening and quite a few posed happily for 'selfies' with members of the crowd.

When Quan hosted a party, she wanted it to be a memorable one. Positively no expense was spared and her team of highly qualified organisers knew that they could give free rein to their creative talents. Tonight, the flowers stole the show. Robbie, her chief florist, had surpassed himself. The previous spring he'd visited a famous wisteria garden festival in Fukuoka, Japan and been overwhelmed with the beauty of the displays. At staggering expense, he'd recreated the theme on board the *Sappho* and achieved a 'garden' of enchantment. Mature plants had been flown in from Japan and trained up and over metal supports to cover the roof of a pergola which had been erected over the Sundeck. Immensely long racemes of Wisteria Floribunda 'Macrobotrys' in white and various shades of purple hung down in a sweetly scented curtain, which swayed in the light breeze, making a magical 'wow' statement and a truly breathtaking sight. It was a major topic of conversation among the blasé crowd on board

Agent Murata had been down to the port and got into conversation with some of the tender drivers. On the basis of what he learned, he'd managed to hire a classic mahogany Hacker-Craft Runabout and was now waiting on the quay to ferry H out to the yacht. Kyuji had hacked into the *Sappho's* computer system and found the guest list for the party. He added two names, so they'd have no trouble getting admitted on board. At short notice, Agent Onishi had managed to come up with a white cowboy hat, a mask and a pair of knee high boots, making the third guest appearing as the Lone Ranger. Only the most discerning eye would have spotted that the guns both he and H wore on the belts at their hips, were the real thing – and loaded with real bullets. Murata offered a seat on the boat to a portly Julius Caesar, who was waiting on the quay and was handing him down when H arrived and jumped gently aboard.

The sun had set and as the evening drew in, the *Sappho* could be seen from miles around, lit up like a Christmas tree and twinkling with thousands of fairy lights.

Chapter 67

The minutes ticked by as Sora sat at her dressing table, waiting for a fashionable hairdresser to finish putting her hair up and fixing a diamond tiara, copying Audrey Hepburn's Holly Golightly look in 'Breakfast at Tiffany's'. The man talked non-stop, gushing about how gorgeous Sora looked and that she'd be the undoubted 'belle of the ball.' He told her long, involved and scurrilous stories of some of the wealthy clients he worked for. Sora nodded and smiled without taking in one word of what he was saying.

When she decided that she'd never be able to get rid of him, she asked if he'd be kind enough to zip up her dress before he left. He finally took the hint and left her alone. She took out a pair of sneakers, jeans and a sweatshirt and left them on the balcony with her bags. The little black dress and stilettos she was wearing would be inappropriate if she had to move quickly. At any moment now Quan might be ready to leave and whisk her away, without H being aware of what was happening.

She needed somewhere to hide and she'd need some help. There was really only one person she could think of to ask. On the voyage from Ireland, she'd befriended Purna Patel and thought she'd be able to trust her. Sora lifted the intercom and asked if she could see her for a few minutes. "Perfect timing," Purna replied. "Javinda has just gone up to join the others and I'm not quite ready yet. Come now."

Purna sat, round eyed, listening as Sora gave her a heavily edited explanation of her predicament and readily agreed that she could hide in her cabin.

"I need you to do something for me and it's terribly important," Sora said. "At the party there'll be a man dressed as Zorro, with a black silk mask and cape. You must speak to him without anyone overhearing and tell him I'm hiding in here and why. Also, if there's any chance you can find out if Madam Quan is still on board, it would be a great help. If she has already left, it'll be safe for me to come up on deck"

"Why on earth would she leave during her own party?" Purna asked, putting the last touches to her make-up and standing up. She looked round and saw that Sora wasn't going to answer. "Ok, I'll do my best with your masked admirer and not ask you any awkward questions, but I'll have to pick my time. Javindar may not want me himself, but he really hates me talking to any other men. This is all quite exciting. Look, lock the door behind me and when I come back, I'll knock three times, then twice, so you'll know it's me. I'll tell your Zorro too."

"I can't thank you enough, Purna, and I hope one day I'll be able to explain it all to you."

It was a beautiful evening and the sea was flat calm, which was a good thing for the musicians and singers who were belting out classic movie theme tunes on their floating platform. With their forged invitations and credentials, H and Onishi were admitted on board without any problems and passed through a security check. After collecting drinks they mingled with the crowd, who seemed to be going through bottles of Cristal at an astonishing rate and demolishing trays filled with caviar and oysters. The noise was rising by the minute and a gay time – in the old fashioned sense of the word – was being had by all.

H was surprised that Quan didn't seem to be there to greet her guests. He asked a couple of the crew and guests, but nobody seemed to know where she was. After two circuits of the deck, he was concerned when he couldn't see any sign of Sora either. At the lunch party, they'd exchanged details on what costumes they'd be wearing, to make it easy for them to find each other, but there was no Holly Golightly look-alike in sight.

The Listers were standing by the rail, talking to a lovely young Indian woman in a lilac sari, which echoed the colours of the wisteria hanging overhead. He'd noticed her earlier at the lunch party, but they hadn't been introduced, so H was a little surprised to see her beckon him over. He joined the group and was glad to see that his mask prevented him from being recognised. Lady Lister introduced herself and her husband and said, "This is Purna Patel, who sailed here with her husband as a guest of Madam Quan's. We've just been asking her what film she's dressed from. Can you guess, I wonder?"

H shook hands all round, smiling down into Purna's face and enjoying the tinkling sounds of her myriad silver bracelets, which rang together as she put out her hand. "I'd get the pronunciation wrong if I tried, but I'd imagine your costume is inspired by one of the popular 'Bollywood' films."

"Very good, Señor Zorro." She turned aside and started to speak softly, rapidly giving him the information Sora had asked her to pass on. He smiled and thanked her sincerely for her help. She nodded and turned back to the Listers.

H, having seen the schematics of the *Sappho,* could instantly visualise where the Patel's stateroom was situated. He was on the point of going to find Sora when he noticed an inflatable dinghy with an outboard motor approaching the Swim Platform in the Stern. His eyes narrowed as he noticed that there was only a single occupant aboard, who was wearing a long, dark coat. H looked around for Onishi and, catching his eye, motioned him over. "This may be trouble," he said, indicating the small craft, which was now only yards from the *Sappho.*

Hands reached to help the newcomer aboard and to tie up the dingy. Once he reached the deck, the man could be seen as tall and youngish, with a short, dark beard. He had a wild look in his eyes and disregarded a junior security guard and the young woman with the clipboard, who was trying to check his name off her list. After brushing past them as if they were invisible, he stood stock still. His eyes were shut and his lips were moving, as if in prayer.

"Shit," H said audibly to Onishi.

As those standing closest to him would later tell the authorities, the man then opened his coat, to reveal to a suicide vest, which looked to be packed with explosives. Those witnesses said that at that moment, they were unsure if this was a guest wearing a costume in impossibly bad taste, or the start of a terrorist attack.

The man opened his eyes wide, took a deep breath and started screaming "*Allahu Akbar.* Death to all infidels." He began to raise his left arm, with a detonator grasped in his hand.

All hell broke loose.

Part Four

Chapter 68

Secret Service HQ – Tokyo

It was just after four o'clock in the morning and after catching a couple of hours sleep on a futon in his private sitting room, Tanaka was back at his desk. Punishingly long working hours were expected in Japan, but, when a crisis was on, Tanaka was on call 24/7. He sat in his shirtsleeves, looking at a note Mai-Li had left on his otherwise virgin desk. The Cabinet meeting was scheduled to start at 8 a.m and he was waiting to brief those of the staff who'd been working through the night.

The note read, 'Brigadier Sir Harry Wetherall of MI6 in London, telephoned at 2.23 a.m. and *insisted* that I not disturb you. He asks you to ring, whatever time it may now be in London.' Tanaka checked the bank of world time clocks on the wall. It would be shortly after nine in the evening. Before lifting the phone he pulled a pad of paper and a Montblanc pen out of a desk drawer and made a note of the date and time, adding Sir Harry's name.

"Tiger, old friend, I have something which may be of interest to you. Early this morning, acting on a tip-off, we raided a house in Balham, looking for a cache of weapons. We netted more than we'd bargained for and arrested four men. One of them is Chinese. We have him in custody and I wonder if you might like us to turn him over to your chaps here? He's not saying much, but luckily, the stupid chap had his laptop with him. It seems he's been exchanging a string of extremely indiscrete emails with his brother. They were using a childishly simple code and I feel you should see them a.s.a.p.

to evaluate them yourself. The brother lives and works in Tokyo and there are some thinly veiled hints about an upcoming wave of terrorist attacks there. This fellow sounds a very small cog in the wheel, but you'll probably be able to make far more out of it than we can."

Tanaka thanked him warmly and spent the next few minutes bringing his counterpart in London into the picture about Madam Chow Lee Quan and what they'd discovered about her plans with the Chinese generals. If Wetherall already knew any of this, he kept quiet and listened. He ended the call by promising to send the emails straight away, saying he'd keep his ear to the ground and keep in touch.

When the tape of Quan's meeting with the generals had arrived, it had been evaluated by several of Tanaka's section heads, who were about to assemble in his office. Before the Cabinet meeting started, they had to have plans in place for him to submit to the diplomats. In regard to the concrete information they had on the future bombings and demonstrations, preparatory work had continued through the night and Tanaka would listen to suggestions for individual scenarios: which services must be briefed and brought into the picture, particular events needed to be co-ordinated and prioritised, all eventualities to be listed and discussed. Proper co-ordination was vital and everyone had to be made aware of the roles they would play and the timings scoped-out. Tanaka also had to be briefed by the researcher who'd been tasked with the job of laying bare the lives of the three men mentioned on the tape. Every contingency had to be covered, if this massive anti-terrorist exercise was to succeed

Tanaka stood up and stretched, wishing he had time to clear his mind with his daily ritual of Tai-Chi exercises. It was shortly after dawn and the sunrise was only minutes away. He looked out through the pearly, misty light at the panorama of Tokyo below. As usual, the view calmed him, but also brought home his massive responsibility to keep this skyline exactly as he saw it now.

Chapter 69

On Board the *Sappho*

Time seemed to stop, like the freeze-frame on a television remote control. Then several things happened simultaneously. Sir John Lister could be heard shouting, "bomb! Everybody get down." With surprising strength, he pulled the two women to the deck and covered them with his body. One of the better trained and more alert security guards started to draw a concealed weapon, but he was beaten to it. In a blur of motion, guns appeared in the hands of H and Onishi. Shots rang out. Unaware of the drama which was enfolding them only yards away, the musicians continued to play.

As the terrorist's body hit the deck, there were several seconds of suspended animation, before the screaming began and the panic set in. It was started by the girl with the clipboard, who suddenly found that her white outfit was splattered with blood and brains.

H and Onishi's accurate shooting had obliterated the hand of the terrorist, and stopped the explosive charge from detonating. They both followed up with head shots to complete the job.

Above the din, Sir John's voice could be heard again, appealing for everyone to keep calm.

The guns H and Onishi were holding vanished back into their holsters with practised speed and they helped Lady Lister and Purna Patel to their feet. Javinda Patel materialised, looking worried and comforted his wife as she fell, sobbing into his arms. Lady Lister was made of sterner stuff and seemed more concerned about her dress being crushed and her tiara being knocked askew.

One minute H and Onishi were there, the next minute they had gone. Once they were out of sight, H said, "Onishi, call Murata and tell him to bring the boat round to the port side and to come in close. I'll go and find the girl. You get aboard and be ready for us to join you. We need to be away from here before the mass exodus begins."

There was chaos on deck. Guests, caterers, crew and bar staff were milling around and making it hard to move. The Captain's voice came over the tannoy system. "Keep calm. The danger is over. Everyone stay where you are. No-one is to leave before the police arrive." His words were largely ignored and it was everyone for themself. One of the officers stepped forward and covered the bloody body with his jacket. Some people behaved well, but many behaved disgracefully: pushing, barging and stampeding for the exit, calling for boats to collect them immediately and shouting into mobile phones.

H fought his way through the throng and headed down a staircase, looking for Sora. Even though she must have heard the gunfire, he was hoping she'd had the good sense to stay put in the Patel's stateroom.

He banged loudly on the door, three times and then twice. "It's me Sora," he called. "Open the door."

When Sora heard the shots, she rushed out onto the balcony to find out what was going on. There was nothing to see, but she could hear a lot of confused noises overhead. She kicked off her stilettos and climbed over three barriers until she reached her own balcony, where she grabbed her two bags. Returning to the Patel's cabin the way she'd come, she started to struggle out of her outfit, catching the zip in her haste. The dress ripped as she tore it over her head and pulled on the clothes she'd left ready.

With relief, she heard H at the door and ran to open it.

"Good girl!" he said, taking in her preparations at a glance. He took her into his arms and kissed her.

"What's happening H?" she asked.

"I'll tell you as soon as we get away from here. Are you ready to jump ship?" She nodded and he picked up her holdall and led her through the glass door.

Agent Murata had the engine of the Hacker-Craft Runabout idling about fifty yards away. He spotted them immediately and came alongside. Agent Onishi stood ready to catch Sora and without hesitation, she leapt into his outstretched arms. H jumped aboard and Murata glanced round to check that they were seated, before pushing back and turning the boat away from the *Sappho.*

"Where to?" he shouted to H, over the noise of the engine.

"Back to Port Hercule." H then turned to Sora, asking the question which was uppermost in his mind. "Where is Quan?" but Sora didn't know the answer.

Once they'd put some distance between themselves and the *Sappho,* H asked Onishi to look after Sora and to get her a thick towel out of a locker, to keep her warm. He moved across the boat and asked Murata to slow down a little, so he could hear better to make a call.

Kyuji picked up at the first ring and H said, "I need you to get the boss and Monsieur de Lamerie on a conference line, right now. Patch me through. I'll hold."

Only eight minutes after the shooting had occurred, H was speaking to both men. Without preamble, he said, "uncle, please listen, as I need to brief Aristide first." He gave a succinct sit-rep. before stressing the fact that as the *Sappho* had moved along the coast for the party, it was currently in French Territorial Waters, anchored near the seaside village of Beaulieu-sur-Mer. The entire situation would now be in the hands of de Lamerie, the police and other French security forces.

"This attack only happened about ten minutes ago. At this stage it appears that it was conducted by one man, acting alone." H went into a detailed description of what the man looked like, what he'd been wearing and what he'd shouted.

"I apologise for leaving the crime scene, but it seems probable that Quan has already gone and I need to get a lead on her. I have

Miss Mori with me and we couldn't afford to get delayed with the aftermath here. I can give you a fuller statement whenever you have time. As to witnesses, both Sir John and Lady Lister and the Patels were standing close to Onishi and me, but as our costumes both had masks, none of them is aware of our identities. With your permission, Aristide, I'll be flying back to Tokyo in the next few hours."

De Lamerie said that, in the circumstances, it wouldn't be a problem and wished him luck, before hanging up.

Tanaka said, "I don't envy Aristide having to deal with the fallout of another terrorist attack, even though you and Agent Onishi managed to avert any loss of life. Now, Hiroshi, our focus remains on Quan. Do you know her current whereabouts?"

"Unclear at this point, Uncle, but Quan told Miss Mori that she would be leaving this evening and returning to Tokyo."

"I'll get Kyuji onto the airport data straight away. If she can be detained by the French, I think there's a valid reason to do so now."

H agreed and hoped they'd be in time. "I have made plans concerning Miss Mori and hope you'll approve. If you can spare Onishi and Murata for twenty four hours, I'd like them to accompany her to Dublin before returning to Tokyo. With Quan's whereabouts still uncertain, I feel Miss Mori may still be at risk from her."

Tanaka appreciated that Sora had been instrumental in facilitating their plans and gave H permission to organise her protection.

As Murata was steering the Runabout into Port Hercule, H had a quiet word with Onishi, allocating jobs for him to relay to the others in the team. They needed to get packed-up: there was a large car to be hired, various plane tickets to be booked and the bill to be settled at The Hermitage.

H took Sora up to his suite. She still had no idea what was going on, but had showed fantastic patience. The boat trip had been too noisy for her to hear H's telephone conversation, so she was still completely in the dark. He got her a small bottle of brandy from the mini bar and sat her down. As he talked, he changed out of the Zorro outfit and quickly packed his things. He described what had happened, and how he'd dealt with a terrorist trying to attack the *Sappho*. When it came to his arrangements for her, he sat down opposite her and took hold of her hands. She listened in growing consternation.

"Can't I stay with you?" she asked, hopefully. "I don't *know* any of these people and I can't face ... "

H cut in, choosing his words carefully. "I wish I *could* take you with me, but it's not possible. I'm in the middle of an assignment and I've been ordered back to Tokyo. Those two guys from the boat, Onishi and Murata will take good care of you and Liam Callaghan is one of my oldest friends." He could see she was unconvinced. "Trust me, Sora. Whilst Quan is still unaccounted for, I don't want to take any chances with your safety. I know it's hard for you, but I hope it won't be for too long. I'll be driving with you to the airport and I'll tell you more about Liam on the way. He's great and I know you'll adore him."

H said goodbye to her at the boarding gate at the airport. She clung to him, with tears on her cheeks. She felt that things were spiralling out of her control and realised – just in time – that she hadn't even thought to thank him for rescuing her. He hugged her to his chest for a long moment and kissed her. "Safe trip, Sora. I'll see you soon." He exchanged nods with Onishi and Murata before turning and walking across the concourse, to where Kyuji was waiting for him.

There was a long wait for the next flight to Tokyo, so it was almost twenty four hours later when they landed at Narita Airport. Tanaka had sent a car, which was waiting on the tarmac.

As H sank into his seat, his aching shoulder reminded him it was time for some more pills. He picked up the direct line telephone and rang Tanaka to find out what had been happening.

Chapter 70

They'd missed apprehending Quan at Nice Airport. She'd boarded her Boing Business Jet, which had taken off fifteen minutes before the alert went out and the pilot had filed a flight plan for Tokyo.

Tanaka had taken a call from Aristide de Lamerie, with an update on the attempted bombing onboard the *Sappho.* It seemed as though Quan herself was not the target. A diary, recovered from the terrorist's dinghy, showed that the venue had been chosen as a means of killing a large number of high-profile non-believers. Although the affair turned out not to have any direct bearing on the Quan case, Tanaka was impressed with the speed with which de Lamerie had gathered so much data on the terrorist. The man's name was Wassim Taleb, a twenty three year old Sunni Muslim refugee from Algeria, who'd been granted asylum in France two years ago. He'd passed several security checks and was not on any 'watch list.' The authorities had so far found no evidence of contact with any radical elements.

De Lamerie sounded tired and dispirited. "However vigilant we are, some will always slip through our nets. We have no idea yet as to when he became radicalised, but the police are at his flat now and they'll be talking to neighbours and staff at a Moroccan restaurant in Monte-Carlo, where he'd been working as a sous-chef." Tanaka congratulated him on compiling a dossier in such a short time and wished him luck with his investigation.

The briefing of the Cabinet had followed predictable, if frustrating lines. Tanaka had known that the one question they'd fixate on, was the date and time of the first planned bombing – the only missing link in the chain of information he'd compiled. He was used to dealing with politicians and had seen many come and go. The fact that the plans of a major series of terrorist atrocities had been uncovered by his service was forgotten in their quest for this one piece of – as yet – uncovered information

One or two of the ambitious, younger members wanted to grandstand, but Tanaka brought them back into line by painting a grim picture. He had to take them all with him and grant him the additional powers he'd need to circumvent the imminent dangers. He spoke well and painted a vivid and ominous picture, explaining that the significant loss of life which was planned, could easily topple the Government. This got their attention. International outrage, he went on to say, would rain down condemnation on a government which failed to protect not only its own citizens, but the thousands of tourists and foreign nationals who lived and worked in Tokyo. He established that the disruptions and panic, which would follow the protests and demonstrations would be catastrophic to the city and to the national economy.

He had persuaded them and was granted every emergency power he requested.

In comparison, his briefing to the heads of the National Security agencies, presented him with no such problems. They understood the wider picture without having to have it explained to them and were right behind him from the start.

Chapter 71

Whilst these events were taking place, Quan was on her way back to Tokyo.

Overall, she'd been delighted with how the meeting on board had turned out. Everything had gone according to plan, with the added personal bonus that General Weisheng had been routed on all points.

The news of Zheng's mysterious death had disturbed her and the *Sappho* had suddenly felt stifling. Although she had already planned to fly back to Tokyo as soon as possible, she felt ill at ease without Zheng at her side, and somehow vulnerable; a feeling which disconcerted her. They had been together for many years and Quan was used to having the devoted, huge mute at her side. The newly promoted head of security was utterly useless, she decided, and would need to be replaced as soon as possible.

The fastest way to travel to Nice Airport was via helicopter, but for some reason which she couldn't define, she felt it inadvisable to go into Monte-Carlo. At the back of her mind floated the image of the ubiquitous Mister Suzuki. There was nothing she could put her finger on, and she shook her head in irritation, but she had a feeling that he could somehow pose a threat to her and to her plans.

Having come to a decision, she glanced at her Cartier watch. With the ball due to start in less than an hour, she decided to leave before the first guests arrived. She called for one of her personal assistants and gave orders for a fast motor launch to take her to Nice immediately and a limousine to drive her to the Airport. Her Boeing Business Jet was to be ready and waiting for her. She expected her staff to anticipate what needed to be done and felt it unnecessary to go into details about organising the flight crew, numbers of who'd be travelling with her, ensuring her personal chauffeur was waiting on the tarmac when she landed, or mundane items such as luggage. She didn't bother to ask that Captain Féng of the *Sappho* be informed that she was leaving and this courtesy was overlooked by her assistant, in the flurry of Quan's departure.

A minor fracas and delay ensued when Sora could not be found. Quan ordered a thorough search to be made immediately, but none of the crew was able to find her. Quan was incandescent with rage and her staff quaked. Eventually, Quan stormed onto the motor launch and left without Sora.

She boarded her plane with a face of thunder, which made the flight crew exchange worried looks. They took off without incident and although the pilot was informed by radio of the abortive terrorist attack on the *Sappho*, Quan had already eaten and gone to sleep in her luxurious bedroom and he felt it was more than his life was worth to disturb her. It preyed on his mind throughout the night, as he flew south towards Japan. He had to second guess his boss and hope that he'd made the right choice.

As soon as she reappeared in the main cabin, the pilot relayed the news.

For once in her life, Quan was speechless.

Chapter 72

Tokyo

When H arrived at the Japanese Secret Service HQ, he was whisked up to Tanaka's suite of offices on the Penthouse Floor. Mai-Li was waiting for him. She tut-tutted when she saw his sling, but he assured her that it was almost better. He kissed her cheek and handed over a large bunch of yellow roses, which he remembered were her favourite flowers. Kyuji had been amused when H had asked the driver to make a brief stop at a flower market on their way in from the airport.

Tanaka was seated at his desk, but he stood up as H came in. They both bowed to each other – a ritual always performed when H returned safely from a mission abroad – then they embraced warmly and Tanaka waved him to a chair.

An hour later, H had enlarged on all the events which had happened since he left Tokyo and Tanaka had brought him up to speed with the latest developments, as well as what had gone on in the briefings.

"Having reviewed all the data, your next job will be to approach this man." Tanaka pushed a photograph across the desk. It showed a full length shot of a well-dressed man in his early thirties, coming out of a building, carrying an expensive looking attaché case.

"Minsheng Gāo," Tanaka said, tapping the photo, "is the only one of the three men mentioned on the tape of Quan's meeting, who we've been able to locate in Japan. He is definitely implicated in their plans and whatever he knows, *we* need to know. Time is something we have very little of and this man seems to be our best shot at finding out when and where the first bomb is due to be detonated. Hiroshi, this *must* be handled discretely. Gāo is a Chinese citizen and works in their embassy in the Minato-ku area of Tokyo. We've had him under surveillance and the details of what we have learnt are in here."

He handed H a file. "In view of your shoulder, I'd like you to handpick a small team to take with you and I'll make them available. Work out how best to confront Gāo, and bring your plan to me first thing tomorrow morning."

Tanaka stood up, stretched and massaged the back of his neck. H knew that he'd been working solidly for almost two days and wasn't surprised that he looked exhausted.

"By the way," Tanaka said, "you'll be pleased to know that Onishi and Murata encountered no problems, and they've handed Miss Mori over into the care of your friend Liam Callaghan, who was there to meet them at Dublin Airport. They are now en route back here."

"Thank you, sir. Liam will take good care of her until this is all over," H said.

"Mai-Li has made you an appointment to get your shoulder checked-out," Tanaka looked at his watch, "in half an hour. A car is waiting for you downstairs."

H knew it was useless to argue. He would have liked to advise his uncle to get some sleep, but he knew that that would be futile too. After slipping the photograph inside the file, he picked it up, said goodbye and left the office. Even before he reached the door, his mind was leaping ahead and forming plans for how to deal with Minsheng Gāo.

Chapter 73

The shoulder specialist gave H a thorough check and some sound advice which tallied with what Doctor Monvert had told him in Monte-Carlo. H was tired and his mind was preoccupied, but he forced himself to listen carefully and intended to take the instructions seriously. It was a 'given' that an active agent had to be in peak physical condition and one with a faulty shoulder would soon find himself either dead, or assigned to a desk job. He signed himself up for a course of physical therapy, where he'd learn the exercises necessary to regain full mobility and range of motion, as well as exercises to strengthen and tighten the joint, so that it would be less likely to dislocate in the future. He was dismayed to hear that it could take between three and six months to recover fully and that he'd need to wait for a couple of weeks for things to settle down, before starting treatment.

As he got up to leave, the Doctor told him, "your age and excellent physical fitness are greatly in your favour. Presuming you follow my advice, the chances of further dislocations are less than 50%."

H read through the file on Minsheng Gāo on his way back to HQ. He was impressed at how much information had been gathered in such a short time and made a mental note to thank whomever had compiled the dossier. He'd decided which two agents he'd most like to use as back up and rang the switchboard, asking for them to be located and ready in one hour, for a meeting in his office.

By the time he arrived, a plan was fully formed in his mind. Three men stood up as he walked in and they all shook hands before sitting down. He'd often worked with Johnny Dashu and Baku Mori before and was glad they'd both been made available. He was surprised to see a much younger man with them. He never forgot a face, though the last time he'd seen this one, was as a schoolboy. He was now a large, heavily built young man, with a deceptively angelic face.

"I apologise for coming here uninvited, but I hoped that you might find a use for me, in some minor capacity, sir. My name is ... "

H laughed and cut in, "I know exactly who you are. Welcome to the major league, Dai Chavet! Forget the 'sir' and tell me how your big brother's getting on?" The 'big brother' was Oki Chavet, a good friend of H's, who'd recently retired from field work and had been promoted to Head of the Paris Station. He'd stepped into the shoes of Tadeo Fujita, who'd died the year before during a terrorist attack in which H had been involved.

H handed Dashu and Mori his file on Minsheng Gāo and asked them to start reading, whilst he caught up with news of his friend Oki.

"My brother is well and sends his compliments. I must mention that it was at his suggestion that I was bold enough to gatecrash this meeting."

"Oki's always been free with advice and sayings. Carpe Diem and Nothing Ventured, Nothing Gained, were always two of his favourites. It's good to see you again and I'm sure I can find something for you to do."

When they'd all finished reading the file, H asked for their thoughts.

Johnnie Dashu was the first to speak. "He seems to have a gambling problem, which might be used as a lever."

"Exactly so," H said. "This seems to be his only weakness, but our people have only had Gāo under surveillance for a very short time." He turned to Dai Chavet and explained, "in an operation like this, I'd hope to have much longer to prepare for what I have in mind. We don't yet know nearly enough about his regular habits and routines. Mistakes can happen when we act on insufficient information, but in this instance, we don't have the luxury of time. Is there anything you want to add, Dai?"

"Well, sir ... I'm sorry, *H*, there's only one small thing. With Gão's relatively lowly position and salary at the Embassy, don't you think he seems to be living rather high?"

H nodded. "Good point."

As H laid out his strategy, they nodded, smiled, and made notes. He wound up the meeting by saying that he'd run it through with his uncle in the morning and if he got the green light, they'd put the plan into operation the following evening. He asked the three of them to make the necessary arrangements and to do a dummy-run that evening and then to have an early night. If any further information came to light, they'd be brought up to speed when they met in the morning.

Chapter 74

Quan's Apartment – Tokyo

Quan rang Captain Féng onboard the *Sappho,* to get a report on exactly what had happened, but found that he was still being interviewed by the authorities. A terrorist attack was something so totally unexpected and she was exasperated that the details were sketchy. Leaving an order for Féng to ring her immediately he was able to do so, she petulantly threw the telephone across the cabin.

When Quan landed at Haneda Airport, one of Tanaka's surveillance teams was waiting and followed her back to the City, where she was driven to her apartment. Her movements would now be under constant scrutiny.

Once she was settled in the car, she picked up her phone and called the Managing Director of her Armstec factory outside Tokyo, saying she'd be in the following morning and that she fully expected her most senior explosive expert to have completed his work on configuring the new weapon from the data on the memory stick.

On entering her apartment, she was greeted by her butler, who announced that there was an urgent call holding for her. Shrugging-off a beautiful and fabulously expensive Loro Piana cashmere shawl and dropping it carelessly on the floor, she marched over to her desk and snatched up the receiver.

Captain Féng sounded tired as well as nervous. He started by saying what a relief it was to him when he'd found out that she'd disembarked before the nightmare.

"Yes, yes," she said, "get on with it."

He listed the sequence of events, and the drama which had unfolded so rapidly. No organisation, he said, had yet claimed responsibility for the attack. She interrupted him several times, being more interested in hearing details about the men who'd shot the terrorist, than in the suicide bomber himself.

"You say that this man was killed, not by my security staff, but by two of the guests?" She asked incredulously. "Who were they and how come they were allowed on board, carrying weapons?" Féng had no answer.

"Where were you, whilst these events were taking place? Sleeping?" she asked unkindly.

He quickly explained that he'd been on the bridge and was not in a position where he could see what had happened. After hearing the shots, he'd appealed for calm and left his bridge to investigate. He'd questioned the eye-witnesses, but there was so much confusion that people's versions differed widely.

"The two guests who did the shooting – have they been identified? What happened to them and are they in custody?"

"According to one of your guests," there was a pause and a noise of rustling papers, "– a Sir John Lister – and confirmed by one of the crew – the two men disappeared right after the shooting. Apparently, both were wearing costumes with masks and the authorities are still anxious to identify them."

"You've told me almost nothing," Quan shouted into the receiver. "I'm appalled at the general inefficiency and lack of facts. You should have been more alert."

Trying to placate her, he said, "whoever they are, we should be thankful that these quick-thinking men were on board. With the large quantity of explosives strapped to the would-be bomber, I gather that without their intervention, many people would have died and the *Sappho* might even have sunk."

"Oh, so we should be *thankful,* should we? It is *not* your place to tell me what I should or should not feel." There was a pause. "Naturally I'm relieved at how things turned out, but you-will-not-rest until you find out who these two gunmen were. The security was lax in the extreme. You will naturally fire those on duty at once – without references. Now I have more important things to attend to. I shall expect a fuller report as… as in yesterday."

When the butler heard the phone crash down, he waited for a few moments before opening the door and beckoning two underlings to wheel-in a trolley containing a bottle of Quan's favourite Cristal and a selection of canapés. This was done in complete silence and Quan did not acknowledge that they were there. He waited until everything was laid-out to his satisfaction, bowed and followed the others out of the room, silently closing the door behind him.

Chapter 75

Secret Service HQ – Tokyo

"I like it," Tanaka said, after going through H's audacious plan with his usual care and consideration. "You have my permission to proceed. Make it clean and make it work, Hiroshi. We can't afford any mistakes. Johnny Dashu and Baku Mori are both good choices, but are you sure young Chavet is ready for something of this importance?"

"I think he is," H replied. "He'll only have a minor role to play this time, but having read through all his training reports last night, I was impressed. Apart from his outstanding scores, his psychological evaluations demonstrate he can keep a cool head. He's shown that he has no problems with authority and obeying orders, but he's also proved himself capable of independent thought. I spoke to Johnny Dashu, who's been keeping a close eye on him, for Oki's sake, and he agrees with me that Chavet shows all the makings of a fine agent."

Tanaka laughed. "I've also been watching his progress with some interest. In many ways he reminds me of you, a few years ago – apart from the 'no problems with authority' part! When are you planning to move on this?"

"I'd like to say that we could do it this evening, but, if you'll allow us one extra day of surveillance, I think tomorrow night would give us a better chance of getting it right."

Tanaka considered the time frame. "I agree. We both know too well how unpredictable these jobs can be. Keep in close contact."

H returned to his office, where he found the others waiting. They went down to Kyuji's domain and sat through the surveillance tapes of the target. The team assigned to watching Minsheng Gāo hadn't found any fresh information overnight and one of them, who'd just come off duty, was there to brief H.

"Luckily," he said, "the target seems to be a man of fairly set habits and routines. He lives close to the Embassy. If I may be permitted to say so, he seems to be living well above his means. We've been inside his flat and a whole load of money has been spent on it." He stopped abruptly, at the sound of laughter and clapping from Dashu and Baku. Chavet was brick-red with embarrassment when he saw that his hero, H was smiling at him, for having his suggestion proved so conclusively.

"Take no notice of us," H said. "Please continue."

The tired surveillance agent got back on track and looked down at his notes. "As I was saying, the target has left his flat promptly each morning at 6.50. He stops at a Starbucks for something to eat on his way in, and arrives at the Embassy at 7.15. He hasn't yet left the building for lunch, or any other meetings. He has left work at 9.30 each evening. The first two evenings he went straight home and didn't go out again. Last night, he walked home as usual, but came out of his flat after twenty minutes and walked to a local restaurant, where he met two men for dinner. At 11.10 all three of them took a taxi to a discrete, private casino. He stayed there for a little over two hours, before catching a cab alone, arriving home at 1.35."

H thanked him and asked; "have you been able to access his home computer or tap his phones?"

Kyuji, who was listening to the conversation, answered, "the answer is yes, but it doesn't get us anywhere. One of the surveillance team managed to bump into him, when he was making a call, and cloned his mobile. We've also put a tap on his home line. I've downloaded the hard-drive of his laptop, but he's either been highly trained or is just naturally discrete. He hasn't had any suspicious conversations, sent any unusual emails or downloaded any incriminating files. It's all innocent family-and-friends stuff. We're still listening, but so far, nothing to help us. It's possible that he has a 'burner-phone' for private conversations, but we haven't found a bill for one.

There are only two points of interest," Kyuji went on. "One new piece of data – which you might need to be aware of – is that he holds a black belt in Karate. We found a series of emails from a martial arts club, which establishes this as a fact. The second point is that we've managed to hack into his personnel file. We've found no evidence to suggest that he has any family or private money, above and beyond his salary."

H took his team into the canteen for a quick lunch, where – sitting in an isolated table – they went over their plans once more. The afternoon was spent walking the route several times between the Embassy and Gão's flat and back again. H decided on the best spot for what he had in mind, and called HQ to arrange for two dark coloured vans to meet them. Whilst they waited, they discussed possible problems and how to overcome them. When the vans arrived, H ordered one to be parked at a particular spot, near a corner and took charge of the keys, asking the two drivers to make their own way back to HQ. He pulled out a note-pad and wrote 'BROKEN DOWN' in large letters on a card and stuck it under the windscreen-wiper.

H asked Baku to ring and inform the local police and traffic wardens that the van with the given registration number (with a note on windscreen) was to be left strictly alone. The team piled into the second van and H asked Chavet to drive. Together they mapped-out several routes, checking that there would be no problems with unexpected road-works or diversions. Once H was satisfied, he called it a day with the reconnaissance work and they returned to their offices.

Tomorrow night they'd be ready.

Chapter 76

Quan checked her iPad and scrolled through the list she'd made on the flight from France. The tasks she'd already done were deleted and she sat thinking if there was anything else to add.

Her private office on the penthouse floor of the Armstec International headquarters had been furnished to impress those she allowed to meet her there. It was obvious that the interior decorator had had a field day and the large room was crammed with museum-quality furniture, pictures, rugs and objets d'art. Individually, the pieces were superb, but nothing gelled or looked harmonious. The modern setting somehow quarrelled, rather than enhanced the over opulent space. Money, not taste was the overall impression. Quan was delighted with it.

Removing the lid from a pale celadon jade Chinese jar of the Quianlong period, she plunged her hand inside and scooped out a handful of coloured, miniature 'macarons' from an exclusive Tokyo patisserie shop. After eating five, she brushed the crumbs from her fingers and made another note on her iPad.

Earlier that morning, her meeting with the Armstec head weapons technician and the computer expert had gone well and she now felt supremely confident that Jiro Nomura's invention would achieve her aims. Naturally, one could never have too much money, but she smiled to herself at the thought of the staggering amounts which would shortly be wired to her various accounts around the world. She closed her eyes for a moment, envisaging a secret room, filled with gold ingots, piled to the ceiling. Now, her ambitions were centred on the power which would soon be hers. She would be invincible.

One of her PAs had scheduled several meetings for that afternoon. They would be strictly compartmentalised, and none of the men would come into contact, or be aware of the others. Taking another handful of 'macarons,' she chewed them as she mentally ran through the list. The first was due in fifteen minutes. Minsheng Gão, from the Embassy, had a small, but vital role to play. He would be followed by those she had selected to plant the explosives. Her head of public relations would be given carefully worded pieces to leak to the press, anonymously. Finally, her chief strategist would brief her on the projected aftermath of phase one of the bombings.

For security reasons, Quan had decided not to be in Tokyo when the action started. A tour of her other offices in Japan would give her a reason to be elsewhere. An idea started to form in her brain and she looked at it from every angle. She was suddenly tempted to visit the site of the first, planned bombings. There she'd see the hundreds of insignificant little ants, going about their pathetic daily business and *she* would be the only one to know what was in store for them. Actually *being* there would give her an enormous frisson of excitement and the feeling of power would be magnified a hundred times. It was irrational and there would be some danger involved, but once the notion was in her mind, it refused to be banished.

Once again, her hand explored the inside of the jade jar, only to find that it was now empty. Remembering, just in time, how astronomically expensive the antique jar had been, she curbed her desire to smash it on the floor.

Her intercom buzzed and it was time for the meetings to begin.

Chapter 77

After the run-throughs with his team, H felt reasonably confident of a successful 'lift.' He was well aware that there were risks involved and unforeseen problems were always a possibility. He spent the early afternoon in his office, catching up with the day-to-day paperwork, which had accumulated whilst he was in Ireland and France.

The phone on his desk rang. He picked it up and heard Kyuji's voice.

"Our man is on the move!"

"Where is he now?" H asked.

"His tail has just rung-in. Minsheng Gāo left the Embassy twelve minutes ago. He's walking in a purposeful way and has a briefcase with him. Our man is following him."

"Who is our man?"

"It's Agent Nin-Po," Kyuji replied.

"Good," H said. "He's one of our best. Look, tell him to do a surveillance check and make sure Gāo isn't being followed by anyone else."

"Will do," Kyuji replied. "I'll let you know as soon as he reaches his destination."

H rang-off and went back to his paperwork. A few minutes later, the phone rang again.

"Gao has just walked up the steps and entered the offices of Armstec International. Nin-Po saw him show a pass to the Commissionaire before he was allowed in. He says the target is 'clean' and no-one was showing any interest in his movements. As

Nin-Po had no pass, he didn't try to follow him into reception, but he's watching the building."

"Get another couple of agents down there straight away, to cover any other exits and make sure they have Gāo's photo."

After thanking Kyuji, H rang off and called for his team to assemble in his office.

The three men arrived with a young, female agent. H had chosen Midori Ito the day before and briefed her thoroughly. She was young and attractive. As per his instructions, she was wearing high heels, an extremely short skirt and a skimpy top, which revealed a lot of cleavage.

"Perfect!" H said, looking at her approvingly. "Are these your props?" he asked, looking at an unwieldy pile of files and books, which she'd put down on a chair. She said that they were.

"Sit down, everyone. We may be moving the timetable up. Are you all ready?"

As they nodded, H put them in the picture.

"It seems probable that he's meeting Quan," he continued. "This is good for us, as it definitely ties the two of them together. I'd love to know how the meeting was set up. Kyuji hasn't found any trace of their communications. Now, *if* he sticks to his routine, we hope he'll walk back to his office and we can pick him up as planned. Any questions?"

There were none. "Right," he said. "Let's get going."

Chapter 78

H and his team had been in position for just under an hour, when his earpiece vibrated. He was on an open channel and heard Agent Nin-Po alert them that Gão had just left the building and was walking back the same way he'd arrived. H listened before lifting his wrist-mike to his face.

"Stick with him. It's almost two miles and will probably take Gão about thirty minutes. Sing out when he reaches the corner by the Azabu Fire Station. Let's hope he doesn't decide to take the subway or jump into a cab."

H spoke to the spotter he'd placed on a nearby rooftop. "In position, with a clear sight of the road," Chavet confirmed, keeping his voice steady and the excitement out of his tone. Next, H checked-in with Kyuji who confirmed that he could hear all feeds clearly and the cameras showed unobstructed views along Gão's projected route. The local police had been informed that the Secret Service was carrying out an operation and had agreed to turn a blind eye.

They waited.

Twenty seven minutes later, Agent Nin-Po's voice came through everyone's earpieces. "Subject still en route and will reach the Fire Station in a little under thirty seconds."

"Subject now in view," Chavet said.

In the dark van parked by the pavement, H nodded to Johnny Dashu, who slid the side door open. They were both wearing white overalls and caps with the logo of a telephone repair company on the breast pockets, matching the decal which had been added to the side panels of the van. H stepped out and stretched, before having a word with Baku Mori, who was sitting in the driver's seat, with the engine idling.

When Gāo stepped into the invisible cordon, two other agents, similarly dressed, moved in behind him and started to close off part of the pavement to pedestrians.

Suspecting nothing, Gāo walked on. As he came abreast of the front of the van, Midori Ito crossed the road and stepped onto the pavement in front of him. Her mobile phone started to ring and she struggled to answer it, whilst holding onto a large pile of books and papers. The unwieldy bundle slipped out of her grasp and spilled over the pavement. With a little cry, she stooped, dropping her mobile as she did so. Gāo, who couldn't fail to have noticed her charms, exposed by her kneeling posture, leapt forward.

"Please allow me to help," he said, bending down to help her back to her feet. She gave him a dazzling smile and he scarcely noticed the prick of a tiny needle on his neck as she grasped his collar. He went down onto one knee and gathered her phone and a few sheets of paper, but his hands suddenly refused to work. He looked up at her in puzzlement, as her face dissolved into a blur. He was unaware of the two pairs of strong hands, which lifted him quickly into the van. The door was pulled shut behind them and Baku Mori drove the van out into the street.

On his rooftop, Chavet had watched the scene unfold through high-powered binoculars. He felt exhilarated and impressed by the slick operation. H had taken him on one side the night before and told him, "if possible, you should always try and take a simple approach, with no fancy touches. This is an old ploy, but it usually works."

Chavet scanned the area, but the incident had happened so rapidly, that none of the passers-by had noticed anything untoward. He panned the binoculars and watched the two agents removing the temporary barrier at the corner. A bright yellow Toyota Aygo was backing into the large parking space vacated by the van and the street had returned to normal.

Chavet laughed as he saw the driver of the Toyota leap out of his seat and start helping Midori Ito to pick up the last of her books and papers.

Chapter 79

Baku Mori drove the van to a safe house belonging to the secret service a few miles outside the centre of Tokyo. Minsheng Gāo was still unconscious when they carried him downstairs to a room which had been prepared for him.

A few minutes later, Midori Ito arrived driving her own car, accompanied by Dai Chavet and another female agent. Following the instructions H had given in the briefing, they set the stage in the basement bedroom.

Upstairs, Johnny Dashu and Baku Mori were also making some preparations. In an open dining area, they pulled down the slatted bamboo blinds, laid out various papers, a large envelope and a pair of garden secateurs on the table. Two chairs were arranged facing each other and the rest were moved back against the walls.

When H was satisfied, Baku Mori went outside to check the perimeter and the others sat in the kitchen drinking Oi Ocha unsweetened green tea, which Midori Ito had had the forethought to bring with her.

H called HQ and spoke to his uncle. "We've arrived at the safe house. All went well and Gāo should be coming round fairly soon. I'll let you know what he has to say, as soon as I can."

"I have some new information, which could be of use to you in your interrogation." Tanaka said. "You'll remember the email data we received from Brigadier Wetherall in London? Kyuji went through the Chinese fellow's laptop and has managed to hack into the brother's computer as well. His name is Yu Hang, which Wetherall seemed to find most amusing. Anyway, as we thought, he's a low-grade cog in the wheel, but one interesting thing, is that he has Minsheng Gāo's cell phone number and has spoken to him twice in the last week. He's a driver for a security company who move money between banks in armoured vehicles. His name – and the fact that we know about him – should give Mister Gāo a jolt. Kyuji's computer team are checking all the other names and numbers, to see if we can find a further tie-in."

H thanked him and was about to end the call, when Tanaka asked, "can you wake him up more quickly? With only forty eight hours to go, we need Gāo's information urgently. The Ministers are still dithering about whether the Emperor and his family and some key government figures should be moved to secure locations out of the City. It has got back to me that they think me 'overly cautious.' Anyway, that's not your problem."

H heard Tanaka sigh as he rang off. Johnny Dashu poked his head round the door. "Our guest is awake," he said.

Chapter 80

Dublin

When H had rung Liam from Monaco to ask if he'd look after Sora for a short while, and keep her safe, Liam had accepted without a second thought. As a keen follower of trends and clothing, he enjoyed looking through international fashion magazines and Sora's face and name were already familiar to him. He thought she looked sensational. H had already told him a certain amount about her and the predicament she'd suddenly found herself in. Liam was innately chivalrous and before even meeting her, his protective instincts were aroused.

Although in many ways an extrovert, he was a naturally modest man, but he couldn't help being aware that women found him attractive; even before he started to become celebrated for his success and staggering wealth. Over the years he'd managed to end most of his affairs gently and remained on amicable terms with his old girlfriends, before moving on. He was popular and had a host of good friends and a handful of soul-mates, such as H.

He dressed with particular care on the day he was due to collect Sora from Dublin airport, shaved so closely that he almost cut himself and splashed on his favourite Dior Sauvage. Breathing in the familiar scents of bergamot and citrus, he ran a comb though his floppy hair, which he wore quite long and made a face at himself in the mirror. He ran downstairs, whistling a tune, slammed the front door behind him and climbed behind the wheel of his Aston Martin DB11.

Sora arrived, conscious of not looking her best. In the rush of leaving Monte-Carlo, she'd had no time to change out of the sneakers, jeans and sweatshirt she'd worn when she'd left the *Sappho* and longed for a bath and the chance to wash her hair. Luckily she'd thrown a small make-up bag into her holdall and felt a little more human after putting on some mascara, blusher and lip-gloss and brushing out her hair.

Onishi and Murata had both tried – without success – to chat her up on the way over. She'd been too tired and tense to respond, although she was grateful that they were with her. Wedged between the two burly men, she sat back in her seat, feeling temporarily safe and closed her eyes.

Shutting her mind to the past, she wondered what would happen when she reached Ireland, and how long she'd have to stay there before being reunited with H. He'd swept her off her feet in Kinsale and for a brief few hours, she'd managed to forget Quan and experienced pleasure and fulfilment in H's arms. He'd come back to the *Sappho* – at considerable danger to himself – and saved her from Quan. She smiled sleepily at the memory. When she'd needed a knight in shining armour, he'd been there for her.

On the borders of sleep, her mind played back over the time since her abduction. She'd been wafted along with no control over what happened to her. She desperately craved some peace and stability. She longed to be able to slow the pace of her life and regain some semblance of normality. Would she ever be able to return to her old life as a model, and… would she *want* to? The thought pulled her sharply awake. Those days now seemed incredibly far away and almost unreal. Her thoughts returned to H and the life he led, with the constant dangers of his profession. She wondered if she was naïve in thinking she could have any sort of a future with this enigmatic man. The plane touched down and she opened her eyes. She had found no answer to her question.

Onishi carried her holdall as they walked through the passport and baggage areas and out into the Arrivals Hall. Liam was there waiting and walked forward to greet them. He carried a large bunch of purple freesias, which he held out to her with a beaming smile.

They looked at each other for the first time. In her he saw the embodiment of his dreams. The fact that this lovely girl looked tired and frail, with dark smudges under her eyes, only added to his immediate feelings. Sora was a tall girl, but she needed to tilt her head back to look up at him. She took in everything about him in a single glance: the way his hair flopped forward over his forehead, the blue eyes, staring at her so intently, the way his wide lips curved upwards, the expensive but whacky clothes. Not a conventionally handsome man, she decided, but there was *something* about him. It was almost as if she recognised him and knew all there was to know.

Chapter 81

The Safe House - Outside Tokyo

Minsheng Gāo was conscious, but completely disoriented and bewildered. For the past ten minutes he'd slowly surfaced, wondering why he was in the dark and why his mouth felt so dry and tasted disgusting. He wondered if he'd got drunk the night before. He tried to look at his watch, but he couldn't move his arm. He flexed his fingers and discovered that his hands were tied together. Panic set in when he tried to move and realised that his ankles were similarly tied. The mists of the drug, which were still rolling round his head, peeled back and he was suddenly afraid.

As he opened his mouth to call out, he heard the sound of a key turning in a lock. A door opened and lights were switched on. He screwed his eyes shut at the sudden glare and then opened them again. Without speaking, two men walked over to the bed and hoisted him to his feet.

"What is the meaning of this? Who are you, and where am I?" He was disgusted to find that his voice shook.

There was no reply and although he tried to hang back, he was half carried upstairs and placed onto a chair. The two men took a step back and stood behind him.

He looked across the table at the man who sat opposite him.

"You, my friend, are in a heap of trouble," H said in a conversational tone.

"Trouble! What trouble? What are you *talking* about? It's *you* and your thuggish friends who are in trouble. I demand to know why you have kidnapped me and brought me here – wherever here is – against my will. There will be serious repercussions. I am an important man, with powerful friends. You have no idea what you have done."

H allowed him to ramble on, until Gāo's bluster started to falter and he ground to a halt, looking baffled and frustrated.

"I find it interesting," H said, as if he hadn't heard the tirade, "that you haven't asked the obvious question, as to *why* we wish to speak to you." Gāo goggled at him, as H continued speaking.

"You are in a very perilous situation. No, don't interrupt," he said, as Gāo opened his mouth. "Just listen. We know a lot about you and your activities," H looked down at some papers in front of him. "As I see it, you have not one, but three problems. Let's get the least important one out of the way first." He selected a sheet from the pile and glanced at it.

"Through your unfortunate gambling habits, I see that you are in debt to the tune of almost four million yen, to a private casino called," H glanced at his notes again, "The Pink Dragon. This is a pretty staggering amount, considering your salary." H indicated a large man seated behind him, who was cleaning his nails with the tip of a commando knife. "Mister Sakai, here, represents your creditors at the casino and is anxious to speak to you when we've finished our discussion."

Gāo showed the whites of his eyes and struggled in his chair. "I can pay it back. I have large funds coming in … "

"Yes," H broke in, "let's come back to those 'funds' a little later." He selected another page from his notes. "You have been conspiring to commit acts of terror on Japanese soil. As you are in no doubt aware, Japan retains capital punishment."

H placed his elbows on the table and rested his chin on his knuckles. "I am a civilized man. In my view, violence should be used only if unavoidable. Unfortunately for you, these gentlemen here with me don't share my scruples." He allowed his words to sink in and watched, with distaste, as Gāo seemed to shrink in his chair. He'd spotted the pair of secateurs which had been left on the table and looked around the room wildly, searching for some way out. "However," H went on, "I would much prefer to conduct this meeting on my terms. If you comply, there should be no necessity for any violence or pain."

The prisoner wrenched his eyes away from the secateurs and tried to gather himself together. In an arrogant, blustering voice he said, "What do you want from me? I need a drink and a cigarette and take these restraints off before we continue."

He looked boldly at H, who smiled thinly. "Yes, I think you may be permitted a drink. Your request for a cigarette is denied. The restraints are there for a reason. We are aware that you hold a black belt in Karate, but if there are to be any demonstrations, we'd rather they came from us."

H nodded to Baku Mori, who poured out a beaker of green tea and held it to Gão's lips. When he'd gulped it down, H said, "Mister Sakai, as this information is private, would you mind taking a walk and waiting for us to finish?" Sakai (who was actually Dai Chavet) lumbered to his feet, stuck the knife in his belt and left the room, patting the bound man on the shoulder and smiling at him as he went. He hadn't said a word, but he left an aura of menace behind him.

"Right, let's get down to business," H said. "I want some information and I advise you to tell me the truth. When you have answered my questions, you will be allowed to leave and return to your embassy; if you still wish to go there. I will hold off Mister Sakai, *if* I get what I want. Please believe me. If you lie to me, I will throw you to the dogs. Do you understand?" Gão nodded.

"I want to know about your dealings with Madam Chow Lee Quan. Tell me how you came to join her and we'll go from there."

"How do you know about…," he cut the words off and snapped his mouth shut. With many promptings, his story came out. H took it slowly, posing his questions carefully and Gão gradually gained confidence. As he talked he became more fluent and for a while he seemed to forget his predicament and almost boasted about what he'd achieved. He'd been tasked with the job as liaison officer and coordinator, recruiting low level Chinese staff as drivers, deliverers and the general workers needed for the smooth running of Quan's 'operation' in Japan.

"Ah yes, people like Yu Hang and," H stopped as Gāo gasped – horrified at the amount of information his interrogator knew about his operation.

H continued, giving Gāo glimpses of the information he had in his notes. When H finally mentioned the date of the opening action, he saw Gāo's eyes widen.

"But the date's been … " He stopped and sucked in his breath.

"Yes, you were saying, the date has been, what?" Gāo remained silent. "Oh dear, we were doing so well. Now, tell me if that date has been moved up or moved back. I need specifics." He shuffled his papers once more and removed one sheet.

"You need to convince me that the information you have given me is correct. I have here the venue for the first bombings. I want you to confirm that to me." He looked up expectantly. The paper seemed to fascinate Gāo, who looked fixedly at it.

In a rising panic, he started to shout. "You're trying to trick me. I don't believe you have that information. I refuse to say any more without my lawyer being present."

"Grow up," H said sharply. "If you remain silent, you'll never see a defence lawyer. You won't need one where you'll be going."

"I won't. I won't say any more. They'll kill me. You can't make me."

H sighed, then picked up the secateurs and turned them idly in his hands. "At the beginning of our conversation, I said that you had three problems, but, so far we've only spoken of two. What do you think would happen to you, if we deliver you back to your embassy? I suppose that they might be prepared to overlook the fact of your gambling debts, but it wouldn't do any good to your career. You can kiss goodbye to whatever sums you were expecting to receive from Madam Quan. It won't be happening. Your superiors will also take a very dim view when they see these."

H opened an envelope and upended it. Colour photographs spilled out onto the table.

"What *is* this?" Gāo shouted, struggling to his feet and swaying unsteadily on his bound feet. "You *bastards*! I never did anything. I never touched her. Who *is* this?" He frowned as he recognised the girl who'd dropped the papers at his feet earlier. The images showed him naked in the bedroom downstairs. He was not alone. Midori Ito – who was also naked – lay beneath him on the rumpled sheets. The shots had been artistically posed and left nothing to the imagination.

"This charming young lady is an agent in the Japanese Secret Service. I think it would be impossible for you to explain these away to your Chinese masters. They'd brand you a traitor and send you home. You probably have a better idea than I have, as to what would happen to you when you got there."

As he realised the full implication of how he'd been tricked and horrific thoughts of what would happen to him flashed through his mind. He sank back onto the chair, licking his dry lips.

"I'll tell you everything," he said.

Chapter 82

To an impartial eye, it seemed as though the architect of Tokyo's Tawā, or The Tower had taken inspiration from a dozen or more of the world's tallest buildings. Having been unable to make up his mind, he'd borrowed elements from all of them. The resulting skyscraper was eye-catching, but few would have called it a thing of beauty. It was a colossal, tapering structure with the inevitable shopping mall covering the whole of the ground level. There were over thirty restaurants and fast-food outlets, a twenty-screen cinema, four art galleries, a theatre and an endless basement car park. The upper levels contained a hotel, a prestige health club, beauty salons, offices and flats. It was topped-off by a circular glass observation area, which was popular with tourists and locals alike.

Quan was in her element as she strutted around the shopping area. She stopped to look at her reflection in a window. One of her staff had been detailed to visit The Tower and to bring back a complete set of the female security staff uniform and shoes. A tailor had made Quan a copy overnight. The truncheon, hanging from her belt and a sidearm completed the picture. When she was satisfied that no-one was giving her a second glance, she stood still for a few moments in the very epicentre, craning her neck to look skywards, through the core of the building, straight up to the atrium ninety two floors above.

She watched everyone going about their daily business: the shoppers strolling around, the smartly dressed businessmen and women, walking purposefully towards the banks of lifts and escalators, talking earnestly into their mobile phones, the discrete cleaning staff with their trolleys, the holidaymakers and students, staring around in wonder.

The image of the carnage to come and the fact that she alone possessed this knowledge excited her and she allowed her imagination to run riot. A million shards of glass would rain down from above, slicing the crowds to ribbons. Hundreds, if not thousands of people would be screaming and stampeding in a futile rush for the exits, before the building imploded and came crashing down on top of them. Those who managed to make it outside would probably die as the rubble and debris hit the surrounding streets. She could almost hear the wails of the fire engines and ambulance sirens.

She blotted her upper lip with a handkerchief, before ringing for her chauffeur to pick her up. Once settled into her limousine, she planned her evening. She deserved a little relaxation and entertainment, she thought, as she rang her apartment. "I want my bath run in ten minutes and have my favourite masseuse – whatever her name is – ready for me in half an hour. I'm expecting a guest, who'll be arriving shortly. Put her in the Dragon Suite." She opened her tablet and scrolled through a file of photographs. Beside each one was a brief physical description. After several minutes of deliberation, she made her choice. From memory, she dialled another number. "The latest consignment of girls at the warehouse; is number 15 still there?" She checked her watch and listened until the voice at the other end replied in the affirmative. "Good. Have her cleaned-up and delivered to my apartment within the hour."

Quan's thoughts returned to what was to come. She smiled to herself envisaging the wave of mayhem and terror, which would shortly rock Tokyo.

The world was about to change. This opening salvo was only the beginning.

Chapter 83

The Safe House – Outside Tokyo

H was now in possession of all the information he needed. Once Gāo realised that he had no other option, he'd folded like a wilting plant and answered all of H's questions. H sat for a few moments, processing what he'd learned. The most vital piece of information was finding out the exact location of the first bomb. When Gāo told him that there was not one, but three bombs, and that they were already in situ, H was appalled. He was also shocked to hear that the time-frame had been moved up and they now only had a few hours.

When H finished the interrogation he gave orders for Minsheng Gāo to be driven back to the City by Johnny Dashu and Baku Mori. There, as per Tanaka's instructions, he would be held incommunicado until a decision was taken about his future.

As soon as they'd left the building, H picked up his mobile to call his uncle, but found there was no reception. Swearing under his breath (in a most un-Japanese way), he shouted to Dai Chavet, Midori Ito and the other female agent. None of them could get a line. Chavet turned on a television set and tuned it to a local station. After several minutes of frustrating delay, they heard that there was a problem with telephone and internet services in the area.

"We need to get back to HQ right now," H told the rest of his team. "Dai, you'll have an opportunity to show me your driving skills."

They all piled into Midori Ito's car and set off. H kept trying his mobile and eventually – after a nerve-wracking twenty minutes driving – he got a line.

As Tanaka came through, H said, "sir, bad news, I'm afraid. Firstly, we no longer have 48 hours. They've moved up the time-frame to tomorrow morning at 9.15. Secondly, there are three, I repeat, three bombs and they are already in situ. However, there's one piece of excellent news – we now have the location. It's The Tawā complex."

Tanaka took a moment to digest the news. "The time-frame will have to be managed. Finding the location was our main objective. Well done. We always knew they'd choose a high profile site, where maximum casualties would occur," he said grimly. "The Tawā was on our list of possible sites and will be a brute to manage. Do you have the exact location of where the bombs are planted?"

"Negative, sir," H replied. "Unfortunately, all Gāo knows is that all three are situated somewhere in the basement garages. It's a huge area."

On this depressing thought, H ended the call, saying, "I'm on my way back and should be with you in just over half an hour and will fill you in with the details then."

When H arrived, Mai-Li showed him into Tanaka's boardroom, where he found a high level meeting underway. Fourteen men and women – several in uniform – sat around the table deep in discussion.

Tanaka made a general introduction, adding that everyone was fully briefed on the situation except for the details of H's interrogation of Minsheng Gāo, and asked H to give them the latest news.

H knew that he was under close scrutiny as he walked to an empty seat next to his uncle, at the head of the table

"Ladies and gentlemen, the situation is this." He had no need for notes and started to speak fluently and succinctly, bringing them up to speed on the information he'd culled. He looked around their horrified faces, when he told them the site and that there were now three bombs to deal with. There were several interruptions and loud demands for further information. Tanaka realised that the meeting was in danger of degenerating into a free-for-all. He held up a hand and requested that Agent Suzuki be allowed to finish before taking any questions.

The last hiatus had come from a woman in civilian dress, who'd risen to her feet, planted her hands on the table and leant forward towards H. In a sarcastic tone, she asked, "and are we *permitted* to inquire what methods were used to *'extract'* this information? Not forgetting that this gentleman is a Chinese citizen."

H had been listening patiently, but now he looked at his uncle and raised an eyebrow. "Would you mind, sir, if I address this humanitarian concern before I continue with my report?"

Tanaka hid the shadow of a smile.

Controlling any sign of irritation, H continued, "I am happy to inform you that Gāo is unharmed and unmarked. He gave his information without duress."

The woman opened her mouth, but was cut off by a much bemedalled general, who recommended, "save your sympathies for someone who deserves it, madam. Let's get on."

H concluded his principal points and took questions. After which, he was congratulated by several of his auditors.

As chairman of the meeting, Tanaka asked each person if they had any more comments to make. Most took advantage as their turns came and they thrashed through various ideas and suggestions. The room became stuffy and several of the men removed their jackets.

Almost two hours later, when every conceivable point had been decided and everyone knew what they had to do, Tanaka wrapped up the meeting.

When the room had emptied, Tanaka called in his heads of departments. Whilst they waited for them to arrive, he and H helped themselves to some iced green tea and reviewed their strategy once more, from every angle.

The next meeting was concluded far more speedily and this time, there were no interruptions.

Chapter 84

H went home to his flat, knowing that it would be sensible to have an early night. There was nothing he could usefully do, but with the anticipation of the following day, he found it hard to settle.

After taking a shower, he pulled on a pair of jeans and prowled around in bare feet. He felt like some music and scrolled through his playlist, finally opting for some Chopin Nocturnes, which suited his mood. After a while, he flopped down into a comfortable chair with a small glass of Louis Royer XO Cognac, which he kept for special occasions. It had been an impulse buy simply because the shape of the bottle had appealed to him. He'd found the taste and the aroma appealing too. He cupped the glass in his hands and brought it to his nose. He could distinguish a honey fragrance, as well as various fruits and nuts. Taking the first sip of the mellow, amber gold liquid and rolling it around his palate, he sighed with pleasure and closed his eyes. He found his thoughts drifting to Maurice Duval, another lover of good cognac and wondered how he was and if he was settling back happily into his life at the bakery. When tomorrow was over, he'd call him to find out.

Finally relaxed, H let his eyes wander over his collection of framed photographs and paintings. Each one gave him pleasure and led his mind back to when and why he'd chosen to buy them. So often, he thought, one walked past one's own possessions without really noticing or appreciating them.

A half-finished 'fiendish' Sudoku lay on the table in front of him and he picked up a pen, but after a few minutes, he hadn't filled in a single square on the grid. He dropped it back onto the table and walked into his bedroom. The emotional beauty of the music was making him feel nostalgic. He looked around the space, thinking back over the women he'd shared it with. Looking down at the bed, he brought up the image of Monique Lavalle; the woman he'd wanted to spend the rest of his life with, but she had died and he'd only realised afterwards how much she'd meant to him. He sniffed the air, but there was no lingering trace of the Jo Malone Orange Blossom scent she'd always worn. He wrenched his thoughts away from the haunting memories and suddenly wondered if he'd ever see Sora here.

The sound of his phone interrupted his thoughts. Liam Callaghan's name came up on the 'caller id' screen. "Thought transference," he said, "I was just wondering how you and Sora were getting on."

"Everything's fine," Liam said. "Look, H, I feel a complete heel and I'm not sure how to say this … "

H interrupted, "don't tell me," he said half jokingly, "you've fallen for Sora and want to marry her!"

There was a distinct pause before he heard Liam clear his throat and say, "you've taken the words out of my mouth."

H listened as Liam apologised for being such a poor friend and went into raptures about how he felt and what a wonderful girl Sora was.

When he could edge in a word, he said, "Liam, you bastard! Congratulations. I think you're made for each other. You are right, she *is* a great girl and deserves someone like you. Take good care of her and keep her safe. I hope she feels the same way about you."

Assured on that point, he wished them well and when Liam asked tentatively if H would consider being his best man, he said he'd be honoured. They promised to meet up soon and said goodnight.

H looked at the antique clock on the wall, which cleared its throat and chimed twelve times. He stepped out of his jeans and slid under the cool, linen sheets. The music had ended and the flat was silent. Telling himself to wake at 5.00, he closed his eyes, turned off his brain, and slept.

Chapter 85

H woke up early. It was not quite five o'clock when he left his flat for a run. A watery sun was starting to herald another beautiful day. The Imperial Palace Park was not open to the general public until nine o'clock, so he had the famous, five kilometre surface almost to himself and revelled in the relative peace and quiet. He had a quick shower and some breakfast when he got back to the flat, before heading down to the Tawā. Pre-warned by Tanaka that the entire parking garage would be closed, he travelled on the Metro Subway, arriving shortly before seven o'clock.

Despite the early hour, the main concourse was already busy. Having checked in with HQ, he went to find Baku Mori, who'd been put in charge and had been on site since midnight. He was in a vacant shop, centrally situated on the ground floor, which had been assigned to the Secret Service.

"What's new?" H asked.

Rubbing a tired hand over his eyes, Baku Mori said, "We have good news and bad news."

"Let's hear the bad first," H said.

"We have a major problem. The good news is that two of the three explosive charges have been located, but our bomb disposal guys have run into a problem defusing them. Quan's expert has used something we've never seen and they can't get the clock to stop. I've told Mister Tanaka and he's sent a SWAT team to arrest Quan's chief weapons designer at the Armstec factory. He's the only one who can stop the timer. We'll have to force him into talking our guys through the process of shutting the damn things down.

So far, we haven't been able to find the third bomb. We've had in the tracker dogs and all the other gizmos, but no joy yet and we're running out of places to look.

After your meeting ended last night, Mister Tanaka spoke to the head man at the complex here, a Mister Higuchi who sensibly offered to help in any way he could. Although he immediately offered this shop as a temporary HQ, he wasn't that thrilled with our first request, to close-off the entire basement sections and parking areas at eleven last night. Since then he's been besieged with angry calls, but he's fending them off. The story he's put out is that a suspected gas leak's been reported and the area has had to be sealed-off until it's sorted. All of the shops were shut by then anyway and most of the office personnel had left, but wow, did he get angst from people whose cars were still in there. The police have also been most co-operative. They've closed several of the surrounding streets and are re-routing the traffic, but by now – with the rush hour in full swing – there'll be pretty good chaos in the whole area."

"Luckily that's not our problem," H replied.

Kyuji and the bomb disposal expert came through the door, looking less than cheerful. Kyuji's expression lightened a bit when he saw H.

"The SWAT team have arrived at Armstec," Kyuji said. "They've persuaded Quan's man to cooperate and, we expect both timers to be dismantled very shortly. We're still looking for the third device. The search has already been most comprehensive, but we're waiting for the architect to arrive and hope he'll be able to pinpoint the most vulnerable places in the structure. We know that when the complex was built, the latest technology was included, in the event of an earthquake, but he may come up with some additional information." He looked at his watch. "We have an hour and forty five minutes to find the third device."

The architect arrived at the gallop, followed by an unmistakable military man in his fifties. Introductions were made and H left them to it.

Quan had enjoyed her evening and slept well. Excitement had made her wake up earlier than usual. She called for breakfast, knowing that her helicopter would already be waiting on the roof to take her away from the City.

The incredible buzz she'd experienced at the Tawā had worn off, but like a heroin addict, she craved for more. Her watch showed 7.16. Would the time frame allow her another quick look? It would be madness, but she told herself that even allowing for margins of error, there'd be plenty of time for her to be well away from the danger zone by 9.15.

Twelve minutes later, she'd changed into the security guard outfit (which she covered with a light coat) made sure that her handgun was loaded and the stolen security pass was safely stowed into a pocket, and was making her way up to the roof, issuing orders and trailing aides and personal staff behind her like a comet. The pilot had powered-up, a marshal had the door opened for her as she scuttled across the roof in a crouch and clambered into her Sikorsky S-76.

Putting on her headphones, she spoke to the pilot. "Change of plans. Put me down on the roof of the Tawā.

Chapter 86

The number of people on the ground floor concourse had almost doubled in the thirty minutes since H had arrived at the Tawā and there was a bustle of activity everywhere he looked.

H decided to head for the car park to get an update on the current situation. He spoke into his wrist mike and told Johnny Dashu where he'd be. At the centre of the concourse, he did a 360 degree visual sweep, looking for anything out of place or suspicious, but his view was limited by the mass of the hurrying throng. Without knowing it, he was standing exactly where Quan had stood the evening before. As she had done, he looked up to the top of the atrium. H took a moment to marvel in the architectural feat, which had been achieved.

He stopped in front of a large board showing the floor-plan, to orient himself and find the nearest staircase. His earpiece pinged.

Johnny Dashu's voice came over, speaking in an exultant voice. "H, they've just located the last device! It's being defused as we speak."

"Fantastic. I'm on my way back."

Feeling euphoric and incredibly relieved, H started to retrace his steps, thinking of the horror, which had now been averted. He glanced at his Rolex and saw the time was 7.45. The margin had been damn narrow, with only ninety minutes in hand before the possible detonation.

Deep in these thoughts, he suddenly halted in mid stride. A small child bumped into him as he stopped and the mother glared angrily at H as he turned to apologise. Something out of place had nudged him into super-awareness. What was it?

His eyes flashed from left to right, trying to pinpoint the anomaly. A sudden gap opened in front of him and he saw what had attracted his attention. A female security guard was about sixty feet in front of him, heading away. He recognised the walk. It was Quan.

Field agents lived by trusting their instincts, but H needed to make certain that he was right. He hurried after the figure, dodging through the crowd. How could it possibly be her? he wondered. She'd be mad to be anywhere in the vicinity.

Moving fast, he'd made up ground, but now he'd lost sight of her. She was short and taller people kept spoiling H's view as the crowds ebbed and flowed. He needed height. Noticing a shoe-shine kiosk, H leapt up onto a platform with a high chair, where an elderly man sat, having his shoes cleaned. H scanned ahead from his vantage point, ignoring angry yells from the old man who'd dropped his newspaper when H landed almost on top of him.

He spotted her! She was making for a security door at the end of a line of shops. At the sound of the loud shouts, she'd turned in his direction.

As their eyes locked, an expression of shock crossed her face. H jumped back onto the ground and raced to cover the thirty or so yards which now separated them. As he ran forward, he lifted his wrist to his face. "Johnny," he said, urgently, "get a team down here *now.* I've just seen Quan and I'm in pursuit." Seeing a sign above the door where he'd seen her, he added, "area C17, security door."

Quan was fumbling in her pockets. H saw her pull out a security key card and swipe it across the reader on the wall. The door swung open and she leapt through it, flashing a triumphant glare at H as she pulled the door closed behind her.

Grinding his teeth, H lost precious seconds finding a security guard who could let him through. Luckily there was one not far away. H flashed his credentials and said, "get this door open immediately."

The man looked at him doubtfully, saying he'd need to ring his superior first. H could hear the sound of running feet, as his team swarmed to catch up with Quan.

"Sorry, out of time," H said, grabbing the security card from around the guards' neck and slapping it onto the reader.

"Here, you can't do that. Authorised personnel only," the man shouted.

The door swung open again, H drew his Browning and prepared to check before exposing himself. The guard tried to bar the entrance. H pushed him to the ground, out of danger and in doing so, left himself silhouetted against the light for an instant.

Instead of escaping, Quan had waited. Her hatred of H and the knowledge that he must somehow have discovered her plans, rooted her to the spot.

Three shots rang out.

H fell to the ground.

Chapter 87

Captain Endo, Quan's helicopter pilot was in a dilemma. He knew that his boss might return at any moment and expect to find him ready to take off, but his bladder was bursting. He'd made his pre-flight checks and had been keeping the rotors turning in 'flight idle' for some time. He decided to take a chance on being back before she reappeared. His co-pilot sat beside him, with his nose in an aviation magazine. Briefly explaining where he was going, Endo made a run for it.

He'd only just gone inside when the lift doors opened and Quan rushed out, heading for the helicopter.

"Take off, take off," she screamed at the cockpit as she scrambled inside. The unfortunate co-pilot quickly explained what had happened. Quan completely lost the plot. The gist of her furious tirade was that Captain Endo was fired and the co-pilot should lift off instantly. "Get me in the air, *now*," she shouted. The man dared not disobey her. He rapidly undid his seatbelt, pulled off his headset and slid across into the Captain's seat. Once he was safely buckled-in, with the other headset on, he engaged 'flight mode', increased power and prepared to 'lift the lever and go'.

Below in the shopping mall, H had hit the ground and rolled away from the open door, dragging the hapless guard out of Quan's line of fire. He leapt to his feet and fired two quick shots through the doorway, but there was no return fire.

Ignoring the furious complaints of the guard who'd been manhandled, and the shouts from some onlookers who'd quickly appeared, H burst through the door at a run, firing as he did so. There was no sign of Quan, but he could hear the sound of echoing footsteps.

He found himself in a short corridor with doors leading off on either side. After checking and finding two empty rooms, there was only one way to go: he followed round to the left, pausing at the turn. He heard shouts and then a single shot, followed by the renewed sound of running footsteps.

The corridor branched left and right. H looked both ways and saw someone lying on the ground. It was one of his agents, who'd been stationed at a door to the car parks.

The man had been shot through the chest. He was barely conscious and called weakly to H.

"She went that way," he gasped, his hand fluttered to the left. "I wouldn't let her through."

H didn't want to leave him, but Quan was getting away and he could tell that the man was dying. "You did well," he said gently. "Agent Dashu is on his way."

Pounding down the left hand corridor, he stopped by a bank of two lifts. He could hear that one was in use and looking at the numbers over the door, he saw see that it was going up. He punched the button and the door to the second lift opened. As it climbed, he called Dashu, who couldn't be more than a minute or two behind him.

"We have a man down, in critical condition. I think Quan's heading for the roof. I'm on my way up. Get a team up there."

CHAPTER 88

As the lift door opened, H boiled out and ran towards the helideck with his Browning at the ready. The helicopter was about to lift off and in order to prevent it leaving, he needed to make a split second decision. Several options whizzed through his brain at 'warp speed'. Shooting the pilot would have the right result, but would involve collateral damage. The second choice was to try and get on board. He knew that Quan was carrying a gun and if she hit him with a lucky shot, she'd escape. He could fire at the fuel tanks, but even if he punctured them, the pilot might still get airborne and fly for a short distance. He went for the fourth option – several shots into the tail rotor gear box, which – if accurate – would mean that the pilot wouldn't be able to control the aircraft in the hover and climb away.

His decision coincided with the return of Quan's pilot and the Tawā deck marshal, who were running forwards on the land side area of the helideck. As they were not in his line of fire, H took aim and opened up at his chosen spot.

The co-pilot had just lifted off and had reached a height of about five feet, when he saw three men converging on him. His headphones prevented him from hearing H's shots, but he immediately realised he'd lost tail rotor control. The aircraft started to spin out of control and he had no choice but to try and put her down.

Quan – who was being thrown from side to side – shrieked, "what are you doing, you idiot? I said get me *away* from here."

The man over compensated, struggling to regain control as the rate of the torque turn increased. His only option was to lower the lever and try to get back onto the roof. From inside the machine, the helideck appeared to rush towards the descending helicopter. One of the main rotor blades hit the concrete, followed almost simultaneously by the other three. The noise was horrendous. H dived to the deck, covering his head with his arms as razor sharp pieces of metal flew over the area, missing him by inches.

The deck marshal was not so lucky and was instantly decapitated. His body stood for a long moment, before crumpling to the ground. The pilot – who was running a few feet ahead of him – narrowly missed a similar fate.

The helicopter lurched as the spin stopped then bounced once before miraculously settling on its wheels. The impact was jarring. The co-pilot's hands were slick with sweat as he fumbled to shut off the fuel master switch.

H ran across the helideck, wrenched the door open and pulled Quan out onto the ground, before she was aware of his approach.

Dazed, but with surprising agility, she rolled and came onto her feet, shaking her head. Normally, there would have been no contest: an overweight, middle-aged woman against a trained operative. It was their guns which levelled the playing field. Somehow, Quan had managed to retain a hold of her weapon.

The rooftop had suddenly gone silent. They stood facing each other, only ten feet apart.

"It's over, Quan," H said loudly. "You've lost. Drop your weapon."

She laughed wildly. "You *maniac*! You don't know what you've done. This building is going to blow up at any minute. We'll both die."

"That's not going to happen. We've found your bombs and they've been defused. We know all about your plans for Japan. You're *finished*. You'll spend the rest of your life behind bars."

Quan's pilot had been standing rooted to the spot and drenched by the deck marshal's blood which had sprayed over him. Although he was unarmed, he belatedly went to his boss's aid and launched himself between H and Quan. A shot rang out and the man dropped where he stood.

Quan, aiming for H whilst he was still talking, had hit her own man in the back. She looked down at the body, as if surprised to see him there. Then she looked up at H.

Unseen by either of them, the co-pilot had crept up behind H. He managed to knock up H's gun hand and jabbed a hard finger into H's back, bluffing that he had a gun. Instinctively, H whipped his head round and saw both of the man's hands were empty. In a single blur of movement he pivoted on his left foot, struck the man's upper jaw bone with his right elbow, following it up with a rapid knee to the groin, which brought his adversary down. Without waiting to see him fall, H was already turning his gun back towards Quan and snapped off a shot.

At the same instant Quan sidestepped the body of her pilot, took aim and shot H twice in the chest.

Seconds later, Johnny Dashu and three heavily armed men pounded onto the roof. The first thing Dashu saw was Quan's body lying spread-eagled in front of him, with blood turning the front of her jacket red. His eyes passed over the ruined Sikorsky, the bodies of the helicopter pilot, the deck marshal and the unconscious co-pilot.

Then Dashu spotted H a few feet away. "Get an ambulance and paramedics," he shouted over his shoulder. Dropping to his knees, he tried to stem the blood, which was pumping from H's chest and making a rapidly expanding pool on the ground. H's eyes opened and Dashu signalled to one of his men to take over the compression as he lifted H's head into his lap.

"Hold on, H," he said urgently. "Help's on the way."

H tried to speak, but his voice was so faint that Dashu had to lean down to hear.

"Did she get away?"

"No – you got her, H. Lie quiet. Just *don't die* on me."

A weak smile flitted over H's face. He opened his mouth and tried to say something else, but a spasm shook him and he began to cough. Dashu watched with horror as dark blood came pouring out of H's mouth.

Chapter 89

Dashu called his boss, knowing he'd be shattered by the news. Tanaka listened without speaking, before asking two questions.

"Will he live?"

Dashu couldn't tell him.

"Where are you taking him?"

It was four o'clock in the afternoon and almost six hours since H had been wheeled into theatre, when Tanaka finally saw what he'd been waiting for.

The doors of the Operating Room opened and a surgeon appeared in wrinkled scrubs. He was pulling off his surgical cap, which was spotted with blood and looked exhausted. Looking up, he found a group of secret service personnel had materialised in front of him, with Tanaka at their head. The tension was palpable.

"We've done all that we can," he said slowly. "It's incredible he didn't die on the operating table. We almost lost him a couple of times, but somehow he managed to rally. One bullet was a through-and-through, causing some muscular and bone damage, but the other did far more damage as it hit the subclavian vein." He broke off, realising that he was getting too technical.

"He seems to be an extraordinarily resilient young man. He's still on the critical list, but at the moment he's sedated and stable and we've taken him off the respirator. *If* he makes it through the next twenty four hours ... " He stopped again and looked at Tanaka before continuing, "look, I feel I should inform you that – in my professional opinion – he has a less than 50-50 chance of surviving."

Tanaka spoke up. "You don't know my boy."

The Doctor looked at him in surprise. "I'm sorry. I didn't know. Is he your son?"

"He is a son any man would be proud of," Tanaka said softly.

Epilogue

H survived the next twenty four hours.
Three days later he was moved out of the Intensive Care unit.
Four weeks after that he discharged himself from the hospital.
H was back on active service five months after the shooting.

THE END

Acknowledgements

In writing this – our second book – I'd like to end my expressing my heartfelt thanks to the following people, who have generously helped me with their expertise.

Firstly, to our editor **Martin Fletcher** who has been an unending source of constructive, good humoured advice, encouragement and support.

Christopher Little, Emma Schlesinger and **Jules Bearman** – of Christopher Little Literary Agency.

Lord Patrick Beresford. Alain de Boisanger – checking my French expressions. **Doctors Catriona and Gerard Corrigan** – hospital procedures and medications. **Christine de L'isle Bush** – proofreading, general advice and support. **Doctor Valerie Dias** – advice on medical details and terminology. **Doctor Deirdre Fanning** – medical help and facts. **Captain Robin Garaway** – information on superyachts. **Patrick Holland** – retired Garda Officer, checking my facts, terminology and procedure. **Robbie Honey** – inspirational florist. **James** – Concierge at the Merrion Hotel, Dublin. **Francis Kluzniak** – proofreading. **Roger Michael** – multi-award-winning nightlife expert. **Richard Muirhead** – Software entrepreneur & investor. **Brian O'Connor** – Aer Lingus pilot. **Virginia, Viscountess Petersham** – Monaco details. **Alex Pownall** – of Parkour Generations UK – for H's Parkour scenes. **Uday Senapati** – Head of Technical Operations, Bentley Mulliner. **Gerry White** – Dublin details. **Ken Wills** – Helicopter expert, Chairman, founder and CEO of Summit Aviation.

Ros Pearl

Printed in Great Britain
by Amazon